THE
House
that
VANITY
BUILT

Mysteries by Nancy Cole Silverman

The Misty Dawn Mystery Series

THE HOUSE ON HALLOWED GROUND (#1)
THE HOUSE THAT VANITY BUILT (#2)

The Carol Childs Mystery Series

SHADOW OF DOUBT (#1)
BEYOND A DOUBT (#2)
WITHOUT A DOUBT (#3)
ROOM FOR DOUBT (#4)
REASON TO DOUBT (#5)

Praise for Nancy Cole Silverman's Mysteries

"With an addictive plot featuring a clever psychic, a young actress from a legendary Hollywood family, and a couple of mischievous ghosts, it doesn't take a crystal ball to predict Silverman's new Misty Dawn Mystery series will be a hit with readers."

— Ellen Byron,
Award-Winning Author of the Cajun Country Mysteries

"A high-speed chase of a mystery, filled with very likable characters, a timely plot, and writing so compelling that readers will be unable to turn away from the page."

– *Kings River Life Magazine*

"The author gives us a terrific story building up to a climax that will please the reader. The old saying regarding 'people are not always what they seem' fits perfectly in this case."

– *Suspense Magazine*

"Will keep you turning pages late into the night and make you think twice about the dark side of the Hollywood Dream."

– Paul D. Marks,
Shamus Award-Winning Author of *Vortex*

"Radio host Carol Childs meets her match in this page-turner. Her opponent is everyone's good guy but she knows the truth about the man behind the mask. Now Carol must reveal a supremely clever enemy before he gets the chance to silence her for good."

– Laurie Stevens,
Award-Winning Author of the Gabriel McRay Series

"Crackles with memorable characters, Hollywood legends, and as much action behind the mic as investigative reporter Carol Childs finds in the field."

– Mar Preston,
Author of *A Very Private High School*

"Fast paced and cleverly plotted, an edgy cozy with undertones of noir."

"Carol is a smart, savvy heroine that will appeal to readers. This is a cozy with a bite."

"A thoroughly satisfying crime novel with fascinating, authentic glimpses into the world of talk radio and some of its nastier stars...The writing is compelling and the settings ring true thanks to the author's background as a newscaster herself."

"Silverman provides us with inside look into the world of talk radio as Carol Childs, an investigative reporter, finds herself in the middle of a Hollywood murder mystery...A hunky FBI Agent and a wacky psychic will keep readers guessing from beginning to end."

"Silverman creates a trip through Hollywood filled with aging hippies, greedy agents, and a deadly case of product tampering. Forget the shower scene in *Psycho*; *Shadow of Doubt* will make you scared to take a bath!"

"I loved the tone, the pace, and the drama which pulled me in immediately...All the while I suspected something was amiss, and when it came to fruition, I knew the author was going to pull a fast one, and yes, she did, and bravo because now I must read the next book to see how it all plays out."

THE House that VANITY BUILT

A MISTY DAWN MYSTERY

NANCY COLE SILVERMAN

HENERY PRESS

Copyright

THE HOUSE THAT VANITY BUILT
A Misty Dawn Mystery
Part of the Henery Press Mystery Collection

First Edition | May 2020

Henery Press
www.henerypress.com

Copyright © 2020 by Nancy Cole Silverman

This is a work of fiction. Any references to historical events, real people, or real locales are used fictitiously. Other names, characters, places, and incidents are the product of the author's imagination, and any resemblance to actual events or locales or persons, living or dead, is entirely coincidental.

Trade Paperback ISBN-13: 978-1-63511-595-6
Digital epub ISBN-13: 978-1-63511-596-3
Kindle ISBN-13: 978-1-63511-597-0
Hardcover ISBN-13: 978-1-63511-598-7

Printed in the United States of America

To my better half

ACKNOWLEDGMENTS

It takes inspiration to write a book, and for that, I thank Misty Dawn, who jumped off from the pages of my Carol Childs books and insisted on her own story, as well as the very special group of fans and friends who helped me bring her to life.

To better understand Misty, I interviewed a number of psychics—not for readings of myself, but to get an idea about the types of people they saw, the questions they were asked, and their experiences with spirit guides. They were, as I expected, varied and intriguing. But this book would not have been as divinely inspired were it not for Patti Negri, a Hollywood psychic, who in the course of my interviews stopped me and told me just to trust myself; that I had this.

I also want to thank my good friend and Sister in Crime author, Rochelle Staab, who worked with me through numerous transitions and believed in Misty and Wilson as much as I did. My Tuesday walking partner, Ellen Byron, who is a wonderful author and who I ran ideas by. Rhona Robbie, who continues to read everything I write and offers me moral support when I need it most. Special thanks to my keen-eyed proofreaders, George Marlowe and Lynn Akers. They caught errors that my less than keen eyes missed. And of course, my husband, Bruce, who has cheered me on throughout the process.

And to the entire staff at Henery Press, my editor Maria Edwards; Christina Rogers, who funneled numerous emails back and forth between myself and Henery's staff, and worked hard to develop the cover for this new series; and most especially, my publisher Kendel Lynn—you make dreams happen. I am forever thankful for your belief in me.

Chapter 1

Sunday mornings around the old Craftsman were slow. I luxuriated on the couch, reading the paper, with my cat in my lap and my tea on the table. But this morning, Wilson, my resident spirit guide, had chosen to tune to a classical music station and was blasting "Flight of the Bumblebee." The sound of manic strings pulsated like a hive of angry honeybees throughout the house. So high pitched and frenzied were the notes that I failed to hear the doorbell. Nor did I think when my cat scurried from my lap, alerting me to the bell's ringing, that there might be a connection between the song and my caller.

Unfortunately, psychics have never been good at reading themselves.

My name is Misty Dawn. I've often been referred to as the Hollywood Psychic to the Stars. Over the years, I'd counseled some of the greats. Liz Taylor. The Gabor sisters. A former president's wife—who had kept my number on speed dial—and hundreds of other celebrities whose names I've sworn to secrecy. I had also worked as a frequent consultant to the FBI and LAPD. Mostly on cases concerning missing persons and various homicides. I was a clairvoyant with a sixth sense about the world. People came from all over to seek my advice.

Standing on my porch that morning were two young women, both twenty-something—one blonde and slightly taller than the other, a curly-haired brunette with a curious smile.

The brunette spoke first.

"Sorry to bother you, I realize it's early, but we were driving by and saw your sign, and—" The girl pointed over her shoulder at the shingle I'd hung out in front of the house advertising my services. "—we need your help. Or she does anyway." The brunette elbowed her friend in the ribs, and the blonde nodded her head, shaking like a bobblehead doll.

I stepped away from the door and, with my hand behind my back, signaled Wilson to dowse the music while I nodded in the direction of the living room. Within a hair's breadth, the music faded, and Wilson returned and peered over my shoulder like a nosy old lady. My guests, oblivious to his presence, entered as far as the foyer and stopped.

"Is that a fainting couch?" The blonde stepped ahead of her friend into the living room and ran her long fingers across the sofa's delicately carved wood trim.

"It might be. However, I tend to think of it as more of a sofa or a lounging chair. It belonged to the former owner." I gestured to the furnishings in the room, the couch, two wingback chairs, and an old Victrola. "It all did. Everything you see here. This room was once part of a stage setting from *Sunset Boulevard*. Wilson was a set designer. He had a flair for design and rather eclectic taste. Women adored him, although I doubt the feeling was ever mutual." I winked and moved on. "He died suddenly in his sleep last year. His sister inherited the house and all that's in it. I'm merely the caretaker until she decides what to do with the property."

In truth, both Wilson and I were temporary residents. Wilson was what we in the psychic world called a "shade" or a person that hasn't fully passed over and was, for lack of a better word, stuck. Kind of floating between two worlds. I'd worked with several shades in the past. They served as my spirit guides, offering communication between our world and the next. Wilson's limbo-state was entirely dependent on what good he chose to do—or not do—while under my guidance. The choice was up to him. But it was all a temporary gig. At some point, based upon our work together, the universe would decide his fate, and he'd move on. Simply put, Wilson would either earn his wings or not.

"*Sunset Boulevard*?" In an overly dramatic fashion, with the back of her hand to her forehead, the blonde looked up to the ceiling. "I'm ready for my close up, Mr. DeMille." Then with a giggle, she slid down on the divan and stretched her long pale legs out in front of her. "I played Norma Desmond in high school. I'm an actress. Or I want to be anyway."

She needn't have told me. I got a lot of wannabes on my doorstep, but for this one, I didn't see any flashing marquee lights in her future.

"You'll have to excuse Amy. She's majorly stressed." The brunette stuffed her purse under her arm and joined her blonde friend on the couch. "My name is Carlene Muller, and this is Amy Hendersen. And the reason we're here is that—"

"I've lost my ring," Amy whined and held up her left hand, wiggling empty fingers in front of me.

Based upon the urgent look on their faces, I sensed this was no ordinary ring, nor insignificant loss.

"Your engagement ring?" I asked.

Carlene lowered Amy's hand to her lap. "It's a five-carat, platinum marquis. Worth thousands. A family heirloom."

"I see." I took a seat in one of the wingback chairs opposite the fainting couch and smoothed my long paisley skirt over my knees. "I assume you've told your fiancé?"

"Told him?" Amy's voice cracked. "I haven't had the nerve. The ring was his mother's. She's passed on, and far as I know, it's the only thing he had left of hers. I can't imagine what he'll do when he learns I lost it."

"You're afraid to tell him?" I didn't get the sense Amy's reluctance to tell her fiancé about her loss was due to any fear of physical violence. Rather, her concern was more of a personal loss. "That he might call off the wedding."

"Oh, no. Not at all. He'd never do that. He can't wait to get married. He's more excited than I am. He even planned the wedding for his birthday. This coming Sunday." Then sitting forward, with her elbows on her knees, Amy's hands slipped from her mouth to the side of her head as though she were trying to contain her thoughts. "It's less than a week away, and I can't find the ring anywhere. Who loses an engagement ring the week before the wedding?"

Carlene leaned across the coffee table. "We were hoping you might be able to tell us something. We searched everywhere. Do you have one of those crystal balls, maybe it could tell us where it is? She's desperate."

I sat back, my hands in my lap. Clearly, these two didn't understand my powers or what a real psychic does.

"I hate to disappoint you, but I don't use crystal balls or cards or any such gimmicks to assist in my readings. They're nothing more than window dressing, and not necessary. As for finding missing objects, people are my specialty, not lost objects like engagement rings. I'm really very sorry, but I don't think I can be of any help to you."

I was about to dismiss them, when Wilson, looking very debonair in pleated pants and oxford spats, slipped in from the entry, where he had been standing watch.

"Oh, she is delicious. So pale and youthful. An ingenue." Wilson leaned against the window and crossed his arms. "Tell them you'll work with them. We simply must. She's so...needy."

After our last case, Wilson had grown weary and shown little interest in my consults, which was of mounting concern to me. Content to rest on his laurels, Wilson felt he needed a break. But if he were to earn his wings, sitting back and pretending time didn't exist for him was a mistake. The universe didn't suffer fools, and Wilson's time, whether he was aware of it or not, was ticking away. This lack of action didn't bode well for him. For that reason alone, I wasn't about to second guess why he was so insistent I take Amy's case, only that I felt this was a case I couldn't turn down, for Wilson's sake.

"But perhaps, Amy, if you were to tell me more about your fiancé, I might be better able to advise you. Why don't you start by telling me his name and how you met."

Carlene nudged her. "Go on."

Amy started slowly. "His name's Jared, and he's smart and handsome, and—" Amy blushed and finished quickly. "And he makes me feel special in a way nobody else ever has."

Wilson put his head in his hands. "I don't believe it. Look at her, would you? The girl's a virgin! An innocent. Little more than a blushing bride-to-be. I didn't think LA had any more of those."

I shot Wilson a warning glance. Shades were not to interrupt during a reading. My eyes tracked back to Amy.

"Is Jared your first love?"

Amy's cheeks grew red. I didn't have to be psychic to know the girl wasn't all that experienced with the physical intimacies of a close relationship, or that she was blinded by passion and more in love with the idea of being in love than actually in love.

"I've never been engaged before if that's what you mean." Amy leaned closer to Carlene, as though she were looking for support.

Carlene spoke up. "He's a nice guy, okay? And if you must know, he's worth a fortune—heir to the Conroy Cosmetics' empire. Everybody knows about the Conroys. You must have seen their billboards. Their "Bee Natural" line is advertised everywhere. It's the new botox." Carlene made air quotes around the b-word. "Made from bee venom."

"Jared Conroy?" I said.

"You know his name!" Amy put her hand to her heart. "You are good."

Anyone who had watched TV or read a newspaper would know Jared Conroy. His youthful exploits had been chronicled in supermarket tabloids along with the Lindsay Lohans and Justin Biebers of the world. When Jared wrapped his daddy's Maserati around a telephone pole on Sunset Boulevard several years ago, his father cut him off and sent him to an expensive rehab clinic in Europe. Rumor had it that until Jared turned thirty-one and proved to his father, the pharmaceutical genius Dr. Elliott Conroy, that he had sobered up and settled down, access to the boy's trust fund had been denied.

Wilson moved from behind the sofa and took a seat on the head of the fainting couch. With his elbows on his knees, he stared at Amy like *The Thinker.*

"Poor baby. Blinded by her fiancé's handsome face. Seduced by his charms and the future of wealth beyond her dreams. What's a girl to do?" Wilson put both hands on his heart, patted his chest, and looked at me pleadingly. "I'm all aflutter."

I ignored him and kept my attention on Amy.

"Aside from Jared's good fortune and handsome looks, what is it about him that makes you want to spend the rest of your life with him? You're very young. What are you, maybe twenty-one, twenty-two? You're certain this isn't just infatuation?"

"I'm twenty-four," Amy said. "I know everybody thinks it's all about his money. That I'm some gold digger, but I'm not. I love him. And more importantly, he loves me. Jared isn't like anybody I've ever known. He's kind, and he's funny."

I didn't for a second believe Amy to be a fortune hunter. She wasn't at all sophisticated like girls her age who had grown up in the city might be. My sense was that she was more down-home. The type of girl who shopped Target, tithed to the church, and worried when she brushed her teeth every night if she left the water running.

Carlene, on the other hand, with her curious smile, was something else. She had grown quiet, her mind elsewhere. I let it wander and returned with my questions for Amy.

"You're not from here, are you, Amy?"

"No, but Jared likes that. He says I'm not jaded. He finds the fact I'm not all Hollywood refreshing."

I wasn't surprised. This salt-of-the-earth innocent had spent her life making others happy—a rare commodity in Hollywood.

"How did the two of you meet?" I asked.

"Carlene introduced us. I'd just moved here from Carp."

"Santa Barbara," Carlene corrected.

Carpinteria, or Carp, as the locals referred to it, was a largely working-class, more agricultural community south of Santa

Barbara. And much less glamorous.

"Santa Barbara, then, but not really. Carlene thinks it sounds better for me to say Santa Barbara. Has a ritzier ring to it she says. But, the truth is, I grew up in Carp. My mom was a schoolteacher, and my dad—he died years ago—was a farmer. But then you probably already knew that. You being a psychic and all."

People always assumed psychics knew more than they really did, and I'd found it easier to let them think what they will, rather than try to correct their illusions. In truth, first impressions are really very shallow.

"You came to the city to pursue your acting career," I said.

"I did. I always wanted to come to LA. Then last year, my mother died from a stroke. At first, I was lost. I mean, for a long time it was just my mom and me, and I didn't know what to do. Then I thought, well, now's my chance. My mom always said I was destined for bigger things. So here I am. I got an apartment in Beverly Hills. A job at Starbucks. And before I knew it, I was taking acting classes and making pumpkin spiced lattes." Amy laughed. "Then one day, Carlene walks in and orders this salted caramel Frappuccino with extra foam, and things just happened."

Carlene smiled. "I work as a party planner, and I have a small matchmaking business on the side. When I met Amy, I couldn't help but think she'd be perfect for Jared."

My eyes clicked back to Amy. "And are you perfect?" I asked.

"Maybe not perfect," Amy said. "But Jared says he loves me, and we have a lot in common."

I wondered about that.

"Is he perfect?" I hoped my question might open her mind to her own wants and desires, if she even knew what they were.

"For me?" There was that blush again. A glow of innocence that warmed the room.

"Yes, you," I said. "Is Jared perfect for you?"

Wilson stood up. "Oh, give me a break. Why wouldn't he be perfect? The man's rich, famous, and heir to one of the world's biggest cosmetics companies. If I could, I'd marry him."

I scowled.

Amy paused.

"I think so," she said. "I mean, isn't that what falling in love is all about? Finding someone who makes you feel special, growing together, and making it work."

Wilson scoffed. "In Mayberry, maybe. This is Hollywood, darling."

I pinched my lips and closed my eyes momentarily as though to shake the thought, then looked directly at Amy. "That is part of it, but love isn't always perfect. There must be something about Jared that frustrates you? Maybe drives you a little nuts?"

Amy shook her head. "No. I don't think so. He's really great."

"Nothing at all?" I sensed if I scratched the surface I'd find something.

"Well, okay, maybe his allergies. He's allergic to everything and has to carry an EpiPen with him all the time. He gets upset if he can't find it. But other than that, he's—"

"I know," I said. "He's perfect."

I leaned back in the chair. Amy was a nice girl in the old-fashioned sense. Believed in love at first sight, was new to the city, and unsophisticated. Perfect for her friend Carlene, the opportunist. A matchmaker who had arranged an all too convenient pairing between Jared and Amy, which I sensed would result in a handsome finder's fee. And Jared, Amy's betrothed, who I only knew from what I had read, had to believe Carlene had found him the girl of his dreams. Someone his daddy would love, and would—if the rumors were true—enable him to inherit his trust fund in time for his thirty-first birthday.

"I'm sorry, I wish I had good news for you, Amy. But I'm afraid I've no idea where your ring is. If it helps, however, I can tell you I don't feel the ring is permanently lost."

Amy sat up and fisted her hands. The look on her sweet face, hopeful.

"What I do think, however, is you have a severe case of bridal jitters, and, as a result, you've misplaced the ring. In fact, I wouldn't be at all surprised if it showed up again, and very soon."

"In time for the wedding?" Amy asked.

"I see it back on your finger sooner than you might expect. As for those bridal jitters, if you feel the need, my door's always open."

Amy stood up and gave me a big hug. At that moment, I knew she felt I had solved all her worldly issues. Unfortunately, I knew better.

I watched from the doorstep as both girls walked back to their car.

Wilson watched from the window. "That's it then? You're not going to work with her? You think she'll find the ring?"

"It's already been found," I said, "By someone close to her."

"Any ideas?" Wilson looked at me, quizzically.

"Not yet. But I do know the ring is the least of Amy's worries, and I'm going to need your help. That girl's in trouble. She doesn't know it now, but she will very soon. And when she does, you and I are going to have a job to do."

Chapter 2

It wasn't yet nine a.m. on Wednesday morning when I heard a heavy rapping at my door. It had a sound of desperation about it. I knew before I looked out the window it would be Amy.

I opened the door, and the girl fell into my arms.

"Jared's dead!" she cried.

"What?" I whipsawed my head in the direction of the study. Wilson stood in the doorway with an expression of complete surprise on his face.

I looked back at Amy. "Come in, dear. Take a seat on the couch. I'll be right with you."

I closed the front door, then took a side step toward Wilson. Out of the corner of my mouth, I whispered, "How could you miss such a thing?"

"So now it's my fault? Who do you think I am? Keeper of the crypt?"

I rolled my eyes. "This shouldn't have come as a surprise, Wilson. It doesn't bode well for you."

"Please, do you have any idea how many voices there are on this side of the veil? It's like the PA system at Grand Central Station around here. All of them trying to get a message through. What do you expect me to do, tune in to every one of them?"

I gritted my teeth. "Only those connected to clients you've agreed to work with. I thought you understood that."

I left Wilson to ponder this missed opportunity and joined Amy in the living room.

"I am so sorry, dear. What happened?"

Amy looked up at the ceiling, her arms wrapped around herself as she gently rocked back and forth on the sofa. Tears welled in the bottom of her eyes.

"I don't know. Dr. Conroy called this morning. It must have been around three a.m. I was asleep when the phone rang." Amy closed her eyes, and the tears began to fall down the side of her face. "He told me he was leaving the hospital. I didn't know what he was talking about. I was so confused. I can't even tell you which hospital. All I remember was that he said something terrible had happened to Jared at his bachelor party, and he wanted to see me at the house right away."

I sat down in the chair opposite Amy and put my hand on her knee. She was trembling uncontrollably.

I blamed myself that I hadn't seen this coming. Not that I always do—even psychics can be surprised. Admittedly, when Amy first told me about the wedding, I'd had my doubts. I didn't see her walking down the aisle. I deliberately chose not to say anything about it. With new clients, I found it best to tread lightly around negative subjects until I knew them better, and I never brought up the topic of death. In hindsight, however, I had felt the presence of someone hovering protectively close to Amy. At the time, I thought it might be her mother, and didn't pay much attention. Mothers who have passed often stay close to their daughters during times of great stress, and for a psychic, time—past, present, and future—could easily blend together, making it difficult to decipher the then and now. I never thought for a moment the presence I felt surrounding Amy might be the shadow of a death yet to be, and for that, I felt an uneasy sense of responsibility.

"You weren't at the Conroy's last night?" I asked.

"No." Amy took a tissue from her bag and dabbed her eyes. "I was at my apartment in Beverly Hills. Jared and I...we...we don't live together. Not yet anyway. We decided it'd be best to wait until we were married. Jared lives—" Amy sniffed and blew her nose. "—or lived, in the guest house on his father's estate in Beverly Park. I was going to move in after we returned from our honeymoon."

Wilson took a seat next to Amy at the end of the sofa. We looked at each other. I felt a tremendous sense of responsibility to do something to help the girl.

"Alright," I said, "let me get this straight, Jared's father called you and—"

"I got in my car and drove over to the house. I had no idea what was wrong, but I knew from the sound of his voice something terrible had happened."

"And when you got there?"

"Dr. Conroy met me at the door. He looked awful. Like he had just been run over or something. So frail and gray. I knew from the look in his eyes, Jared was dead. He didn't have to tell me, I just knew." Amy fisted her hand tight beneath her nose, her pretty face contorted with grief.

I took another tissue from a box beneath the coffee table and offered it to her.

"I lost it. I don't know who grabbed who first, but we just stood there and held one another. Then Dr. Conroy took me into the great room, and we sat on the couch, I told him I couldn't believe it. I had just seen Jared before the party. He was so excited. The doctor said Jared had had an allergic reaction to something at the restaurant. By the time his friends called paramedics, and they rushed him to the hospital, he was...he was...dead."

Amy blew her nose.

"What about the EpiPen? You said he always carried one with him."

"It didn't work. Dr. Conroy said it's not always 100 percent."

I took Amy's hand and held it in my own. "I'm so sorry."

"I couldn't believe what he was telling me. I had just seen Jared before his party, and he was fine. I didn't know what to do. I was numb. I went into the kitchen to get a glass of water, and when I came back, the doctor was pacing the room. He couldn't sit still. He said we needed to do something. He wanted to plan a memorial. The biggest memorial the city had ever seen, and he wanted me to do it. Next Saturday, he said. At the church where we were going to be married."

"Whoa!" Wilson put his hands on his hips. "Now that's a new one. Asking the bride-to-be to plan her fiancé's funeral at the same church she was about to take her nuptials. Got me!"

Amy went on. "I couldn't believe the doctor was talking like that. It was like he had pushed aside that Jared had just died, and we needed to move on. The whole thing, Misty, it's like a nightmare. I keep thinking I'm going to wake up, and this is all nothing but a bad dream. But it's not! Jared's dead."

I had seen people react differently to the sudden death of a loved one. Some were in total denial; others so overwhelmed with grief they required months of counseling. And some, like Amy, showed up on my doorstep. There was never any accounting for how one should act or what one might say.

"You're both going through a lot right now. And I'm sure the doctor's overwhelmed," I said.

"No, no, it was more than that." Amy squeezed the tissue in her hands until her knuckles turned white. "When I told him I didn't know if I could plan anything right now, he got angry. I've never seen him angry. The look in his eyes, it was like he was somebody else. I didn't recognize him. He said he was going to call the police and demand a thorough investigation. That he knew people, people high up in the department, and he was going to get answers. All of a sudden, it was like he didn't believe Jared's death was an accident. That somebody wanted Jared dead, and he was going to find out who it was."

I took Amy's hand. Was this the trouble I had sensed coming her way?

"And did he," I asked, "call the police?"

Amy nodded. "He did. And just like he said, the cops came right over. They were there before sunrise."

"What happened when they arrived?" My eyes searched Wilson's. We were both glued to Amy's response.

"When the cops came in, Dr. Conroy was inconsolable. He was sobbing one minute and talking to himself the next. The cops tried to calm him down, but then he'd start yelling and screaming like there was somebody else in the room. He insisted something wasn't right about Jared's death. That he wanted a full investigation, and he wanted the police to question everybody at the party. Including me."

"You?"

"Yes, me. He pointed right at me, as though he had never seen me before, and called me a gold digger. He said he wouldn't talk to me again until I had spoken to the police and told them everything I knew."

Amy's face paled, her eyes pleaded with mine for answers.

Wilson got up from the couch and went to the fireplace. "That's it, the man's insane. Who'd think she'd do such a thing? Just look at her. The girl's clearly innocent."

I ignored Wilson.

"Did you talk to the police?"

"What else could I do?"

"Do?" Wilson started to pace the room. "She should have called a lawyer, that's what she should have done."

I narrowed my eyes, a reminder of the rules; shades weren't to interrupt.

Amy continued. "I didn't think I could refuse. One of the officers suggested we go into the kitchen. He made me a cup of coffee, and we talked."

"What about?"

"Mostly about Jared and our relationship. He wanted to know how we met. How long we'd been together. That type of thing." Amy dabbed her eyes. "I was afraid he'd notice I wasn't wearing my engagement ring and ask me about it."

I glanced at Amy's empty ring finger. "About that," I asked, "were you in the habit of taking the ring off?"

"Not at first, but it got to be tight on my finger. Jared said his mother and I were about the same size, but lately, my fingers swell at night, and I—" Amy shook her head.

"It's alright, dear." I patted her knee. "Did you tell the

investigator you thought you had lost it?"

"No. I haven't told anyone. Just Carlene and you. Dr. Conroy doesn't even know. I was afraid if the police found out, they'd think maybe I had stolen it, and based on how the doctor was acting, think even worse. That maybe I had killed Jared."

I scoffed. "That's a ridiculous thought. Why would anyone think that? You were about to be the next Mrs. Jared Conroy. That comes with a lot of perks, my dear. If you were to kill Jared, you certainly wouldn't kill him for the price of a ring, no matter how valuable it was."

"But I didn't kill Jared!" Fresh tears started to roll down Amy's face. "I loved him."

"Forgive me. I'm quite sure you did, and I can't imagine why Dr. Conroy would think any different. He's understandably upset. Probably in shock. In time, I'm sure he'll come around. You'll see." I wasn't certain I believed my own words. I didn't know the doctor, and without his being there, I couldn't get a read on him. But the sudden death of a loved one brings out odd reactions in those closest to the departed, and I was anxious to comfort Amy.

"I guess, but right now, I don't know what to do." Amy wiped the tears from her face with the back of her hand. "After I finished talking to the officer, I went back into the great room to check on the doctor. He had made himself a drink, and he looked calmer. I told him I thought maybe I should go home, but he said no. He wanted me to stay. He insisted I shouldn't be alone at a time like this, that we needed to support one another. I could go home if I wanted to get some clothes, but he made me promise to come back so we could begin to plan the memorial." Amy shook her head as though she were trying to clear the vision from her head. "To be honest, I don't know what I'm doing. I'm not comfortable going back to the house and staying with him. Not alone. When I left, I just started driving. I didn't know where to go. I didn't want to go back to my apartment, and I don't have many friends in town. You were so easy to talk to the other day, it just seemed right I come here. I hope it's okay."

"I'm glad you did," I said. "Have you spoken to Carlene?"

Amy pushed her hair out of her face. "I tried to call her, but it went to voicemail. I know she had another event last night. She's probably not up yet."

"Another event?"

"A quinceañera, I think. She had planned Jared's bachelor party at Mastro's in Beverly Hills, but she didn't go. I told her to call me as soon as she got my message."

I stood up and told Amy I would put on a pot of tea. I didn't think she should go anywhere until she had spoken to Carlene and maybe had a plan to get together. What Amy needed was a friend, and Carlene, duplicitous as I suspected her to be, was as close as it was going to get.

"You look pale," I said. "And I'll bet you haven't eaten anything. How about I make something. A little toast, perhaps?"

Amy put her hand on her stomach. "I don't think I could. I haven't been able to keep anything down for days."

Wilson must have read my mind. Our eyes locked, our thoughts in sync. Nervous stomach? Forgetfulness? Swollen fingers and a missing ring? It could only mean one thing.

"Are you—"

"Pregnant?" Amy nodded. "I'm about three-and-a-half, maybe four months along. I hoped my stomach would have settled by now, but nothing helps. Jared told me it's why he wanted to rush the wedding. He didn't want me to waddle down the aisle."

My suspicion there may have been a greater financial reason behind Jared choosing the date of his birthday for the wedding was growingly apparent. "Does the doctor know about the baby?"

"He's thrilled. Jared insisted we tell his father right away. Dr. Conroy said he couldn't have been happier. We were all going to be one big happy family, and he couldn't wait to be a grandfather. It's why I have to go back. What else can I do?"

Amy's phone buzzed. She glanced down at the screen. "It's Carlene. You mind?"

I waited while Amy explained what had happened to Jared.

Even though Carlene wasn't sitting on the sofa, I could feel her worried response. What I didn't feel was a sense of surprise.

Amy said goodbye to Carlene and stood up.

"I have to go. Carlene wants me to come by her place, but before I go, can I ask a favor?"

"Anything," I said.

"When I left Dr. Conroy this morning, I agreed to help plan the memorial. Would you come? I'd feel a whole lot better if you were there. Saturday. The Methodist Church on Wilshire in Beverly Hills. I don't know the time yet, but—"

"Don't worry. We'll—" I stopped and corrected myself. "—I'll be there. You can count on it."

Chapter 3

Amy rushed down the front walk to her car. With her keys in her hand and her head bowed, she was the image of a young woman whose world had fallen apart, and one who I feared was about to fall even farther.

I pulled my phone from my skirt pocket. Dr. Conroy wasn't the only one with contacts deep inside LAPD. While I waited for someone from LAPD's Robbery-Homicide division to answer, I told Wilson to ready the Rolls.

"Put a little speed on," I said. "We don't have a lot of time."

Wilson had two vintage automobiles parked in the garage: a Rolls Royce and a classic '54 Jaguar. The Rolls was a black-and-gray Silver Wraith, like Princess Kelly had once owned, complete with leather interior and blacked-out windows. Perfect for what I had in mind.

"We need to visit the Conroy Estate," I said.

"The House that Vanity Built? In Beverly Park? Are you kidding?"

"You know it?"

"Doesn't everybody? It's been tabloid gossip for years. Maybe not so much lately, but it didn't get its name by accident. I would have loved to have gotten into one of those parties. But," Wilson sighed and fanned a hand skyward. "I was much too young back then to have made the guest list. Believe me, I would have given my ruby slippers to have even been a lowly busboy. Can you imagine? I've heard the bathrooms have gold-plated toilet seats."

Wilson's reference to Conroy's wild parties and The House

that Vanity Built didn't surprise me. Even today, city bus tours made regular stops along Mulholland Drive to point out the infamous house, a twenty-thousand-square-foot mansion that included six master suites, an indoor-outdoor pool, theater, solarium, and guest house. All of it made famous by the doctor, his wild parties with Hollywood stars, anorexic models, and monied men who came to party and believed Conroy's cosmetic empire offered a promised fountain of youth.

"No offense, Old Gal, but they're hardly going to throw open the gates for you, even if your name is Misty Dawn."

"We'll see about that, won't we? But for now, we need to hurry. Amy's gone to visit with Carlene, and if I'm right, the doctor's been up all night. With a little luck, he'll be napping when we arrive and will never know we've been there."

"Might I ask just how you intend to do that?"

"I'll explain later, Wilson. What's important is that I get inside that house to see whatever it is the police saw, and what they didn't."

In many ways, my mystic talents worked like those of a bloodhound. Timing was of the essence. The sooner I could get inside the Conroy estate to see where Jared lived, the more likely I'd pick up a scent that would help my investigation.

While Wilson readied the Rolls, I left a message for Detective Cesar Romero. The two of us had recently worked a case concerning the drowning of a Hollywood starlet. The detective—a look-alike for his Hollywood namesake—was a senior investigator with LAPD and a lonely widower. That was until I introduced him to my landlady and Wilson's sister, Denise Thorne. The two picked up immediately, as I knew they would, which elevated my relationship with the detective from professional consultant to that of friends and family, which allowed for a few favors.

"Detective. Hi, it's Misty Dawn. I need your help. I have a client who may be involved in a homicide investigation. The victim's name is Jared Conroy. Heir to the Conroy fortune. I'm sure by now you've heard." I explained how Amy, my client, had come by to tell me Jared had died at his bachelor party at a restaurant in Beverly Hills, and that his father, the renowned Dr. Elliott Conroy, had called the police and insisted on a thorough investigation. "Anyway, I need you to call. I have an uneasy feeling about Jared's death and think we should talk."

Before we left the house, I returned upstairs and grabbed a hat, a black-brimmed fedora, and one of Wilson's double-breasted jackets from his closet. The blazer fit me like a duster, a bit tight over my rounded middle, and because I was a good foot shorter than Wilson, hit midway down my long paisley skirt. The hat, with my gray hair tucked beneath the brim, provided enough of a disguise that when I looked in the mirror, I didn't recognize myself. *Not bad.*

I met Wilson in the garage. He looked at my choice of wardrobe suspiciously. "A change of persona? You think that's really necessary?"

"It is if I hope to convince people I've come from the mortuary."

"The mortuary?" Wilson snickered and slipped behind the driver's wheel. "What is it you have in mind?"

"Just drive, Wilson. In good time, if things work out, I believe you'll be impressed."

We arrived at the guardhouse, a small brick building covered with ivy, that could have easily passed as a private residence were it not for a kiosk next to it, manned by a uniformed guard.

With my hand on the steering wheel, so it would appear I was behind the wheel of the English drive Rolls, I scooted across the seat until I was sitting on Wilson's lap.

"Ugh!" Wilson groaned and pulled the Rolls forward. "Gonna half to watch all that late-night snacking, Old Gal."

I poked him in the ribs and smiled at the security guard as he leaned his head out of the kiosk.

"May I help you?" he asked.

"I'm here from Sunrise Mortuary." I used the name of a local funeral home and hoped the guard hadn't heard any different. "Dr. Conroy requested I come by to pick up a suit for his son for the viewing on Saturday."

"I see." The guard stepped back into the kiosk and checked his records.

Wilson leaned back into the seat. "You really think this is going to work?"

"It will if you hush up!"

"Why? You think he can hear me?"

"That's not possible, and you know it."

"I didn't think it was possible I'd have a woman sitting in my lap either, but—"

"I'm warning you—"

"Pardon me?" The guard returned from the kiosk.

"Sorry," I said, "I'm muttering to myself."

"I'm sorry, ma'am. I can't find any record of the doctor's call, and I can't let you into the Park without it."

"Roger, right?" I pointed to his name tag. "Perhaps he's forgotten. I'm sure he's distraught. Tragic news about his son. I assume you heard?"

"About Jared?" Roger stepped back to the kiosk. I had little doubt the guard had waved Jared through the residence's private entrance just opposite his duty shack numerous times. "Yes. Terrible loss."

"Perhaps if you ask for the housekeeper, she might be able to help. In fact—oh, for heaven's sake, I believe it was the housekeeper who called. You'll have to forgive me. I must be having a senior moment. How could I forget? She said she was calling for the doctor. Her name was Lola or Lolita. Spanish, I think."

A Spanish name was an easy guess. There wasn't a house in the park that didn't have a housekeeper and figuring the Conroy's employed a Hispanic housekeeper was hardly a long shot. As for guessing the housekeeper's first name might begin with an "L," that was a bit of a stretch. But I used a trick a lot of less-than-authentic psychics use when trying to convince someone of their connections with the spirit world. I picked an initial and went for it, knowing the guard would fix on a name and fill it in.

"You must mean Lupe," Roger said.

I blinked. "Yes, that's it. Lupe."

Roger took a step forward and studied the Rolls. His eyes combed the vehicle from the flying goddess hood ornament on the front to the trunk.

"Nice ride," he said.

I patted the open window frame. "Yes, isn't it? I'm lucky. The mortuary's owner lets me drive it for things like this. She's a beauty. Not a scratch on her, and she purrs like a pussycat."

Wilson growled, and I punched him again in the ribs.

Roger walked back around the car and gave it one final look, then slipped back into the kiosk and picked up the phone. I put my hand on Wilson's leg and tapped my fingers nervously while Roger checked out my story. Minutes seemed like hours.

Finally, Roger appeared from the kiosk. "I suppose it's fine. Lupe didn't remember the doctor saying anything about someone coming by to pick up Jared's suit, but she'd prefer not to interrupt the doctor now. He's napping." I winked at Wilson. *Told you so.* "She said she'd meet you in the courtyard. You know the way, right?"

I told Roger this was my first call to Beverly Park. He placed a sticker outside on the windshield, then took a map from within the kiosk and marked the Conroy estate with an "X."

"Straight ahead, two miles. When you reach a four-way stop, turn left. Go three blocks and take a right on Ridgecrest. Can't miss it. Driveway's about a mile long. Have a good day."

I rolled the window up so the guard couldn't see the car drive itself away.

Wilson looked over at me. "Score one for the Old Gal."

I punched his shoulder. "And you didn't think I could do it."

Chapter 4

Jaw-dropping. That's the best way to describe the Conroy mansion. The home—if one could call it that—looked like a small version of Versailles. Built to impress. White stone and red brick with tall arching windows and a gray slate roof. Under California's cloudless blue skies, the manse looked as out of place as the gilded statue of Aphrodite, the Greek Goddess of beauty, that graced the twenty-foot marble fountain in front of the home's center motor court.

Lupe, or the woman who I assumed to be Dr. Conroy's housekeeper, stood beneath the mansion's huge columned portico and waved for us to pull the car around to the side of the motor court.

"We've been getting floral deliveries all morning," she said. "I'm not sure if they're for the wedding or the memorial, but I'd prefer you not to block the entrance."

Wilson pulled the Rolls to the side of the house, and I got out. Quick as I could, lest Lupe got curious about the Rolls and came too close and realized the seat of the English drive was set too far back for a short, plump senior like myself.

"You must be Lupe." I shuffled across the gravel drive toward the front door. The woman looked to be about my age, late sixties, early seventies. Hispanic with dark, graying hair, and a pleasant round face. "The doctor told me to talk to you. My name is Annie Johnston. I'm from the mortuary."

My fictitious name for the day rolled off my tongue as easily as I extended my hand to shake hers. I wasn't about to use my own name. My plan to infiltrate the Conroy Estate was dependent upon

Lupe not knowing my real identity.

"I apologize for my intrusion," I said. "But my boss insisted I come by and pick up a suit for Jared's memorial."

The second she heard Jared's name, Lupe dropped my hand, squeezed her eyes shut and covered her mouth with a clenched fist. I had hit a nerve.

"I apologize. I didn't mean to appear insensitive. This must be a very difficult time for you."

Lupe brushed her eyes with the back of her hand. "Jared was a good man. And it's all been so sudden. One moment we were planning a wedding. Everyone here was so happy, there was so much to do and look forward to, and now—ugh! It's awful, Jared's dead, and we're planning a funeral." Lupe swallowed hard. "I've been fielding flower deliveries all morning. If you give me a moment, I'll go find a suit."

I glanced back at Wilson. He stood with his arms and legs crossed and leaned casually against the front of the Rolls, and smiled knowingly. My plan to get inside the Conroy house had hit a snag, and he knew it.

"Now what are you going to do, Old Gal?"

"Excuse me." I trailed after Lupe. "Would it be too much for me to ask for a glass of water? I've been running from place to place all morning. I forgot my water bottle. It's a little warm, and I need to take a pill." I patted my chest. "I'm afraid my heart likes to bounce around like a tennis ball if I don't take my pills regularly."

If I had eyes in the back of my head, I would have seen Wilson smile. Score two for the Old Gal. He knew full well my medical remedies amounted to nothing more than what I could grow in my garden, and my erratic heartbeat was a thinly veiled guise designed to gain access to the mansion.

"Follow me." Lupe led the way back beneath the portico and through a set of glass and wrought-iron front doors with gold-leaf filigree insets that must have been ten feet high. They opened onto a marble hallway, and soon as she shut them behind us, Wilson left my side. Like a bee to honey, he disappeared down the long hallway ahead of us.

I worried the echo of our footsteps across the marble flooring might alert the doctor to my presence, but Lupe assured me we were alone, or as alone as one might be in a house where the servants outnumbered the occupants. The doctor couldn't hear us. He was in the east wing, in his study, napping.

"Wasn't always so quiet around here," Lupe said. "But since I've been here, the doctor's wild party days with celebrities and lots of beautiful people...they're long gone."

I followed Lupe into an expansive kitchen with a twelve-foot center island that opened onto a sunroom with hanging ferns and potted palms. Lupe stopped in front of a double-wide sub-zero refrigerator and took out a bottle of water and handed it to me.

"I've coffee if you'd like," she said.

I accepted the bottle and glanced casually at my watch. "That'd be nice. I do have some time, and I have to admit, I am curious. One hears such stories."

"Hard not to. The house had quite a reputation. In its day, it was right up there with Hugh Hefner's Playboy Mansion. But that was well before I started working for the doctor."

I took a seat at the kitchen's island, and with my water bottle in hand, feigned taking a pill.

"These days it's only the doctor here in the house and a few staff. Jared lived out back in the guest house."

"Must get lonely, a big place like this with just the doctor around." I scanned the kitchen and the adjoining sunroom. The light showed brightly through the windows and danced silently through leaves of several potted palm trees and onto an empty settee. "If only the walls could talk, right?"

"I take it you've heard the rumors." Lupe took a cup from one of the kitchen cabinets and poured me some coffee. "Cream? Sugar? Or maybe something a little stronger?"

From a drawer beneath the island, Lupe pulled out a silver flask and splashed a swig of what looked like rum into her cup. I covered my own. I suspected this wasn't her first morning brew, and I planned to use it to my advantage. The poor woman had no one to share her grief with, and I sensed she would welcome a gentle ear.

"Can't avoid hearing a thing or two now and then," I said. "In the eighties, this house had quite the reputation. Sex, drugs, and rock and roll, right?"

"I wouldn't know. I don't trade in gossip. The doctor wouldn't like it if I did. But between you and me, there's still plenty of evidence around here things were wild back in the day."

I glanced back into the sunroom. Wilson had taken a seat on a small couch beneath a palm tree. And he wasn't alone. Seated next to him on the settee were two gray-haired ladies, women my age, dripping in jewels. Made up to the max, and dressed in long, jewel-colored silk robes, like goddesses. I had seen their kind before—restless spirits. A less experienced psychic might have mistaken them for ghosts, but I knew better. These were luminaries: pests identifiable by a slightly greenish tinge about their silvery-shadowed selves, and in my opinion, much less respectable than ghosts.

"Do you think the house is haunted?" I asked.

Lupe laughed. "I don't believe in ghosts. The doctor, however, he'd tell you differently. I hear him sometimes. He still talks to his dead wife. As for me, I think the doctor's only haunted by her memories and mourns her loss. Poor soul's a broken man."

"You don't believe in ghosts?"

"Do you?"

"I work in a mortuary," I lied. "Sometimes I wonder."

My eyes shifted back to Wilson and the luminaries. The three of them finger-waved and mouthed hello. I glanced back at Lupe. Did she not see the two women sitting on the settee, or had she merely chosen to ignore them?

"Besides, the doctor keeps me too busy for such nonsense." Lupe poured herself a second cup of coffee, topped it off with another jig from the flask, took a sip, then offered me a swig.

I shook my head.

"Don't mind telling you it's nice to have someone to talk to. Doctor's not much for chitchat." Lupe pushed the flask to the center of the counter and raised her cup to mine. "If you change your mind."

I raised my cup and took a sip of my coffee. Between her inebriated state and need for company, I planned to get as much information from her about Jared and the house as I could.

"How long have you worked here?" I asked.

"A couple of years. The last housekeeper didn't last. Actually, the last several housekeepers were in and out of here pretty fast. The one before me went running out of here like a madwoman. She said the doctor frightened her."

"I've heard he can be difficult." I looked down at my cup, best not let her think I was too curious.

"I've known a lot worse. But if it's stories about the doctor you're looking for, you won't hear any from my lips. Far as I'm concerned the man's a saint. It's just a matter of accepting his moods."

"You like it here then?"

Lupe took another sip of her coffee. "It's a job."

I sensed not much upset Lupe. Job security obviously trumped the doctor's mood or the fact the house was haunted. It was clear Lupe had chosen to either ignore the luminaries or was totally unaware of their presence. Which can happen. Luminaries are very specific about with whom they make contact, and how much of themselves they will allow to be seen or heard. Either way, I felt certain Lupe was hiding something about herself that might explain her loyalty to the doctor. And I felt I knew what it was.

"And a green card?" I asked.

Lupe put her cup down. The color drained from her face.

"How did you know?"

"A good guess. You wouldn't be the first housekeeper in Beverly Hills guaranteed a green card in exchange for loyalty."

Lupe sat back from the counter, her hands outstretched to her cup. "I needed a place to go to. Somewhere safe."

"You're not legal?"

"I am now. I was a schoolteacher, educated in the US. I came here on one of those student exchange programs years ago, then I went home like you're supposed to. I taught English in Guadalajara."

"Which explains why you speak so well." Lupe's English was pitch-perfect, without a trace of an accent. "But not how you ended up here, working for the doctor."

"Things happened. I needed to get out of Mexico. One of my students got himself mixed up with a cartel. I made the mistake of trying to interfere. The boy's father smuggled me across the border. If he hadn't, I'd be dead." Lupe reached for the flask and added another jig of whatever was inside to her coffee. The third or maybe fourth since we'd sat down. "Dr. Conroy employs a lot of people. One of them happened to hear of me and knew the doctor was looking for a housekeeper and put me in touch. Dr. Conroy took care of the paperwork, and here I am. And grateful to be so. I suppose you could say he made me an offer I couldn't refuse."

Or walk away from, I thought. I wanted to keep her talking. I told her I'd accepted a few offers like that myself.

Lupe grabbed her cup and held it tight between her hands. "A girl's got to do what a girl's got to do, right? Sometimes the choices aren't so easy."

"And now you can't leave. You're stuck," I said.

"Hey, I'm safe, and so far, I haven't wanted to leave. So things worked out." Lupe swallowed the last of her coffee and stood. "But enough about me. You wanted to see the place, and the doctor won't nap forever. I'd prefer he not find me chatting in the kitchen. Come with me. I'll show you around. I'll text the guard at the gate to call my cell if we get deliveries."

Parked behind the kitchen's back door was a small, red, canopied golf cart, big enough for two. Lupe told me to jump in, and with my hand on my head to keep my hat from flying off, and the other holding onto the grab rail, and Wilson balancing like a bag of clubs on the back, we took off like we were late for tee time.

With one hand on the wheel, Lupe pointed to the estate's sculpture garden—a large, peaceful-looking green expanse with a marble fountain in the center—surrounded by tall hedges and accented with Greek sculpture. Or what I thought was Greek sculpture. On closer look, as we whizzed by, I realized those marble-looking figures I thought resembled Greek goddesses, weren't Greek at all, but chiseled, life-sized copies of former Hollywood stars. Nude statues. Copies of their namesakes posed to look like the gods.

"Whoa!" I yelled at Lupe to stop the cart. "Is that—"

"Marilyn Monroe?" Lupe laughed. Directly in front of us, the star was posed as she had been for the famous shot of her above the subway grate with her skirt flying in the wind. Only here she stood naked, like a nymph, with her hands on her legs and a perpetual smile frozen on her face.

"There are twelve in all. It's the doctor's own Hall of Fame. Next to Marilyn there's Mansfield, Bardot, and Taylor. I'd stop and walk you through, but there's not time. However, you might notice the statue in the fountain." Lupe pointed toward the water feature in the center of the yard.

"Is that?"

"Steve McQueen," Lupe said. "The doctor has a rather odd sense of humor."

"Or is an equal opportunist." Wilson poked me on the shoulder. I grimaced. A reminder shades were to be neither seen nor heard by either me or anyone else while I was investigating. "Just sayin'," he said.

"Is the doctor bi-sexual?" I asked.

"Not that I'd know. But he's definitely bipolar, never know what his mood's going to be." Then directing my attention to an arched opening in the hedge, Lupe added, "There's a pathway leading from the garden through to the tennis court, pool area, and the doctor's private gardens. I won't bother showing it to you now, time being what it is, but I will show you the guest house before the doctor wakes up. I wouldn't want to risk him knowing I invited company in for the nickel tour. We'll take a shortcut past the garage. There's not much to see there."

As we zipped past the garage, I did a double take. Was it my imagination, or were my eyes playing tricks on me?

"Stop." I pointed at the trellised garden area, just beyond the garage. "What's that?"

"That?" Lupe laughed, and with her foot to the accelerator kept going. With the wind in our faces, I held tight to the grab bar and steadied myself. "Did you think you saw a spaceman?"

"I'm not sure. Did I?" I strained to look over my shoulder.

"No. That's Billy, the beekeeper. He's got his beekeeping suit on today. Must be working with his hives."

"A beekeeper?" I stared over my shoulder as Lupe pressed on toward the guest house. "Are the bees part of the doctor's new Bee-Natural product line?"

"Hardly. These here are more of a hobby. The doctor's business, the bee part of it anyway, is done in Europe. Something about European bees being better for what he needs. But bees, in general, are endangered, and the doctor, priding himself on his garden as he does, felt he needed his own hives. And Billy, well, he needed a safe place for his bees. Kind of like me, I guess. Everybody's got their secrets. But I don't ask."

While Lupe may not have wanted to ask, I sure did. My questions about the beekeeper and the doctor were just beginning to form as Lupe pulled up in front of the guest house. I was momentarily stunned by the elegance of the cottage. Similar in design to the main house, but covered in ivy and much more serene. A mood I felt more reflective of its former occupant.

"Wasn't Dr. Conroy at all concerned about Jared getting stung? I mean, with all his allergies, I'd think that might be a problem."

"For you and me, maybe. But it was never much of a concern to Jared. In fact, it was Jared who suggested Billy to the doctor.

Billy's a friend."

Lupe got out of the cart and headed to the front door of the guest house.

"For how long?" I asked.

"Jared and Billy?" Lupe paused with the key in the door. "Oh, I don't know. Billy started hanging around here about the time Jared and Amy met."

"Before or after?"

"After, I think."

"Why?"

"Just curious," I said.

"Well, there's nothing to it. In fact, I remember being in the kitchen when Jared and the doctor agreed the bees were no riskier than it might be if Jared was to go to the beach. Supposedly, the bees aren't the aggressive kind, and behind the garage, where Billy keeps them, neither the doctor nor Jared thought it'd be much of a problem. As you can see, it's a fair distance from the guest house. Must be about half a mile. Plus, Jared always carried an EpiPen with him. The doctor insisted on it."

Chapter 5

As I waited for Lupe to unlock the door to the guest house, I asked why Jared hadn't chosen to live with his father.

Lupe said she didn't ask those kinds of questions. "The doctor wouldn't like it if I did. But, a year ago when Jared came back from Europe, the guest house was empty, and Jared had it redone. I suppose he decided it was close enough without being right under his father's nose. A long time ago, there was a housekeeper who lived here with her daughter. Since then, several more, but only temporarily. Nobody long term."

"And you never wanted to move in?" I asked.

"Me? No, not at all." Lupe's response was quick and stilted. "You live with the rich, and they think they own you. Never stop asking for things or pushing for more, if you know what I mean."

I sensed a me-too history and an opportunity to bond over our life experiences. Most women my age have had something akin to work-related harassment issues.

"I hope that hasn't been a problem," I said.

Lupe may have been pushing her late sixties, but I had little doubt despite the job security the doctor offered that any unwanted advances and Lupe would have decked him.

"Not for me, it's not. I may have needed this job, but I told the doctor before I started working here I wouldn't put up with any funny business. I'd heard the rumors. I told him if he wanted me to work here, he'd have to get me a place of my own. He must have been as hard up for a housekeeper as I was for a job because he didn't put up much of a fight. I have a small apartment fifteen minutes away. Not that it matters. I'm here dawn to dusk, and these days the doctor's more bark than bite anyway. Nothing but a frail old man. Hardly much to worry about."

Lupe opened the door, and I filed in behind her with Wilson silently next to me. Inside, the house appeared to have been professionally furnished. Neutral colors. Oversized furniture. Sans any personal touches. In the living room, a large, leather sectional with geometrically shaped pillows, all earth tones—round, square, and cone-shaped—faced a stone fireplace. In front of it, a glass table with remnants from last night's party. Napkins. Paper plates. Chips. A few beer bottles, wine glasses, and a small cheese dip that looked as though it had hardly been touched. Above the mantle was a large black-and-white photo of Marilyn Monroe, hugging the lip of a pool with the tips of her fingers, her head and shoulders just above the water, as she smiled suggestively into the camera. All in all, the seductive tone of the living room, and from what I could see of the rest of the house, screamed bachelor pad.

Lupe looked around the room, pulled a crucifix from around her neck, kissed it, then crossed herself with the sign of the cross.

"God bless his soul. I still can't believe he's gone. Poor boy."

"You okay?" I asked.

"I'm fine. It's just all so sudden and unexpected." Lupe picked up several napkins from the table and stuffed them into the pockets of her apron. "I was in this very room last night. I would never have guessed it'd be the last time I would see Jared."

"You were here before the party?"

"Not before, but during. I'd come down to put fresh towels in the bath. At least that was my excuse. I always stop by to say goodnight to Jared before I leave. We have—had—a very special relationship. Jared's what made this place tolerable, made me laugh when I didn't think I could anymore. I liked him, and I wanted to see him before he left to go out for his bachelor party."

"And now, here I am," I said. "Picking up Jared's suit for his memorial. Can't be easy for you."

"Yes, but that's the way the doctor wants it. He's old-fashioned that way. He wants the funeral within three days, or close as can be. He thinks it's best for all of us, including Amy." Lupe picked up the beer bottles, stuffed them under her arms, and took them to the kitchen.

"I can't imagine what it must be like for her," I said. "Young bride-to-be like that, losing her fiancé so close to the wedding."

"More than you know." Lupe returned from the kitchen. "The police were here when I came in this morning. Don't know why. I think because the doctor's so upset. He's not making any sense. He said something about an investigation. And the two of them, Amy and the doctor, I've never seen them act so strangely."

"Did the police come down here to the guest house?" I asked.

"They did. But if they found anything, nobody told me, or I wouldn't be showing you the place."

Lupe moved quickly from the living room into the bedroom. I followed and took a seat on the bed.

"You think the doctor really believes Jared's death was murder or is he just understandably upset? In shock maybe?"

"I don't know, Dr. Conroy's a strange man." Lupe flipped on a light in the walk-in closet and began to search through Jared's clothes. "But Amy and Dr. Conroy, they had quite a row this morning. It's fine now, but I don't envy her putting up with the doctor all by herself. The man can be a handful. Very unpredictable, and now with Jared gone—well, good luck with that."

I scanned the room. Like the rest of the house, the bedroom was furnished with heavy, oversized furniture, with a black silk down comforter on the bed, a handsomely mirrored armoire, and dresser. It all felt staged, and out of sync with Amy's lighter, less sophisticated nature. And nothing, other than a single picture of Amy with Jared together on the dresser.

Lupe reappeared from the closet with a black tuxedo on a hanger. "I suppose this will have to do. Jared was going to wear it for the wedding on Sunday. Now he'll have to wear it for his memorial on Saturday instead." Lupe sighed and folded the tux over her arm.

"Come. Sit down." I patted the side of the bed. "This is upsetting you."

Lupe sat and hugged Jared's tux to her body. "It's going to take me some time. I still can't believe it. All those boys, they all seemed so happy last night. Who'd have thought today we'd be prepping for a memorial?"

"Do you recall who was here?"

I had a sense of youthful male energy in the house—young men goofing on one another. Nothing dark or ominous about their gathering, and yet, there was something about the house that didn't feel right. Something out of place. Something off.

"Just Jared's friends. He liked to call them his rat pack. He was a big fan of Sinatra." Lupe smiled. "I think they all thought they were the next generation."

"Party boys, huh?"

"I don't see how Jared could have grown up as he did and not be. In my opinion, he was more like his father than his father wants to admit. Jared's best friends were all his fraternity brothers, and you know how they party. I didn't know them all, but Raul, he was going to be Jared's best man at the wedding. He was here, and so was Billy."

"The beekeeper?"

Lupe shrugged. "Yes. Like I said, they were friends. That's the nice thing about Jared. He may have been born to money, but he wasn't a snob."

"Anyone else?" I asked.

"Matthew, Jared's cousin. He was here, too. Not that they were close, but Matthew had come by to drive over to the bachelor party with them at Mastro's. The doctor had insisted. He'd hired a party bus for them."

"Because Dr. Conroy knew they'd be drinking? Jared as well?"

Lupe exhaled. "You've heard about Jared's troubles, I'm sure. It's no secret he had a problem. The flask on the kitchen counter? It was Jared's. A gift from Raul. I found it one morning under the sink in Jared's bathroom. At first, I didn't know what to do. Who my loyalty was to, the doctor or Jared? But then I thought, the doctor's my employer, I owe it to him."

"And did you tell him?"

"I did. I thought the news would kill him. It hit him so hard he had to sit down. I told him how sorry I was, but he said I was right to tell him and not to worry about it. That it would be fine, it was probably nothing more than a slip-up. Wedding nerves, he said, but nothing we wouldn't get through."

"Was that the last you heard of it?"

"It was the only time the doctor and I discussed it. The wedding was approaching, and I put it behind me."

"Was the doctor pleased about the wedding?"

"I'd never seen him so happy. Before Jared returned from Europe, this house was like a morgue. Quiet and suffocating. It felt as though the walls were closing in on us. When Jared came home, everything changed. And when he met Amy, she breathed new life into this house."

"Happy times, huh?"

"More than happy. I probably shouldn't be saying, but it'll be public soon enough anyway—what with the press and all. Amy's pregnant."

I smiled. Not so much for the news. I already knew about Amy's condition, but because it was clear the alcohol Lupe had been tipping that morning had loosened her tongue, and it was to my advantage. Another housekeeper might not have been so forthcoming.

"Is the doctor okay with that?"

"More than okay. He kept saying they were all going to be a family again. That this was a new start, and things were going to change. The doctor insisted on family dinners. He wanted music piped throughout the house. He even started working in his garden again. And Amy? That girl's amazing. For the doctor's birthday, she baked him a cake. Homemade. Girls just don't do that anymore."

"She sounds perfect," I said. Too perfect for her own good, I thought. Carlene had chosen well. A more sophisticated girl might have been more aware she was but a pawn in a game of chess between a father and his son's desire to achieve financial independence and played along for her own selfish gain.

"We all couldn't wait for Amy to move in. She'd stay over, but she didn't want to move in until after the wedding. She was old-fashioned like that and wanted to wait until it was official." Lupe paused. I could feel she was holding something back. "I just wish…"

"Wish what?" I asked.

"I can't help but think things might have gone differently if she had moved in."

"Why?"

"Maybe Jared wouldn't have started drinking. Amy wasn't a drinker. She knew Jared couldn't handle liquor. She would have stopped him if she knew. It might have been different."

"Do you think Jared was drinking last night?"

"I can't be sure. There was a lot going on. I try to stay out of the way, but when I went into the master bath to hang the towels, I passed Matthew in the bedroom. He was standing in front of the dresser with a drink in his hand. I asked him if he needed anything, and he said no. He had just come in to use the bathroom."

"Not the hall bath?"

"No, but Matthew's family, and it wasn't my business where he was in the house. However, I was worried he might have hidden another flask for Jared."

"Did you look?"

"I didn't have time. The doorbell rang, and Matthew left. Dr. Conroy had come down to say goodnight. I could hear the doctor and Matthew in the other room, talking and laughing together. I didn't want the doctor to know I was there, so I stayed in the bath and busied myself polishing the faucet and rearranging the towels."

"Were you worried if the doctor knew you were there, he would be upset?"

"He didn't feel it proper if I got too close. He preferred I keep it professional."

"Employers," I said. "If they only knew how important that

personal touch could be to those we work with."

Lupe smiled. "Not enough of that these days."

"Don't I know it. The world's just too busy."

"Amen to that."

I smiled and touched her shoulder, convinced I had persuaded Lupe of our shared values and had earned her trust, exactly as I wanted.

"Was Jared surprised to see his father?" I asked.

"I can't be sure. I think the doctor was looking for an excuse to see if Jared was drinking. But a few moments later, they came into the bedroom, and Jared went over to the dresser and splashed some cologne on his face. Then Dr. Conroy patted him on his chest like he was checking for something."

"Like what?" I asked.

"A flask, maybe? I'm not sure."

"Did he find anything?"

"No. But then the doctor put his hand on Jared's back, and the two of them turned and looked in the mirror." Lupe pointed to a full-length mirror next to the armoire. "They looked so handsome together. Almost like they were posing for a portrait."

I stared at the mirror and noticed Wilson standing directly behind us, in front of the dresser. In his hand, he had a bottle of cologne.

I shook my head. I didn't have time to make this a learning moment and stop him from what I knew he was about to do. Shades have a tendency toward kleptomania, and there was nothing I could do about it. I had worked with Wilson long enough to know that when it came to our joint investigations, Wilson had free rein. Any problem I had while on the job I would have to take up with him later at home.

I scowled. *Don't you dare.* Wilson grinned back, his eyes locked on mine. *Watch me.* He spritzed the cologne about his head and shoulders and dabbed his neck. Then looking at me, as though he couldn't help himself, opened his jacket, slipped the bottle inside his coat pocket, and shrugged.

Lupe looked over her shoulder. The hint of Jared's cologne wafted throughout the room. I could sense she was troubled by the scent. Before she could comment, I diverted her attention.

"Did the doctor say anything else?"

"He asked Jared if he had remembered his EpiPen."

"Had he?"

"No, in fact, Jared had forgotten it."

"Where was it?"

"In his dresser. Jared kept at least two there all the time. Just in case."

"Dr. Conroy always looked out for him like that?"

"He did. In some ways, I suppose that was part of the trouble between the two. The doctor was always hovering about, second-guessing his son. Jared hated it, but the doctor never stopped. Always wanted Jared to look good and do well. Even after last night. When the cops came, the doctor asked me not to say anything about Jared's drinking. He didn't want it to get back to the media that Jared had slipped up and was drinking again. He said it didn't matter, and there was no reason to ruin his name."

Lupe's cell buzzed. She pulled the phone from an apron pocket and took the call.

"It's the guard gate. There's another flower delivery. I can't keep track of whether they're for the wedding or the memorial. Terrible, isn't it? I'm sorry, but I have to get back to the house. I don't want them to disturb the doctor. You'll have to excuse me."

Lupe stood up and started to hand me Jared's tux, then stopped. "Oh, I almost forgot Amy's ring! It's in the pocket."

I glanced back at Wilson. *I told you so.* I didn't want to miss the opportunity for him to know how accurate my prediction about Amy and her ring had been.

"I found it on the bathroom sink. Amy must have left it there after she took a shower. I gave it to Jared for safekeeping. Poor girl, her fingers have swollen so much from the pregnancy, I suspect it had become uncomfortable to wear, and she took it off and forgot it. Jared insisted I not say anything. He put it in his tux pocket. He was going to surprise her with it at the wedding on Sunday."

Lupe slipped the ring into her apron pocket. I leaned in to take the tux and hug her goodbye. The woman had been through a lot and needed a little extra hug.

"I'm sorry," Lupe said, "I'm going to have to leave you here, but there's a shortcut up the walk to the motor court in front of the big house where you parked. It's flat and shouldn't take but a minute." Lupe pointed out the bedroom window to the path outside the front door.

"Don't worry about me," I said. "I can let myself out. You go on ahead."

Chapter 6

There were times when I felt like Wilson and I had slipped into a pattern, like an old married couple. Days when there was a comfortable silence between us, and we went about our respective roles with neither of us feeling the need to speak. Then there were times when his very presence irritated me—and we bickered.

Today was one of those bickering days. Wilson had crossed a line at the Conroy guest house, and I was feeling testy. As we drove home, there was a chill between us. Wilson was tight-lipped. His hands gripped the steering wheel. I was biding my time, waiting for the right opportunity to let him have it.

I got as far as the front door then exploded.

"How dare you steal that bottle of cologne. You know the rules."

"Rules?" Wilson stepped ahead of me into the house. "There you go again, Old Gal. Muttering on about your rules. As though something terrible would happen if I broke one now and again."

I stomped into the living room. This wasn't the first time Wilson had returned home with a souvenir from one of our investigative missions. While I had tried to explain to him the importance of leaving a site untouched—if for no other reason than to not disturb evidence—he appeared not to care. After our last big case, I discovered an Emmy hidden beneath the desk. The award belonged to Zoey Chamberlain, a young actress we had been helping. I was upset he had made off with it, and even more concerned, he appeared to show no signs of remorse. I tried the old, *you-can't-take-it-with-you* line, the title from one of his favorite plays. To which he replied that he didn't believe it made much difference, particularly in the case of an actress who had so many, it would hardly be missed.

Despite his obstinance, I continued to argue my case. "They're not my rules. I don't make them up."

"Oh, that's right. They're from a much higher power." Wilson turned and made air quotes around the word as he spoke. "The universe!"

"Which," I reminded him, "could change its mind about you and your situation at any moment." I had seen shades whisked away for lesser offenses than Wilson had committed that afternoon.

"Obviously the universe isn't concerned about me, is it? I'm still here, rules or otherwise." Wilson took a seat on the wingback chair closest to the fireplace, stretched his legs out in front of him, and put his hands behind his head.

I exhaled. "Stealing, no matter what side of the veil one is on, is just plain wrong. You're a shade, and it's my job to point it out to you. You should know better."

"Well, I know this." Wilson took the cologne bottle from within his jacket and spritzed himself. "Jared's not going to miss it. Besides, I'm not the only one who brought back a souvenir today, am I?"

I turned my back and began to smooth out the wrinkles on Jared's tux. "I don't know what you're talking about."

"Oh? You'll excuse me if I say I think differently. I saw what you did when Lupe handed you Jared's tux. You may have tried to make it look like you were giving her a hug. Offering her a little emotional support. You do that so well. Always there with a hug for those in need. But, in truth, what you did was slip your hand into her pocket and take Amy's ring. Admit it. You're busted, Old Gal, I saw you!"

I sat down on the edge of the couch, took the ring from my pocket, and held it against my chest. Damn, I hated when a shade was right.

"Relax, your secret's safe with me. Lupe didn't see, and I don't count, being as I'm not mortal. So what are you planning to do with it? Sell it?"

"Please. I'm not a thief, Wilson. What I want to do is see if I can get a read off of it. Maybe learn something more about the Conroys before I give it back to Amy."

"Because you don't trust Lupe to give it back to her, right?"

"Not entirely. Lupe assumed she and Jared were the only two people who knew the ring was missing. She had no idea Amy had visited with me or that Amy had told Carlene about losing it. With Jared gone, and the doctor not exactly easy to work for, I was afraid the ring might be too tempting for her."

"May I see it?" Wilson put out his hand.

I watched as he held the ring into the light, and like a jeweler, examined it.

"Extraordinary. It's at least three karats, maybe four if you count the smaller baguettes around it. And in an art-deco platinum setting like this, definitely one of a kind. Early twentieth century, I'd say."

Wilson placed the ring back into the palm of my hand. I folded my fingers over it and held it tightly against my chest. With my eyes closed, I waited until I felt I could get a sense of the spirits that surrounded the ring. Objects, particularly jewelry worn for a long period of time, absorb the wearer's energy. What remains is like a shadow, and has a story to tell. For a fleeting second, I sensed Amy and the blush of a newly excited bride. I pushed my thoughts of her aside and invited what other spirits once attached to the ring to come closer.

When I felt I had made a connection, I opened my eyes and moved the ring from the palm of my hand to the tip of my left thumb. The ring had a complicated past. With the tips of the fingers on my right hand, I rotated the ring counterclockwise toward my body so that I might go backward in time with its history.

"The ring belonged to Jared's mother. Before that, it had been his grandmother's wedding ring." I paused. My chest felt heavy. My breathing difficult. Not an unusual sensation when in the presence of an anxious spirit. "The grandmother was a brilliant woman. High energy, but strange and impulsive. I sense she suffered from long periods of darkness, and I'm not sure they were self-imposed. Her husband found her difficult and had her institutionalized. It wasn't a happy marriage." I paused again and closed my eyes. The metal felt cool between my fingers. "It's a family heirloom, passed down from generation to generation. Dr. Conroy's father gave it to him shortly after the doctor met his bride. It was her engagement ring. Her name was—"

"Elenore." Wilson paused. "Elenore Leroy Conroy, to be exact. Eli for short. She was the face of Conroy Cosmetics, right up until her death. Ageless. And very beautiful. I was sitting with her and her friend in the solarium today."

I wondered when Wilson would get around to mentioning the women in the sunroom, but I didn't want to break my concentration. I held my hand up.

"Unfortunately, the ring didn't bring her happiness. Things started out well, but Elenore and the doctor had a rocky relationship. She didn't like to wear the ring. I feel as though it felt tight on her finger." I continued to twist the ring around the tip of my thumb. "Telling, isn't it? Amy felt the same thing. In fact, I believe Eli gave the ring back to the doctor at one point."

"Because there was another woman living with them," Wilson said.

"The woman sitting with you in the sunroom?"

"Christina Munoz, his paramour. They had a baby together. Eli may have been the face of Conroy Cosmetics, but she was never the doctor's only love."

I put the ring back in the palm of my hand and folded my fingers over it. "Conroy kept Christina and the baby close. Like a second family. I get the feeling they may have even lived with them."

"She lived in the guest house with her daughter. She was the Conroy's housekeeper. They lived together until the girl graduated high school. Christina died the following year."

I stopped reading. "And these two women, were they friendly with each other?"

"They are now," Wilson said. "However, they were quite content to say it wasn't always so."

I fisted the ring in the palm of my hand and put it in my lap. "We need to talk, Wilson. These women—"

"You mean my lady friends?"

I rolled my eyes. Under the best of circumstances, shades can be difficult. "You need to be careful. They are not ghosts. They're luminaries."

Wilson moved to the couch and sat facing me. "You mean to tell me there's a difference?"

"Quite," I said. "A luminary is more than a shade and less than a ghost."

"There's a hierarchy?"

"Yes," I said. "But for now, all you need to know is a luminary is not a ghost. In the ancient world, they were considered to be a group of dispossessed spirits who refused the laws of the universe and remained close to the veil for self-serving purposes. Though sworn to do no harm, luminaries have been known to plant thoughts in the heads of mortals and use their powers to get lesser souls to do their bidding."

"Like me?" Wilson pointed to himself. "You think I'm a lesser soul, and that I'm being used? Oh, what a delightful thought."

"There are times when you can be incorrigible. What you need to know and understand is that a luminary can be either good or evil. And in your current state as a shade, I'm not so sure you'd know the difference. But it's important you believe me when I say they may try to use you. And you need to remember, you're in a very vulnerable position." I put the ring down on the coffee table. "Did they tell you why they were here?"

Wilson shook his head. "I assume they're just having fun with the doctor. Doing what they could to torment the old man."

Chapter 7

The next morning I was still thinking about Wilson and his lady friends when I was disturbed by the sound of an impatient rapping, like a woodpecker, on my front door, followed by an even more incessant hollering.

"Misty? Misty? Are you home? I have bagels."

The voice belonged to Wilson's sister, Denise Thorne. Realtor. Wannabe actress. And psychic junky. I did regular readings for Denise in exchange for her allowing me to live in her brother's home. At the sound of his sister's voice, Wilson slammed the door to the study.

The love lost between the two siblings could fill an ocean. Wilson had made it very clear, despite his limboed-state, he preferred his sister's visits to be short, if not at all.

In a voice barely above a whisper, I put my head against the door to the study and said I'd do what I could to get rid of her. But I knew if I didn't hurry, Denise would let herself in and burst through the front door like she owned the place. Which, in reality, she did.

I managed to reach the door as she inserted her key.

"Oh, good, you're home." Denise entered talking, like she always did, and with little attention to me or the house, brushed by me and made her way to the kitchen. "A client sent these over as a thank you. Way too many for our small office. And since I was showing a house down the street, I thought I'd drop them by."

I followed behind, and as Denise unloaded the bagels onto a cake plate on the counter, I put a teakettle on the stove for hot water.

"Tea?" I sensed Denise had come for a reading.

"Not today. Cesar's taking me for a late lunch. He has something important he wants to talk with you about, so I told him I'd meet him here. We're trying out a new restaurant."

Denise gave the kitchen a quick once-over, repositioned one of the copper pots above the stove, then walked back to the dining room and swept the table with the tips of her fingers. Brushing her hands together, as though she had just completed a white-glove inspection, she moved on to the living room and stopped in front of the couch.

"Is that my brother's?" Denise pointed to Jared's tux that I had laid out so neatly.

"Wilson's? No," I said. "It belonged to a friend."

"Belonged?" she asked. "Or belongs?"

I could see Denise's mind working through a long list of possibilities.

"Just a friend," I said.

Denise fingered the silk lapel. "Expensive. I'll bet he's handsome. Are you doing a reading?"

"You know I wouldn't tell you if I were," I said.

"Humph." Denise's eyes moved from the couch to the coffee table where Wilson had left Jared's cologne. "And what about this?" Denise picked up the bottle. "Is it your friend's as well?"

"No comment." I pressed my lips together, mimicked turning a key to lock them shut, and smiled.

"I'll bet it belongs to your friend." Then holding up the bottle so that she could see the label, she read, "Naked Nectar. Not exactly cheap stuff, Misty." Like her brother, Denise was unable to resist the urge to sample the cologne and spritzed it behind her ears and wrists. "Umm, such a masculine scent, don't you think? I wonder if Cesar would like it?"

Denise held out her wrist for me to smell. Instead, I grabbed the bottle and tucked it into the pocket of my skirt.

"I'm sorry, Denise. You can't be doing that. And this," I pointed to Jared's tux. "is not something I can talk about."

"Why? Has it something to do with the case you and Cesar are working on?"

"We're not working a case, Denise."

"Well, you're doing something, or Cesar wouldn't be coming by to see you in person. And I'll bet I can guess who it is. It's got something to do with that cologne." Denise stared back at the suit, and then, as though she had suddenly put two and two together, snapped her fingers, whirled around, and pointed directly at me. "Ah, ha! I know who it is. It's Jared Conroy. His death is all over the papers. Am I right?"

"I'm sorry, Denise. I'm not talking about it." I picked the tux up and was about to hang it up in the front closet when I was interrupted by a knock on my front door.

Romero stood on the front porch, freshly shaved and showered, the hair around his collar still damp.

"Denise told me you'd be stopping by." I opened the front screen, and Romero stepped inside. His eyes, like a lost puppy, went immediately to Denise, then back to me.

"I wanted to talk with you in person, Misty. After you called yesterday, I met with the detectives who interviewed your client and her fiancé's father. I also talked briefly with the coroner. I'm afraid it doesn't look like there's much of a case there."

Denise stepped between us and shook her finger at me. "I knew it. This explains the cologne and the tux. You two don't have to use code around me. I read the papers. You're talking about Amy Hendersen and her fiancé, Jared Conroy. It's everywhere in the news. Don't deny it. He's the case you're working on. Am I right?"

My secret was out. I folded my arms across Jared's suit and took a step back.

Romero closed the door behind him and pointed to the suit in my arms. "Tell me that doesn't belong to Jared Conroy."

"I probably should have called you back yesterday, Detective, but after I hung up, I realized I had to get inside that house."

"By yourself? You didn't trust I'd get back to you?"

"I didn't feel I could wait around. And for the very reason you're telling me now: The police don't think there's a case. I suspected you'd come back to me with as much. And quite frankly, I don't agree."

"You don't?" Romero smirked.

I didn't appreciate his authoritative tone. Despite my sterling reputation with LAPD and my previous experience with Romero, the man remained on the fence as to my abilities.

"No, I don't," I said. "Call it a psychic-hunch or whatever you like, but after visiting the Conroy estate, I agree with the doctor. I don't think his son's death was accidental. Not at all. I think he was murdered."

I couldn't put my finger on how or why Jared had died, but my sense of whatever had happened to Jared had begun inside that guest house. Like a drop of black ink in clear water, the die was cast. I could feel it in my bones. Something evil had taken root there, and my mind began to swirl with the possibilities. After talking to Lupe and learning about Jared's rat pack, and their pre-party, I had at least three probable suspects. Two from Jared's so-called rat pack, Raul and Billy, and the third, Jared's not-so-distant cousin, Matthew. All of whom might have been jealous of Jared, benefited in some personal way by his death, and who I wanted to know more about.

"How about you and I have a little talk." Romero nodded to the couch, then asked Denise if she'd bring me a glass of water.

Romero waited until Denise disappeared into the kitchen.

"I don't suppose you'd like to tell me how you managed to get into the Conroy mansion? Or how it is you happen to have Jared's suit?"

"Not particularly." I focused my attention on Jared's tux in my lap and gently whisked a piece of non-existent lint from the lapel. "I consider that a trade secret. But if you would like to tell me what the coroner had to say, I might consider sharing it with you."

Romero grimaced. "It's nothing you won't hear on the news

tonight or read in the obits tomorrow morning."

"So then, tell me, Detective, what does the coroner think?"

"The report shows Jared died from anaphylactic shock, a reaction to something he either ate or was exposed to. Ultimately, whatever it was caused his heart to stop. The coroner's running more tests now to determine the exact cause, but for the time being, Jared's death is considered to be accidental."

"Could it have been as simple as a bee sting?"

"Don't know yet. The coroner told me there are all kinds of allergic reactions. Jared could have just as easily eaten something as been exposed to something topically. Whatever it is, the doctor's understandably upset, and not particularly rational. He's lashing out at anybody close to Jared. He's convinced someone wanted Jared dead, and he's demanded a thorough investigation. And the doctor, being who he is, we're looking into it."

"I assume someone from your department has talked to Jared's friends at the party?"

"Detective Williams was on call that night. He got the call from the police commissioner right after Jared died. He was at the Conroy estate all night. Interviewed both Amy and the doctor. Amy provided him with a guest list."

"And?" I didn't feel it necessary to share with Romero how upset Amy had been about that interview.

"And this morning, Williams and another detective interviewed several of Jared's friends, including his best man, Raul Santos. He was there when Jared started having trouble breathing and called 911."

"What about the EpiPen?" I asked. "Amy said Jared always had one on him."

"According to Williams, Raul said he saw Jared shoot himself with it, but it didn't seem to help. In fact, he thought Jared got worse. By the time the paramedics arrived, Jared was unconscious."

"That fast?"

"That's why Dr. Conroy's so upset. That and the fact that the paramedics appear to have lost the EpiPen. They don't recall seeing the pen. But then again, they were so busy doing CPR and getting Jared on the gurney they wouldn't have been looking for it. Between the missing EpiPen and waiting for toxicology to get back to the coroner's office with their reports, and the doctor's insistence, we can't close the case out. Not just yet, anyway. It's my thinking the coroner's initial report finding Jared died from an allergic reaction makes this a pretty open-and-shut case."

"I'm not convinced."

"No?"

Not many people ever disagreed with the detective. "I agree with the coroner that Jared may have been exposed to something he was allergic to, peanut dust from the bar maybe. But I don't believe it was accidental. In fact, I feel as though it was a deliberate act. I don't know how Jared was murdered, but I will."

"If you're trying to tell me Jared died because someone deliberately exposed him to peanut dust, I'm going to need more than a psychic's feeling to prove murder."

"And I believe I'll find that, Detective. You remember the case in the paper last year, where the young woman died after kissing her boyfriend?"

"The one where he had just eaten a peanut butter sandwich?"

"Yes, and like Jared, she was highly allergic to peanuts. The poor girl had no idea when she kissed him it would be her last kiss. And while the young man had no intention of murdering her, there is a history of such. The transference of poisons is not unusual. Have you ever heard of India's mysterious death maidens? The venomous *visha kanyas*?"

"The venomous what?" Denise put a glass of water on the coffee table in front of me, then took a seat on the chair opposite Detective Romero.

"I'm afraid I've no idea what you're talking about, Misty, but I have a feeling you're going to tell me." Romero smiled at Denise and reached across the arm of his chair to take her hand.

"Legend has it that in ancient India, there was a king who stole female babies from beautiful young women. The king's purpose was to create a generation of assassins who he would later gift to his enemies. From the time the girls were very little, he exposed them to deadly poisons—the bite of a cobra or a deadly black widow spider—until they built up a resistance. Those that lived, grew to be beyond beautiful. One look into the eyes of a death maiden and a man might be struck dead. One touch of her smooth velvet skin and his body would begin to sweat and writhe uncontrollably. And one kiss and his heart would explode within his chest. There are those who believe Alexander the Great was gifted with one such maiden and died after attempting to make love to her. Whether it's folklore or not, the theory that poison might be transferred from one to another by the mere touch of another's hand exists. And makes for a perfect murder weapon."

Romero laughed. "That's a good story, Misty, but hard to prove."

"No harder than it was for me to get inside the Conroy estate without making a scene," I said.

"Which you agreed to share with us." Denise put her hand on Romero's arm.

"I will. Just not now. However, there is one thing the two of you could do for me."

Romero glanced over at Denise then back at me. "Which is?"

"I need someone to take Jared's tux to the mortuary. They'll need it for viewing, and I don't believe that someone should be me."

"You want us to do it?" Denise asked.

"Why not? You're on your way out to lunch anyway. How hard could it be?"

Romero stood up. "Hold on, Misty. It's not that simple. I can't be seen showing up at a mortuary with the victim's suit."

"But you don't think he is a victim," I said, "And it's really not your case. You're just checking it out for me."

"Nice try, but even so, I haven't a clue which mortuary the Conroy's are using."

"Please, Detective. It's your job to find these things out. As for walking it in and leaving it with some receptionist, you can have

Denise do it for you. I'm sure she'd love to."

I stood up and handed the tux to Denise.

Denise put her arm through Romero's and drew him close to her side. "Come on. It'll be fun. Besides, I'm getting hungry for that lunch you promised me."

Chapter 8

The following morning, I meditated in the living room. With my back to the window, I let the midday sun warm my head and shoulders as I revisited the facts in my mind. Jared was dead. Amy had been a pawn, a plant by Carlene and Jared to secure his inheritance. Dr. Conroy was beyond consolation and had insisted upon an investigation. The police were biding their time, waiting for an official coroner's report to write off the entire case as nothing more than an accidental death. And I was uncomfortable, convinced the doctor was right—Jared had been murdered. But by whom?

I had three possible suspects: Raul, Billy, and Matthew, but no evidence. Furthermore, why the luminaries? Why were the doctor's late wife and his former lover still in the house? What was their mission? I doubted they had anything to do with Jared's murder. Luminaries, like ghosts, don't kill. They solicit others to do their bidding. I found it difficult to think a parent, particularly a mother, would seek to murder her own child.

My mind was swirling with possibilities when my cell phone rang. I didn't need to look at the caller ID to know it would be Amy. I had sensed an anxious energy around her all morning, and while I felt she was troubled, I didn't feel she was in any danger.

"Hello?"

"Misty, it's Amy. I wanted to remind you about Jared's memorial tomorrow. I need you there. Please, tell me you'll come."

Amy's voice was fragile and thin. I pictured her alone inside that big Conroy mansion, in a room the doctor had prepared for her, still fighting back the tears.

"You really want me there? It sounds more like a family affair. I'm not sure I belong." I didn't want to disappoint Amy, but convincing me to come was easy. Just not for the reason she thought.

"It's just—" I heard a catch in Amy's voice, the tears weren't far behind. "I don't have that many friends in town. After we talked, I felt like you understood me. Jared and I were so busy. I never had time to make friends of my own. Only Carlene and Billy."

"Billy?" Amy hadn't said anything about a Billy? "Who's Billy?"

"An old friend. It's a long story. I'll explain later, but I really need you at the memorial. Please? Ten o'clock. The Methodist church on Wilshire in Beverly Hills. Promise me you'll be there."

I promised and as I hung up the phone, closed my eyes. Amy was hiding something, maybe something of which she wasn't even conscious. The feeling, like a blanket over my head, hung heavy about me.

Wilson sat opposite me, in the wingback chair with the paper in his lap.

"Still no word from the other side on Jared?" I asked.

I had hoped that among the spirit world news of Jared's sudden passing might have sparked some chatter. Some clue I might use to prove to Detective Romero that Jared's death hadn't been accidental, but the result of something much more sinister.

"You mean other than the poor boy's officially dead? No." Wilson folded the paper and placed it back on the coffee table. "In fact, things are oddly quiet on this side of the veil."

I closed my eyes. Usually, spirits, or newly departed spirits anyway, return for a short spell after passing. Sometimes they'll even leave some kind of signal to those they've left behind to reassure them. I have seen it dozens of times. My own mother flicked the lights off and on in the room where she died when I returned to pay my final respects. It was her way of reassuring me she was still with me. The perfect signal, since she was forever yelling at me to turn off the lights. Thinking about it still brings a smile to my face.

"I find it odd that there's been no signal," I said. "Don't you?"

"Unless there's no one left behind who Jared felt needed reassuring."

"There is Amy."

"Who's to say Jared hasn't tried? Perhaps in her grief, Amy's blocking him."

"Or maybe it's more than grief," I said. "It might be she's relieved she doesn't have to marry him after all, and she's feeling guilty." I never felt Amy was truly in love. Jared had done everything he could to convince the girl he was in love with her. Travel. Gifts. But was she really in love with him? I had my doubts. "Could be she doesn't want to hear from him, or she's afraid to."

"If there's no one left for a spirit to reassure, there's no need to return. I was hardly inclined to do so for my sister."

There was a knock at the door, a familiar *rap, rap, rap,* followed by my name.

"Speaking of whom," I said.

"Again?"

I smiled.

Wilson returned to the study and slammed the door behind him.

"Oh good, you're here." Denise barged through the door with a bunch of large purple flowering chrysanthemums in her hands. She pressed past me and went directly to the dining room and placed the flowers on the table. "I thought I'd bring these by. A client sent them over. I've been sneezing all morning. Look at this, will you?"

Denise held her arms out for me to see. She had red scratchy bumps everywhere. "I've got them on my arms. My neck. My chest. I'm either coming down with something, or I'm allergic to these beauties."

I adjusted the flowers in a vase on the table and centered them so the light hit them just right.

"I made an appointment with an allergist. I have to do something. Whatever this is, it's ruining what I planned to wear tomorrow for Jared's memorial."

"You're going?" It hadn't occurred to me Denise might go.

"Of course I'm going. Cesar invited me. I'm to be his cover. He can't show up at a memorial looking like a cop, not if he's supposed to be looking for a murderer."

"I thought Detective Romero wasn't working the case and didn't think Jared was murdered."

"He doesn't, but Jared's father does and insisted LAPD keep investigating. The doctor's convinced whoever murdered Jared will show up at the memorial. You know how money talks in this town. If the doctor wants a detective, the doctor gets a detective. So Romero's going. Detective Williams asked him to help out. How about you? You going, too?" Denise asked as though Jared's memorial was going to be the big social event of the year.

"Amy insisted," I said. "She—"

"Trouble is," Denise prattled on, "I have this fabulous, frilly, little lavender number I want to wear. Scoop neck. Sleeveless. And now what am I going to do? I can't go all broken out like this. People won't want to talk to me. They'll think I'm contagious or something awful."

"It's a memorial, Denise. You really think a sundress is appropriate?"

"Why?" Denise looked at me. "What are you going to wear?"

"Really?" I gestured with my hands open and looked down at my uniform, my tie-dyed t-shirt, long skirt, and Ugg boots.

"You're missing the point, Misty. It's Jared Conroy. His memorial. Do you know what that means? The entire Conroy clan will be there, and so will Elizabeth."

"Elizabeth?"

"Ugh!" Denise tossed her head and looked at the ceiling. "For someone who used to read for some of Hollywood's biggest names, you amaze me. Elizabeth Conroy?" She looked at me, shaking her head, her hands in the air. "The doctor's sister? President of CTA?

Do I need to spell it out for you? Conroy Talent Agency? One of the largest talent agencies in the world?"

"Ahh, of course." I sat down. "And you're hoping to use Jared's memorial as an opportunity to introduce yourself?"

"Don't judge me. An actress has to seize the moment. Which, by the way, is escaping me as I speak. And if I don't hurry, I'll miss my appointment with my allergist. Cross your fingers that this, whatever it is, is nothing I can't cover with makeup. See you tomorrow."

Chapter 9

I was relieved when Wilson and I arrived at the church and saw Jared's memorial was not an open casket. Detective Romero explained that upon the coroner's release of the body to the funeral home, the doctor had decided to scrub the idea of a viewing. While the final results of tissue and blood tests were still pending, the coroner had finished with the body, and the doctor had arranged to have it cremated. The doctor felt Amy wouldn't be able to withstand the shock of seeing her fiancé laid out to rest. So, rather than an open casket at the front of the sanctuary, the altar was surrounded by large bouquets of fresh flowers and a life-sized color portrait of Jared.

The church, which I estimated to easily seat several hundred people, was standing room only. A few veiled, old Hollywood stars, former conquests of the doctor's who wouldn't dare let the sun touch their faces or want the paparazzi to take their photo, and business associates from the cosmetics world, all dressed in traditional black funeral garb, tight-lipped and unapproachable. The rest of the crowd, Jared's friends—his rat pack—were dressed in sportscoats and jeans. Most were longer-haired, some tattooed, some not, but all definitely hip, and they hung together in their own group.

Romero, Denise, and I stood in the back of the church with me on my tiptoes so that I could get a better view of the crowd. Denise had forsaken her decision to wear her fancy, frilly frock in favor of a high collar, long-sleeved black dress. A decision I felt she had made not so much because she thought it appropriate, but because of the allergic reaction she had to the flowers the day before. I couldn't help but smile as I stood next to her and noticed her incessant scratching. Sometimes the universe dishes out a little bit of poetic justice to those overly ambitious, self-absorbed souls.

Finally, just as the organ music started, I spotted Amy as she joined the doctor and several members of the Conroy family in a small, private section that had been reserved for them to the right of the nave. Amy sat next to the doctor, who I recognized from his billboard ads and magazine photos. Next to the doctor was his sister, Elizabeth; his brother, Edward; his wife, Madeline; and two adult children, Mathew and Marilyn. A complex snarl of personalities who I felt mourned more for the loss of a free Saturday morning than that of Jared's life.

Unlike the other mourners in black, Amy wore a long white organza dress and looked paler than when I had last seen her. While Dr. Conroy, despite his loss, looked as distinguished as ever with a gray goatee, and silver-framed glasses. The doctor was not nearly as handsome as his son. It was obvious Jared had his mother's good looks and bone structure.

A program prepared by the church listed less than a handful of speakers: Jared's aunt and uncle, Dr. Conroy, and Raul Santos, the young man Jared had picked to be his best man. I was struck by the fact that Amy wasn't on the list. But from the look of her, seated next to the doctor, with her head rested against his shoulder, she was in no condition to address anyone.

My eyes swept the chancel area for any sign of Jared's spirit. Why wasn't he here? The fact I didn't feel his presence affirmed my belief that Jared's death had been no accident. Spirits frequently attended their own memorials. However, if there was a sense of fear or anger among those present—like guilt—they may choose not to let their presence be known. It's only when the living were clear of their negative feelings, washed away with tears and hugs from well-wishers, that a spirit would feel safe to approach.

But I was wrong.

When Raul stood up to speak and began to talk about his

relationship to Jared, it was then I sensed that Jared might be present after all. There was a change in the room. A non-believer might have said all those bodies packed into the sanctuary on a warm summer's day had kicked up the heat, and as a result, caused the air conditioning to click on. But when Raul's notes began to flutter and took flight like butterflies, scattering to the floor in front of the pulpit, I knew this was no accident. This was Jared's signal. He was here.

Rather than pick up his scattered notes, Raul spoke from the heart. "I don't need my notes to share with you all how I felt about Jared. He was my best friend. He wasn't perfect. He had his faults, and he could get on your nerves. But, Amy, when Jared first started bringing you around, none of us could believe how perfect you were. And I don't just mean pretty, Jared dated lots of good-looking girls. But you were more than another pretty face. You made Jared a better person. You brought out a better side of him. He really loved you, Amy."

Raul paused, then pointed to one of the men in the front row. "And, Billy, you were new to our group–our rat pack–but your friendship meant a lot to Jared. He loved you, man. He loved us all."

It was the third time Billy's name had come up in connection to Jared. I made a mental note of it, then scanned the sanctuary for Carlene. Where was she? Jared's friends were all sitting together. I would have expected Carlene, one of Amy's only friends in the area, to be there. But I didn't see her anywhere.

It wasn't until the church emptied, and Detective Romero, Denise, and I were standing outside on the patio that I noticed Carlene off to the side of the church by herself. Had I not been looking for her, I wouldn't have recognized her. She was dressed in a long, black caftan and wearing a large, straw sunhat that covered most of her face and dark glasses.

I moseyed over in her direction, careful not to attract attention. "Carlene?"

"What are you doing here?" Carlene looked nervously at me,

then cast a quick glance over her shoulder.

"Amy insisted I come, and I felt I should." Sensing Carlene didn't want to be seen, I put my hand on her elbow and led her further away from the crowd, to a semi-private garden area off the patio. "Pardon my curiosity, dear, but may I ask why you weren't sitting with Amy?"

"I'm not what you might consider a friend of the family," Carlene said.

"But you and Jared were friends."

"Jared's father would disagree with you about that, and he wouldn't be at all happy to see me here today. Amy knows that."

"Knows what exactly?" I asked.

"Only that Jared and I were friends in high school, and Jared's father didn't approve. And he wouldn't like it if he saw us talking either." Carlene exhaled and looked away. Several of the mourners had begun to gather near us. Carlene looked worried they were getting too close.

I pulled her closer to me and lowered my voice. "What's going on? There's more to this, isn't there?"

"No, it's nothing. Just leave me alone." Carlene tried to back away.

I sensed a secret. Something beyond what Amy understood or what Carlene had shared with me.

I held tight to her arm and whispered. "Did you plan Jared's party?"

"Yes, but that's not what this is about. And I can't talk about it here." Carlene pulled away. "Please, don't make a scene. Let go of me."

I let go. Whatever was going on, now was not the time.

Carlene stepped away, then turned back and grabbed me by the shoulders and whispered in my ear. "I'll call. I promise. Just look after Amy, okay? I'm worried about her."

Carlene slipped through the crowd, avoiding contact with anyone, and disappeared into the parking lot. Whatever secret the girl harbored, I felt it weighed heavily on her soul. I could feel her pain within my chest as though each breath was hard to take. The girl had much to say and no one to say it to.

I was about to rejoin Denise and Detective Romero in the courtyard when someone grabbed me from behind. Before I could respond, my attacker spun me around, wrestled my wrists together, and held them tightly in front of me.

"You! You thief, you." Lupe's voice was barely above a whisper. "How dare you show up here."

Anyone noticing and not hearing Lupe's muffled words might have mistaken the action as nothing more than an embrace. Two old friends holding tight to one another in a moment of shared grief.

"Lupe, please."

"I've got you now."

I tried to free myself from her grasp. Clearly, my previously attempted disguise as a mortician's assistant had failed. Not only had I been recognized, but Lupe believed me to be a thief, a con artist who had made off with Jared's tux and Amy's engagement ring. Like a rabid dog, she was mad and wanted her pound of flesh.

"Hold on. Give me a moment, I can explain."

If Lupe could have hit me without drawing attention to herself, I knew she would have. But because of the crowd, she restrained herself.

"Please." I opened my fists, palms exposed. "I'm working with the police."

"You're what?" Lupe took a step back, my wrists still tight within her grasp.

"I'm undercover with LAPD."

"You're lying." Lupe tightened her grip. She wasn't about to be fooled twice.

"Look, the police are investigating Jared's death. I know you know that. They were at the house the night Jared died. Dr. Conroy insisted the police look into Jared's death. But so far, they haven't been able to prove anything. That's why I'm here."

Lupe released my wrists. My ruse appeared to be working.

"You really think he was murdered?" she asked.

"I do."

"That's why you were at the house? You were snooping around?" Lupe put her hand to her mouth. "Oh my God, do the police think I did it?"

"No. Of course not. Relax, nobody thinks you've done anything." I reached into my bag, found my business card, and pressed it into her hand. I wanted to move away from her before she had a chance to ask me about the ring. "Here take this. It's my number, call me. We can talk."

Lupe stared at the card. "This says you're a psychic."

"That too," I said. "Call me."

I left Lupe and wandered back through the sea of mourners in search of Detective Romero, hoping he might have seen someone or something that might reveal a clue concerning Jared's murder. I had come up empty. Jared's presence when Raul got up to speak made me wonder if perhaps I was wrong. Maybe Jared's killer wasn't here among us. Why else would Jared be here? Unless, when Raul's papers had flutters and landed on the floor in front of Billy, it had been a signal.

Billy? I scanned the crowd for the young man whose name was coming up more and more and for whom I had no answers. A man Amy claimed to be an old friend, who I suspected might be more, and whom Lupe had identified as Conroy's beekeeper. Despite the number of young men dressed in jeans and dark jackets, none appeared to be the man I was only able to get a glimpse of in the front row of the church. I would have to find another way to meet Billy, so I abandoned my search in favor of finding Amy.

I wanted to offer Amy my condolences and let her know she had my complete support. Instead, I spotted Denise. She had cornered Conroy's sister, and with arms flailing, was in the middle of what appeared to be a pitch. From the look on Elizabeth's face and her wandering eyes, it wasn't going well. Not wanting to interrupt, I backed away. As I did, I heard my name.

"Misty?" I turned around and saw Amy as she pushed through the crowd. "You came. I hoped you would."

I put my arm around Amy's thin shoulders and hugged her tight, then noticed Wilson, several feet behind her. "Where've you been?" I mouthed.

Wilson shrugged.

I narrowed my eyes. I suspected he had been off with his lady friends. It's not like we were tethered together. There was no till-death-do-us-part clause in our relationship. Still, he did work for me. And I had warned him.

I whispered in Amy's ear. "How are you doing?"

"Numb," she said, her eyes looked glassy.

I sensed she had taken something to help her through the day. "It's never easy."

"I still can't believe it. I was supposed to be married here, in this very church, and now this." Amy looked around as though she didn't recognize the church or any of the mourners, who under different circumstances would have greeted her joyously.

"Where are you staying?"

"With the doctor. He insisted, he thinks it'd be a good idea if I moved in for a while. It feels strange to be there, but everything does right now."

Wilson nudged a sharp elbow to my mid-section, as Dr. Conroy approached.

"Amy, dear, where have you been? I was worried about you. You mustn't wander off like that."

The doctor leaned onto his silver cane; his veined hands all that showed his age. His tanned face lineless. No doubt due to the wonders of the cosmetic king's empire.

Amy squeezed her eyes shut. "I'm sorry, Doctor, I didn't mean to upset you."

"Not at all." The doctor's eyes met mine. "I don't believe I know your friend." He extended his hand, and in the nanosecond it took for him to scan me head to toe, I knew I had failed his evaluation.

"Oh, this is Misty Dawn, the psychic I told you about." Then turning back to me, Amy added, "I told the doctor about our visit. How you didn't think the ring was lost."

I shook the fingertips of the doctor's hand and hoped the surprise I felt hadn't registered on my face. Last we had spoken, Amy said she was too afraid to say anything to anyone about the ring. I had been left with the idea that the only people who knew the ring was missing were Jared, Amy, Carlene, myself, and, after my visit to the Conroy Estate, Lupe.

"I shared that you thought my ring was just missing, and I needn't worry," Amy said.

The doctor dropped my hand. "I do hope you're right, Ms. Dawn. Amy's been terribly upset about it. It'd be a shame to lose such a valuable heirloom at a time like this. But let's not worry about that now."

"Elliott?" From behind the doctor, Madeline, the doctor's sister-in-law approached. Trim, with a short blonde bob, and deep tan that could only come from hours in the sun, she grabbed the doctor's arm. "We need to be going. Elizabeth is waiting with the car."

"In a moment, Maddie." The doctor looked annoyed, gave me one final look, a curt nod of the head, then slipped his hand beneath Amy's elbow. "Shall we? You know how Elizabeth hates to be kept waiting, and you do need your rest."

Amy kissed my cheek. "Thank you for coming, Misty. I'll call. Later."

The doctor pulled Amy away from me and handed her off to Maddie like he might a piece of baggage, and waited until the two of them were out of earshot.

"Let me make myself very clear, Ms. Dawn. Amy doesn't need the advice of some fortune teller. If she calls again, tell her you're busy. You understand?"

Chapter 10

I was upset. Whether it was Dr. Conroy's dismissive attitude or that Wilson had slipped my bounds and disappeared for much of the ceremony, I wasn't sure. I settled myself into the passenger seat of Wilson's vintage Jaguar, unable to hold my tongue and lashed out.

"I don't like that man," I yelled to Wilson, my voiced buffeted by the Jag's angry roar. "There's something off about him. I find him—"

"What? Controlling?" Wilson's response smacked of sarcasm. "You think he might be a tad-bit overprotective?"

I dismissed the remark, and with the flick of my hand, sank further into my seat. Maybe I was a bit controlling, but it was for his own good. "I don't want to talk about it."

"You sure?" Wilson gripped the wheel and sailed through a yellow light. Our second in as many blocks.

I grabbed the canvas handgrip above my seat and shouted over the noise of the motor. "Protective is one thing, Wilson. Convincing Amy she needs to stay with the doctor is another."

"Do you hear yourself?"

And there we were, back to bickering. Wilson acting smug, implying my own actions weren't much different than those of the doctor. And me, trying to keep my human feelings for Wilson in check with my psychic-self who knew better.

"Are we going to argue about this?" I asked.

"We already are." Wilson smiled.

"Fine, I'm not your keeper. You're perfectly free to come and go as you like. You always have been. But I'll warn you, your lady friends, those luminaries you've befriended, don't have your best interest at heart."

"That's what this is about? You're worried about them?"

"Concerned," I said.

"You needn't be. Do you honestly think I don't know my way around a few wily women?" Wilson shifted the car from second into third gear, and I fell back against the seat.

We traveled on in silence. Or as silent as one can be strapped into a vintage roadster with a fearless shade at the wheel. Wilson was right. I was going to have to make peace with the fact he was a free agent. I could only hope he'd be careful.

Finally, I said, "The problem is, unlike you, I don't believe Amy has free will. She's much too vulnerable. The doctor's trying to convince her that she's incapable of making it on her own. And under the current circumstances, I'm afraid she'll believe him."

"You think he intends to keep her there?" Wilson asked. "Like he did his wife and paramour, trapped behind the walls of the house that vanity built?"

"I don't know, but he did tell Amy and Jared that having a baby would be like starting over again. A whole new family."

Wilson glanced into the rearview mirror. His expression darkened. "Did you invite anyone from the memorial to follow us back home?"

"No, why?"

I was about to turn around, but Wilson put his hand on my arm. His eyes focused on the rearview mirror. "Because, Old Gal, we've got company. We're being followed."

"By who?" I couldn't imagine why anyone would follow us. Lupe had my card. If she wanted to talk, all she had to do was call. As for Carlene, for the time being, I felt the girl wanted as much space between us as possible. Amy had left with the doctor, who made it very clear he wanted Amy to have nothing more to do with me.

"I don't know. But I'm not about to let whoever it is ride my bumper. Any closer, and he's going to clip us."

Wilson put his foot to the floorboard, and, like a flag that had just been dropped at Le Mans, we took off down the boulevard. Ahead of us, a car had come to a stop. Wilson veered left, just missing the car's bumper, and into on-coming traffic. With one hand on the dashboard, I glanced behind us. A small gray sedan was glued to our fender.

"Game on, fella. Let's see how good you are." Wilson's eyes narrowed at the rearview mirror. In a quick defensive move, he took a sharp left, cut the corner, and swung the Jag wildly up LaCienega Boulevard.

The sedan stuck with us like a mad hornet.

"Hang on!" With both hands on the wheel, Wilson took a hard right onto Fountain Avenue, laid rubber down the narrow street, and then pulled left on Laurel Canyon Boulevard. Just in time to beat the red light, we sailed across Sunset Boulevard and up the canyon road.

"Got you!" Wilson smiled into the rearview mirror.

For the moment, we were safe. I sighed as we entered the canyon, then caught my breath. Ahead, a long line of cars worked their way up onto the mountain. Sloth speed. Bumper to bumper. We were stuck. I glanced back over my shoulder—the light behind us about to change.

"Maybe not," I said.

Wilson's eyes clicked back to the review mirror. "Hold on tight."

With my hand pressed against the dashboard for balance, I glanced back. Whoever was following us had jumped the light, and within seconds was gaining on us.

Wilson yanked the steering wheel to the left. Suddenly the Jag was straddling the center lane, dodging cars in either direction.

At what felt like warp speed, Wilson took a wicked right. I slammed into the passenger door and held onto the grab strap, my body curled into a fetal position. With one eye open, I watched as Wilson weaved the Jag up a series of narrow, twisted streets with stilt-houses overlooking hundred-foot drops to the valley floor below.

"It's you or me, baby." Wilson pressed his foot to the floorboard again.

I peeked back over the seat. Whoever was in the car behind us, his intent was clear. One of us wasn't coming off this mountain alive. I looked ahead. No escape. And then, I couldn't believe my eyes. Ahead, on a street barely passable for one car, was a slow-moving trash truck.

Wilson was about to play chicken.

"No!" I yelled.

With his hand on top of my head, Wilson pushed me down into the seat. I closed my eyes. I felt the Jag veer right. All sense of gravity escaped me. Were we falling, or had we somehow miraculously scraped by the truck, escaping a thousand-foot fall?

"Eat them bananas," Wilson stopped the Jag momentarily and looked back in the rearview mirror.

Still shaking, I peered back through the Jag's ragtop vinyl window at the trash truck. With its big lift arms in the air, it dumped a can full of garbage into its bed, some of it falling into the street, blocking all access to the road behind us. The gray sedan, stuck like a pig in a pen, was unable to move forward.

Wilson started slowly back down the mountainside, toward Ventura Boulevard and home. For now, we were safe.

Or so I thought.

As we pulled in the driveway at home, Wilson kept his hand on the gearshift, his foot still on the brake.

"What's wrong?" I asked.

"He's back." Wilson pulled the key from the ignition. "And it's too late to lose him now."

The small, gray sedan slowed to pass the house. Honked. Then sped away.

"That's it," I said. "I'm calling Detective Romero." I slammed the car door and huffed my way across the yard, back to the house.

* * *

Romero and Denise arrived within minutes.

I opened the door and grabbed Bossypants before she could escape into the streets. The cat's natural instincts had picked up on my jangled nerves, and with her warm body next to mine, her soft purr began to settle my heart's rapid beating, as I paced the room.

"I don't understand what's happening, Detective." I exhaled deeply and scratched behind the calico's ears. "Someone followed me home from Jared's memorial and tried to run me off the road."

Denise insisted I sit down on the couch, and volunteered to make tea. Wilson, who I had expected to retreat to the study, stood with one elbow on the mantle. Both of us curious about the mystery driver who had followed us home.

Romero sat in one of the wingback chairs. "You're sure it was someone from the memorial, and not someone else?"

"Someone else?" The question was preposterous. "What do mean someone else? Who else could it be?" I couldn't believe Romero might think it was some random stranger who had followed me home, intent on running me off the side of the mountain for no apparent reason.

Romero's eyes shifted to the floor.

"Go on, Detective, tell me."

"I'm sorry, Misty, but you drive like a little old lady."

Thump!

Wilson pushed a candlestick from the mantle. I pinched my eyes shut and opened them as Bossypants jumped from my lap and scurried across the room and back to the study.

Romero looked at me, and I shrugged as though nothing had happened.

"You've got a lead foot. Half the time, I doubt you even see what's around you. Maybe you accidentally cut someone off in traffic. Truthfully, at your age, you probably shouldn't even be driving."

"My age! Cut someone off? Me?" I scowled at Wilson.

"It could have been anyone. Were you able to get a license plate?"

"No. We, I mean, I was driving. How could I possibly get a number?"

"Could have been a former client. Maybe someone who was unhappy with your work spotted you and wanted to scare you."

"I don't have unhappy clients. Not like that, I don't."

That wasn't 100 percent honest. Every psychic has someone who's not happy with their work. Over the years, I had a few situations, experiences with people close to my clients who felt I had talked their loved ones out of a relationship. Something I couldn't possibly do, but those unfamiliar with psychic powers frequently believed we had more power than we do.

"You're sure?" Romero raised a brow.

"Of course I'm sure. This was someone from the memorial. I know it. You must have seen something or someone at the memorial that caused you to pause. That was the purpose of your being there, wasn't it? To check for a murderer?"

Romero picked up the candlestick and replaced it on the mantel. Wilson put his hand behind it, ready to give it another shove. I shot Wilson a warning look and shook my head.

"It's not that easy. As I told you before, the coroner's not convinced Jared's death was anything but accidental. And, if it weren't for the fact that Dr. Conroy is as insistent and as close to the department as he is, I wouldn't have been there today, and we would have closed out this investigation and moved on."

Denise returned from the kitchen with a cup of tea for me.

"That may be, Detective, and for reasons you may never understand, I believe that's what our killer wants you to think. But whoever followed me home wasn't just some random driver with a bad case of road rage. I'm certain he, or she for that matter, was at the memorial and is concerned I might be getting too close to something."

Romero stood up. "I'm sorry, Misty. If it makes you feel any safer, I can have a car swing by tonight. Make sure things look okay in the neighborhood. You have my number. If you need anything, call."

"Thank you." I picked up my tea. "If you don't mind, you and Denise can let yourself out. I'm feeling a little spent."

After the door closed, I leaned back into the fainting couch, my hand to my head, my mind full of the day's activities, our harrowing ride home through the canyon, and a growing list of possible suspects.

Wilson interrupted my meditative state.

"It's four now is it?"

I opened an eye. Wilson stood at the mantel, the candlestick in his hand. "Are you reading my mind?"

I knew full well he had.

"It's not hard, Old Gal. You're thinking the killer's either Jared's best man, Raul. Or maybe it's Billy, the beekeeper. Of course, there's always Matthew Conroy, the doctor's nephew. Or after this afternoon, you're wondering if perhaps it's Madeline Conroy. You thought she was overly close to the doctor."

"All possibilities," I said.

"But something else troubles you?"

"And what might you think that is?"

"Amy. The fact she hadn't shared with you about her relationship with Billy. You're concerned about it. And you're wondering if you're not the only one who didn't know about it. Or if it might be some type of trap."

"Now, you' re not only beginning to think like a little old lady, but you're also beginning to sound like one."

Wilson put the candlestick back on the mantle.

"You could have gone all afternoon without saying that."

"I could," I said. I closed my eyes and put my head back down on the couch. Wilson was changing. A year ago, he wouldn't have been as sensitive to my remarks.

"If you'll excuse me, I'll leave you now to your reverie."

Wilson disappeared into the study and slammed the door behind him.

I smiled. Shades could be so thin-skinned.

Chapter 11

I didn't sleep well Saturday night. I lay in bed while pictures flashed through my mind like an old-fashioned black-and-white movie, with screenshots of the gray sedan chasing us through the canyon. I felt vulnerable, like a target. More than once, I thought I heard the sound of a car outside. A door opened. Footsteps. Someone on the porch. Was it my imagination? The wind in the trees? A branch brushing against the house perhaps, or maybe a premonition? I went to the window several times, but each time, I could see nothing. No parked car. No mysterious shadows. Wilson, who I rationalized would rouse me if someone were trying to break in, remained silent in the study. I assured myself the advantages of a live-in spirit guide trumped any home security device. Few intruders could match the energies of an angry ghost, particularly one like Wilson, who was so protective of his personal property. Even so, I reached under the bed, where I kept my trusty Louisville Slugger and hugged the bat to my chest until sleep finally overtook me.

It was close to ten by the time I woke, hours later than my usual time. Anxious to get back into my routine and dismissive of my late-night terrors, I dressed and hurried down the stairs. I was on the couch, reading the paper when Wilson appeared from the foyer with the cat in his arms.

"Sleep well?"

"As well as can be expected," I said.

In the light of day, my fear seemed to have evaporated. Perhaps Romero had been correct. Maybe Wilson had cut someone off, and the crazed driver, being what drivers are in LA, had reacted poorly and wanted to frighten us. No point in harboring fears for which I had no evidence.

"Anything interesting in the paper?" Wilson sauntered into the room, paused at the window, and glanced outside. For the moment, I wondered if he was checking for the gray sedan.

I was about to close the paper when my eye caught a headline on the front page of the business section: "Cosmetics King Names Nephew VP."

"Maybe," I said.

Wilson settled himself on the couch and with the cat in his lap began to stroke her. "Now that is news. Read on. I can't wait to hear."

"Dr. Elliott Conroy, founder of Conroy Cosmetics, announced late Friday afternoon he had named his nephew, Matthew Conroy, as the company's new incoming vice president. The announcement was not unexpected. The recent death of Jared Conroy, the doctor's only son and sole heir, had left investors anxious for Conroy to name a successor to the long-held family business. Sources close to the doctor, who asked not to be identified, claim in-house fighting among members of the board had reached an all-time high. Dr. Conroy said, 'I feel as though my hand has been forced to make this appointment prematurely, but I abide by the board's decision and look forward to working with my nephew, Matthew, in his new position.'"

The article went on, but I paused.

Undisclosed sources? I wondered if on a board made up primarily of family members if that undisclosed source might be Madeline Conroy, Matthew's mother. In my mind's eye, the picture of Matthew standing in front of the dresser in Jared's bedroom seemed more than a coincidence. Had Matthew planted something to cause Jared's allergic reaction? Replaced his EpiPen with one that wasn't working? Was it possible Madeline and her son were working together to wrest control of Conroy Cosmetics and force the doctor out?

Wilson stood up and paced the room, the cat, purring contentedly, still in his arms. "I wonder how long that's been in the works?"

"Good question," I said. I was about to return to the article when we heard a knock at the door.

"You expecting someone?" Wilson put Bossypants down and peeked out the window.

I glanced at the old grandfather clock in the entry. The hands showed it was precisely 10:59. Despite my restless night's concern about the man in the gray sedan, I had the distinct feeling someone close to me was about to reach out for further consultation—a feeling I frequently have when in the midst of a case.

"I am," I said.

I looked up at the clock and waited for the big hand to hit the top of the hour, listened for the chime, then promptly answered the door.

Carlene entered as far as the entry, her arms wrapped tightly across her midsection, as though she were trying to hold herself together.

"I promised myself I wasn't going to come today, but Amy called last night, and—"

"You couldn't help yourself." I pointed to the couch.

"I'm concerned." Carlene sat down. "Dr. Conroy insisted Amy stay with him. He's not allowing her to leave."

From behind me, I heard Wilson. "Here he goes again, keeping his women behind those hallowed gates."

I raised a brow. "She did mention to me she was staying there. But I'm not surprised." From the way Conroy had hoarded over Amy at Jared's memorial, I knew the doctor had no intention of letting Amy out of his sight.

"You have to do something, Misty. Amy can't stay there. Not now. Not without Jared. Not ever."

"Why not?" I glanced at Wilson. Carlene wasn't just rattled; she was frightened. "Does it have something to do with why you weren't sitting with Amy at the memorial yesterday? Or why you were in such a rush to leave before anyone noticed you?"

Carlene exhaled. "It's a long story."

"I have time, and if you like, I could make a pot of tea. I haven't had any myself this morning, and it might help to settle your nerves."

"No." Carlene shook her head. "I don't need anything. I just need to talk. I've never told anyone what I'm about to tell you. If I did, I'm afraid it could come back to haunt me."

"Does this have anything to do with Jared?" I asked.

"I didn't kill him if that's what you're thinking."

"Ahh," Wilson looked up to the ceiling. "Here it comes. The girl's been schtupping Amy's fiancé."

What? I winced. Carlene thought I was reacting to her statement. Wilson looked at me like I didn't know what he was talking about.

"You know, fooling around? Doing the dirty." Wilson gestured with his hands.

I shook the vision from my head. In no way did I feel that was the case.

"What is it then? What's haunting you that's driven you back to my doorstep?"

"I wasn't a hundred percent honest with you or with Amy about how I knew Jared. I told her we had been buddies in high school, but—"

"It was more than that, wasn't it?"

Carlene closed her eyes. "Jared wasn't just a friend. He was my—"

"Brother," I said. The vision of two toddlers playing together hadn't fully formed in my head before the words had escaped my mouth.

"Whoa, I didn't see that coming." Wilson sat down.

"My real name's not Carlene Muller. It's Carlita. Carlita Munoz." She pronounced it perfectly with a Hispanic accent. An accent she had managed to hide from me. "I'm the daughter of Christina Munoz, Dr. Conroy's former housekeeper." Carlene went on to explain that her mother had lived in the guest house, and she and Jared had grown up together, like best friends. "It wasn't until I graduated high school and went away to college that things changed."

Carlene put her hand to her head. The memory was painful. I could feel a deep stabbing in my heart.

"Your mother died," I said.

"It was right before Christmas. Dr. Conroy called and told me my mother had an accident. She had fallen while stringing holiday lights and broke her neck. She died instantly. He invited me home for the funeral, but after that, he told me it would be best if I didn't come back. Ever. That I didn't belong there. That's when I got curious about my father and why he never came to visit. All those years and never once did I hear from him. I decided to do one of those DNA tests, and—"

"You found out your real father was Dr. Conroy." The vision of the doctor's secret family hidden behind the estate's gate was coming together. "Did you ask him about it?"

"When I told him I had found out, he got angry. He said I was nothing but a big mistake. He accused me of trying to blackmail him. Told me there was nothing I could do about it, and if I tried, I'd be sorry."

I locked eyes with Wilson. "That had to be tough."

"It's not like I had any illusions about the doctor being a great father. He was verbally abusive to Jared. It's no wonder Jared was an alcoholic. I remember, when I was little, there used to be these big family parties on the estate with the Conroy's—the doctor's sister, Elizabeth, his brother, Edward, and his wife Madeline and their kids. The only one I really remember was Matthew. The doctor always seemed to favor him. I never could understand why, but looking back on it, it's odd."

Carlene paused.

"Because?" I asked.

"I don't know. I've often wondered if maybe I weren't the only illegitimate child. Maybe Matthew might be Dr. Conroy's too.

Anyway, to give you an example of just who the doctor was, for Jared's fifth birthday, the doctor hired somebody to come give pony rides in the backyard. Jared hated horses, he was afraid of them, but Matthew was all excited. The two of them were each on a pony, riding around in a circle, and Jared fell off and started to cry. The doctor called him a big sissy right in front of everybody, and Jared ran inside the house and wouldn't come out again. Some party."

"Was it always like that?"

"Pretty much. There weren't a lot of good times between Jared and his father. Far as I can remember, Jared grew up angry with the doctor. He never wanted to go to work for him. He hated the business. He didn't want anything to do with it, but his father insisted. I think that's one of the reasons Jared started drinking. And then there was the accident."

"When he drove his father's Maserati off a cliff in Malibu?"

"It was front-page news everywhere. And after the accident, Dr. Conroy sent Jared to Europe to rehab."

"Why Europe?" I asked. "There're lots of rehab centers here."

"I don't know. Europe was always the doctor's playground. Growing up, I remember he'd be gone for months at a time. It's where the company has all its research facilities. I guess Dr. Conroy thought it was the best place. But Eli didn't."

"Jared's mother?"

Carlene nodded. "Sending Jared away like that, after nearly losing him in the accident, put her over the edge. After she died, I remember reading about it in the papers. They said she took her own life, but I never believed that."

"You think the doctor had anything to do with it?"

"I wouldn't dare say if I did. But I always thought if maybe I'd stayed in touch with Eli, things might have been different. Unfortunately, it was a whole part of my life I couldn't go back to. My mother was dead, and Dr. Conroy had made it very clear I never come back. I had no idea if Eli ever knew about Dr. Conroy and my mother, but by then, the past was the past, and I didn't think I should try."

Bossy jumped into my lap, and I stroked her. "And as far as you know, Dr. Conroy had no idea you and Jared were still in touch, or that you had planned Jared's bachelor party?"

"No way. If he did, he would have done something to make sure I wasn't in the picture. The doctor thought Jared's old friends were a bad influence. He blamed them for Jared's drinking, and forbid them to ever come to the house. The only friend he ever permitted Jared to stay in touch with was Raul, and that was only because Raul's father owned some land Dr. Conroy wanted to buy, and he gave him a seat on the board of Conroy Cosmetics with the rest of the Conroys."

"What about Jared's cousin Matthew, were they close?"

"They tolerated each other. They weren't at all alike, and Matthew's name wasn't on the guestlist. Amy, Jared, and I put it together for the party."

"And Amy, she has no idea about your past relationship with Jared?"

"Jared didn't want her to know. He told her the doctor didn't like him staying in touch with his old high school buddies, and that it would just be easier if Amy never mentioned anything about me to the doctor."

"Even though you had changed your name?"

"Why risk it, right? Far as Amy knew, Jared didn't want her to mention anything about his friends to the doctor, and she didn't."

"I'm curious, after your mother died, why didn't you reach out to Jared? He would have been off to college, out from under his father. Didn't you ever try to reconnect?"

"By then, Jared was in his own world, and I didn't trust the doctor wouldn't find out if I did reach out. It wasn't until I accidentally ran into him in Beverly Hills that we started talking."

"And did you tell him about his father then?" I asked.

"Not at first. I mean, those weren't exactly the first words out of my mouth, but it did come up."

"Was he surprised?"

"I suppose you could say he was more angry than surprised.

He said things between himself and the doctor—that's what Jared called his father—were as frosty as ever. After Jared came back from Europe, he moved into the guest house, but what he wanted to do was move out and get as far away from his father as he could. But without access to his trust fund, he didn't have many options. The rich, you know, they're hobbled by their money. Without it, they don't know how to function, and the doctor had threatened to cut Jared off unless he went along with his conditions."

"Which were?"

Carlene counted on her fingers. "Stay sober. Settle down. And go to work for the company. If he could do that, by the time Jared turned thirty-one, he'd come into enough money he would never have a worry about anything again."

"So, you came up with a plan."

"I prefer to think Jared and I came up with an answer. I'd just met Amy a couple of weeks before. She was new to the city. Didn't know anyone, and she was perfect. The doctor wouldn't know anything about her, and I knew Jared would like her. I mean, look at her. What's not to like? The girl's like vanilla ice cream."

"And for this, you got a finder's fee?"

"Jared offered me fifty-thousand dollars."

"That's a lot of money."

"I would have had more if I were able to inherit, but since I couldn't, I agreed. Jared said if Amy worked out, and he collected his trust fund, he'd find a way to set the record straight. That's how Jared was. He was a decent guy, and he played fair."

"And what about Amy? Was he playing fair with her?"

"Initially, all Jared needed to do was convince his father he'd changed. Marry Amy and then somewhere down the line, he planned to tell Amy it wasn't working out. Only—"

"Only what?"

"Only Jared fell in love. For real."

"And the doctor?"

"Jared said he loved her too. Amy changed things inside that house. So much so the doctor and Jared started to get along. And when the doctor learned Amy was pregnant, Jared said he'd never seen the doctor act so paternal. That it was like they were all starting over again. It was a fresh start for them all."

"And after Jared died, did you try to talk to the police?"

"What could I say? That Amy was a setup? I don't need them checking into my background. I didn't kill Jared. If the police told the doctor about me, that'd put me right back in his crosshairs. Besides, since when was it a crime to set someone up?"

Crack!

Bossy jumped from my lap.

Suddenly, the pane glass window behind the couch shattered. A rock sailed through the window, and just as quickly, Wilson shot from his seat. With one hand he caught the rock like a baseball, diverting a trajectory that surely would have hit me, then sprang to the window. Outside, the sound of tires squealed. My eyes followed Wilson. He looked back at me and dropped the rock.

"The gray sedan," he said.

I put my hand on Carlene's knee. "Are you okay?"

With her eyes wide, Carlene responded. "I'm fine. What was that?"

"A warning," I said. "Did you tell anyone you were coming here today?"

"No, nobody. But that rock—" Carlene pointed to the rock on the floor. Her eyes from me and back to the rock. "It stopped mid-air. Did you do that?"

I shook my head. "I'm sure you're wrong, but whoever threw that rock intended it to be a message. I think it best you leave, and I wouldn't mention to anyone about your visit here today. I promise you I won't and that your secret's safe with me."

I hustled Carlene to the door. I wasn't sure if I was more concerned about the rock or that Wilson had interfered, something a shade must never do. His actions had put his future in peril, and his time with me in question. While I was thankful the rock hadn't hit me, I had a mess on my hands. In front of me, shards of glass had scattered, like pieces of a puzzle I needed to put back together.

Chapter 12

I called Detective Romero immediately after Carlene left. He came by, surveyed the window, noticed I had patched it neatly with a piece of cardboard and masking tape, and packaged up the rock. He said he doubted his forensics team would find any prints, but it was worth a try and promised to increase patrols in the area.

I didn't hold out much hope.

Meanwhile, things on both sides of the veil had grown quiet. Too quiet. Wilson had yet to make contact with Jared, and Amy, who had promised to call, had yet to reach out to me.

By Monday, I was beyond impatient. The police investigation, which I knew was little more than a babysitting assignment designed to make Dr. Conroy happy, had produced nothing. The thoughts in my head had grown to include a cast of potential suspects along with a voice screaming at me like the headlines of a supermarket tabloid. "Jared Conroy Murdered!" In theory, I agreed with the doctor; Jared's death was no accident. The question was, who killed him, and why? I tried to focus on Jared's last night, surrounded by his friends, including Raul and Billy, and his cousin Matthew, all growing possibilities, but still no proof. The only other person of interest, at least to me anyway, was Madeline Conroy. Like the others, however, I had no evidence, no smoking gun.

Finally, I decided it was time I prompted Wilson. I found him in the study sitting by the window with Bossypants, purring like a lioness, in his lap.

Ahem. I stirred my throat. "Sorry to disturb you, but you need to try harder. You have to make contact with Jared. Time in a murder investigation is of the essence."

Wilson's hand came to rest on Bossy's back. "You think I'm lollygagging?"

I walked over to Wilson's desk. On top, his notebook computer was open to a Wikipedia page about The House that Vanity Built, with pictures of Dr. Conroy and his wife Eli in the corner.

"What I think," I said, "is that your past proclivities, your nosy-need-to-know-how-the-other-half-lives, has caught up with you." In life, Wilson had been a notorious busybody, part and parcel of what made him a successful stage designer. He knew all the particulars of how the rich and famous lived. How they dressed. Spoke. What they liked and didn't like. And now, as a shade, with carte blanche to wander through the homes of people like the Conroys, the temptation to dally among their personal effects was too much. "It's awfully easy to slip. Old habits die hard."

"What are you trying to do, guilt me?" Wilson strode across the room with the cat in his arms and slammed the notebook shut.

"Is that what you think I'm doing? Trying to bore into your conscience and guilt you into action?" I whipped the cat from Wilson's arms. Rather than nestle against me, Bossy sprang from my hands and disappeared beneath the stairs. In my angst for information, I had repelled my own cat. I had nobody to blame but myself. I was full of worry about the man in the gray sedan and frustrated with the lack of information Wilson had revealed to me. Animals, like spirits, flee negative emotions. Bossy's reaction reminded me that fear or anger would cause a spirit to retreat. Rendering the most powerful of spirits inert or unable to respond in the presence of such negativity. No wonder Wilson hadn't heard from Jared.

I had my own answer. I put my hand on top of Wilson's notepad.

"It's guilt, Wilson. That's why Jared hasn't made his presence known."

"His or someone else's?" Wilson asked.

"I'm not sure." I paced the room. In order for a spirit to

communicate with a mortal, there had to be trust, and Jared had every reason not to trust those closest to him. I paused at the window and tapped my finger against my lips. "However, I do believe we're about to find out."

"Another psychic prediction?" Wilson held his hands up and shook them.

"More like a caller," I said. Outside Amy was coming up the walk. My heart quickened. "And I do believe she has something to share with us, something you may find helpful."

I took five deep cleansing breaths, a trick I used to clear myself of my negative emotion, and answered the door.

Amy looked better than I had expected. Her shoulder-length, blonde hair was neatly combed, parted in the middle, and she had put on makeup to brighten her cheeks. She was wearing a mid-length yellow summer shift that camouflaged her barely-there baby bump. A dress I suspected she had planned to wear on her honeymoon. The color was good for her.

"I'm so glad you're home. May I come in?"

"By all means," I said. "I've been expecting you."

Wilson slipped from behind me and into the living room. Bossypants, forever the curious calico, was at his heels.

"You have a cat?" Amy went directly to the couch, and Bossy jumped into her lap.

"She must have been hiding when you were here last," I said. "She's not always so welcoming of strangers."

Amy snuggled Bossypants to her cheek and stroked her. "I love cats. I guess you could say I'm a cat person." Bossypants pressed her head against Amy and purred while Amy scratched her ears. "I would have come yesterday, but I couldn't get away."

"How's it going?" I asked.

"Okay, I guess. A lot's happened since the memorial. The doctor offered to let me live in the guest house after the baby's born." Wilson and I exchanged a knowing look. "He's even changing Jared's trust fund and naming the baby as the beneficiary."

"That's good news," I said. I measured my words carefully. Based on my conversation with Carlene, I was suspect of the doctor's motives. I didn't want to appear surprised or least of all shocked.

"Of course, Dr. Conroy will be the executor until the baby's old enough to inherit. But if he dies before then, the doctor's named me as executrix. And he's planning to give me a monthly allowance. He said the mother of his grandchild shouldn't be scraping by, trying to make ends meet as a single mom working as a barista."

"That's very generous of him," I said.

"I guess, but then, Jared always said the doctor could be a very unpredictable man." Amy looked down and stroked the cat. "It's just—"

"What?" I leaned forward and put my hand on Amy's knee. There was more she wasn't telling me.

"I don't know. I just never expected any of this. In a way, I feel guilty."

And there it was. Guilt. My eyes met Wilson's. Guilt not only blocked Jared from reaching out to Amy, but also stifled Amy's ability to share with Jared her own grief and truth. The one constant that would have allowed them both to move on.

I ventured forward. "Because you didn't want to marry him?"

Amy's hands froze on Bossy's back, and her eyes began to fill with tears. "How did you know?"

"Lots of brides have doubts." I handed her a tissue. "It's not unusual. When you told me you'd misplaced the ring, I suspected it was more than just bridal jitters."

"I'm so confused. It all happened so fast. Jared, the baby, and now this." The cat jumped from Amy's lap and scampered back into the study. "Billy thinks I need time to absorb everything that's happened. I'm still spinning from the shock of it all."

"Billy?" I sat back and put my hands in my lap. Billy was definitely more than a friend.

"He was my boyfriend all through junior high and high school." Amy sniffed and dabbed her eyes. "I never dated anyone else. After my mother died, things fell apart. I wanted to leave, move to LA, and take acting lessons. Billy's from Carp, he's homegrown. He was never going to leave. When I did, I broke his heart."

"He followed you here?"

"He came into Starbucks one day and told me he wanted to get back together. That he'd do anything. But by then, I had met Jared, and it was too late."

"And Billy couldn't compare."

"Strange, that's exactly what Billy said. Anyway, I introduced him to Carlene, and they started to get along. Before I knew it, we were a foursome. Carlene and Billy. Jared and me. Doing things together. It felt nice. I told Jared all about Billy and our past. It was fine, and Jared wasn't worried, he wasn't the jealous type. When he learned Billy was a beekeeper, he invited him up to the house to meet his father. The doctor had been complaining bees were threatened, and his garden was suffering. I mean, who knew, right? It just all worked out. Dr. Conroy liked Billy, and before I knew it, the doctor asked Billy to move a couple of his hives onto the property, and everybody was getting along."

"That had to be nice for you," I said. "Since you were so new to the area and all alone."

Wilson put his hands across his heart. "Poor baby."

"It was nice," Amy said. "I mean it was a little strange, Billy being so close and all, but he understood I was in love with Jared and supported me."

"He sounds like a good friend."

I glanced back at Wilson and wondered if we had the same thought. Was Billy more than a friend? Perhaps a vengeful lover in disguise, waiting for the right opportunity to win back Amy's love? Wilson shrugged. No help there. I tabled my thoughts of Billy. Until I could speak with him, I'd have no idea. I turned my attention back to Amy.

"Amy, there's something I need to talk with you about. I wanted to call you to tell you to come by, but I knew I didn't need to. I sensed you'd be here."

"Really?" her eyes brightened.

"Yes, you see, I've had a bit of luck, and it concerns you."

Amy's brow furrowed. She had no idea what I was about to tell her.

"Lupe found your ring."

"The housekeeper? But how...how do you know Lupe?"

"I met her the other day," I said.

"At the memorial?"

I nodded.

Wilson crossed his arms and waited. No doubt curious how I planned to explain how I had tricked Lupe into letting me into the Conroy mansion for Jared's suit. I saw no need for an explanation, and instead, I went with a reasonable facsimile of the truth—or as close as I felt I could get—and hoped for the best.

"I told her I was a psychic, and that you had come to me about your ring. She got very excited. She said she didn't really believe in psychics, but if you did, that might be an answer to her problem." I paused and reached into my skirt pocket. "She found it in the guest house in the bathroom. She had given it back to Jared for safekeeping, and—"

"And she gave it to you?"

"She was afraid the ring might cause a problem between you and the doctor if he knew you'd misplaced it. She said she's been waiting for the right time to return it to you."

Amy reached for the ring, her hands trembling.

"I can't believe it."

"Jared planned to give it to you at the altar." I put the ring in the palm of her hand and squeezed it shut.

"I don't know, Misty." Amy held the palm of her hand to her heart. "Something about it doesn't feel right."

"Jared wanted you to have it."

"It's just I feel awful about Jared. I didn't want him to die, but you're right, I didn't want to get married. I was pregnant with Jared's baby, and I didn't know how to get out of it."

I wiped a tear from Amy's face. "You don't have to feel awful. Jared's death isn't your fault. And you don't have to wear the ring if you don't want to, but you should find a safe place to keep it."

Amy stood and hugged me. "Maybe I'll put it away for a while. I need to think about it. But first, I have to go back to my apartment and get some clothes. Dr. Conroy's expecting me back at the house this afternoon."

I walked Amy to the door.

"Whatever you decide, dear, it's entirely up to you. But it might be best if you didn't mention to the doctor that you came to see me today. I sensed when you introduced us that he wasn't a fan." I saw no reason to tell Amy the doctor had stated as much before leaving me at the memorial. "As for the ring, a word of caution: If the doctor were to learn Lupe had found the ring, and didn't tell him, she's afraid it would jeopardize her position. If you say anything at all, perhaps it might be better if you said you found the ring yourself. That with the pregnancy your fingers had swollen, and you'd taken it off and misplaced it."

"I understand." Amy hugged me goodbye. "And don't worry, I know he can be difficult, but I think he means well."

I closed the door.

Wilson slipped up behind me. "That's what you mean by guilt, is it? Why Jared's not making himself available to us, because he feels guilty about using Amy to secure his trust fund."

"Partially," I said. "The other half of that is Amy wouldn't be open to his visitation. She blames herself for getting pregnant and not wanting to marry Jared. I believe today is the first time she admitted it."

"Meanwhile, all this time, Carlene and Jared have been duping Amy into a marriage of convenience. And she had no idea."

"She wouldn't be the first person to be blindsided by the bling of Hollywood."

I felt my cell buzz, and I took the phone from my skirt. I didn't recognize the number, but the caller's voice, that perfect English with only the slightest trace of a Mexican accent, was all too familiar.

"Misty, it's Lupe. I need you to come by the house right away. The doctor and Amy are out, and you and I need to talk. I'll tell the guard at the gate to expect you."

Chapter 13

Lupe was standing beneath the portico of the Conroy mansion when Wilson and I arrived. As we entered the motor court, she pointed at a place for us to park around the side of the house, next to a bright red Tesla.

"Go on inside. I won't be a minute, I've got business to attend to in the garden. I'll meet you in the kitchen."

Wilson and I got as far as the door to the kitchen when I noticed a half-finished cup of coffee on the counter, along with the flask from which I knew she had sweetened her drink. While the kitchen appeared empty, I knew better. Sitting in the sunroom at a small café table with a deck of playing cards between them, were Wilson's lady friends, his luminaries, Eli Conroy, and her housekeeper, Christina Munoz.

"Ah, look who's back. That handsome young shade." Eli finished dealing out the cards then slapped the remaining deck on the table between them.

"And he's brought his psychic charge with him. How charming," Christina said.

"Yes, isn't she?" Eli picked up her cards, fanned them in front of her overly made-up face, and flashed me a pasted smile. "Quite a piece of work as well, don't you think?"

I'd never been called out by a spirit, particularly in such a demeaning fashion. I had to fight my instinct to respond. Any reaction on my part—anger, frustration, or heaven forbid, the green-eyed monster of jealousy that I felt creeping about me, the result of my overprotective nature concerning Wilson—would have interrupted my ability to communicate. I took a deep breath and reminded myself to keep my emotions in check. These two were nothing but pesky luminaries. Temporary beings, whose only interest was in themselves and whatever else they could get from those around them.

Wilson intervened. "Misty's a classic from the sixties. Peace beads and all. Got to love her. She means no harm."

Eli folded her cards. "I suppose you're here to see Jared. Well, you're out of luck, sweetheart. He's not here, and I doubt he ever intends to be. Poor boy spent his life wanting to escape this place and his father and finally has. Sorry to disappoint, but you won't find him here."

I took a step forward. Eli's condescending attitude wouldn't defeat me.

"I didn't expect to," I said. "You, on the other hand, I'm more curious about."

"Why?" Eli returned her attention to her cards. "You think it odd the doctor's wife and his former mistress have taken up residence? I assume your shade explained our *situation?*"

"He did mention something," I said.

"Then you have to understand, Jared hated it here. His father made his life miserable. In the end, he was more interested in his freedom than settling any score with the man. And now he has that. Bless his heart."

The fact Eli hadn't mentioned anything about Jared's impending marriage, Amy, or his sudden death didn't come as much of a surprise. Luminaries can only focus on themselves. Their self-centeredness makes it impossible for them to be concerned about anything that happened after their *being.* Everything beyond the expiration of their mortal existence was considered inconsequential. Beneath their bother. I smiled to myself. Knowledge was power, and despite their presence in the house, I felt as though the cards were stacked in my favor.

"And you?" I asked. "You weren't interested in leaving all this behind?" I gestured with my hand to the room around me. "This house with all its history—the rumors about your drinking, the jealous rages, the doctor's numerous affairs—you had no desire to escape it?"

Eli discarded a Jack of Spades. "On the contrary, it's what keeps me here. Christina and I, we never felt things were entirely finished between the doctor and ourselves. And we can't leave until they are."

"Can't or won't?" I asked.

Eli laughed. "I suppose that's up for interpretation."

"But, if you insist upon knowing, we're here until we've settled things with the doctor." Christina picked up the Jack of Spades and reshuffled the cards in her hands.

"How is it you intend to do that?" I glanced back at Wilson, straddled backward on a Windsor chair, his eyes tracking our conversation like a tennis match.

"That all depends." Eli reshuffled her cards. "As I'm sure you know, we're not capable of doing much more than creating, shall we say, an irritant."

"Such a shame." Christina shook her head.

"The fact is, we're hardly able to inflict any bodily harm—"

"Although," Christina interrupted, "we are able to create a few minor situations where that might be an issue."

"Like what?" I asked.

Eli snickered and nodded to the window.

Outside, I could see Lupe talking with a handyman. She pointed to the doctor's private garden and looked upset. At the same moment, I noticed Madeline Conroy, dressed in a short tennis skirt, her racket in her hand, powerwalking up the path toward a gate leading to the motor court.

"Are you referring to the doctor's sister-in-law or the handyman?" I asked.

"That old battle-ax?" Eli tsked. "Any more time in the sun and she'd be shoe leather. We needn't bother with her. She has her own issues with the doctor and does quite well with them. No, look again. The handyman he's here for the gophers. You can't imagine how problematic they can be."

"Or how easily influenced they are," Christina added.

"Would you believe, this is the third time this month that wretched handyman's been summoned. Those nasty little rodents keep digging up the doctor's garden. Poor Elliott, he twisted his ankle in a hole last month. Hate to see that happen again, but those dear rodents, they just keep coming back." Eli covered her mouth with the cards and fluttered her lashes.

"And bird droppings. You can't forget the bird droppings. They're my favorite." Christina leaned forward and tapped her long index finger on the deck of cards and waited for Eli to make her play. "Particularly when they land on the doctor's new Bentley. He left the top down last week. Do you know what bird feces can do to fine Italian leather?"

Eli drew a card from the deck, and with a quick smile, discarded the King of Hearts, then placed her cards on the table. "Gin! I believe I've won. Again."

I noticed a luminous green halo-like hue about the two as they picked up their cards, and like schoolgirls who had pranked their teacher, giggled.

"And what about Amy?" I asked. "Now that she's moved in, won't that be a problem for you?"

Neither answered. Instead, their eyes slid from me to the back door. We were no longer alone.

Lupe walked in and stomped her feet on the kitchen floor. "Are you talking to yourself?"

"No." I scowled in the direction of the luminaries. "But I swear, sitting here all alone in this big house, I hear voices."

Eli and Christina shrugged and returned to their cards.

"It's the Santa Anas. The wind plays tricks with you this time of year. Howls like a wild animal sometimes, a baby's cry the next. You should know that if you're from here. Makes you think you see and hear things that don't exist." Lupe walked to the kitchen counter, reached for the flask, and sweetened what was left of her coffee. "You want some?"

I shook my head.

"You ask me that's what got the doctor talking to himself. Some may say the man's got a guilty conscience. Me, I think it's just the wind driving him a little crazy."

"You don't think he's done anything to be guilty of?" I asked.

Lupe put her cup down on the counter. "There are those who think his wife didn't die by her own hand. But all that's in the past and none of my business. What I think is the doctor's stressed. That he misses his wife and people talk. Nothing but tongue-wagging by people with nothing better to do."

From the solarium, Eli chuckled. "God forbid anyone ever do anything more than talk."

Christina sniggled.

Eli put her finger to her lips and smiled at me.

My gaze slid back to Lupe.

"Heaven knows the man isn't easy." Lupe picked up her drink, swirled what was left in the cup, then gulped it down. "Probably never was. Genius is like that."

"I suppose," I said.

"Yes, well, I didn't invite you up here to talk about the doctor. If you're interested in the doctor's past, you'll have to find that out on your own. Not from me. What I want to know is what you were really doing here the other day? And don't tell me you're a cop. I don't believe you. You're with border patrol, aren't you? You're an ICE agent. Admit it. You're here to deport me."

"What?" Of all the things I thought Lupe might ask, the last thing I imagined was that she would think I was an ICE Agent.

"Either that or you're working with the cartel. You've found me after all these years, and you're here to drag me back to Mexico."

"Wai—wai—wait a minute." I raised my hands above my head. "You've got this all wrong, Lupe. I don't know anything about any cartel, and I'm certainly not some ICE agent here to check on your immigration status. I came here the other day because of Amy."

"Right. And your name is Misty Dawn. And your card says you're a psychic. I'm sorry, but I don't believe you."

I sat down at the counter. I couldn't blame Lupe for doubting me. I had deceived her, not once but twice, and gaining her trust wasn't going to be easy.

"You've every right to wonder," I said. "But the truth is, Amy came to me for my help. She was upset over Jared's death. I thought if I could get inside the house, I could get a read on it. See if there were any uncomfortable spirits about that might shed some light on what happened."

I glanced back in the direction of the sunroom, where Wilson sat with his two lady friends. The three of them watching me talk with Lupe like we were some hot new talk show. They smiled and shrugged innocently. Clearly, neither Eli nor Christina had made any attempt to interact with Lupe and had no intention of bothering her. I turned back to Lupe.

"Well, as you can see, there are no spirits in this house, uncomfortable or otherwise. It's all nonsense," Lupe said.

"Maybe so," I said. "But on Saturday, when I saw you at the memorial, I wasn't lying to you. I'm not a cop, but I have worked with LAPD, and I was working with them then. A detective and I were there to check out the crowd."

Lupe picked up the flask and poured herself another drink. "Then why did you steal Amy's ring? And don't tell me you didn't, because I know you did."

I reached across the counter for the flask. I don't ordinarily drink, but now seemed like a good time, particularly with what I was about to tell her. I grabbed a wine glass from the rack above my head and emptied what remained of the brown liquid in the flask into it.

"I didn't trust you'd give it back to her, and I knew I would."

"You thought I'd take it?" Lupe put her hand on her heart and sat down.

"I knew you were tempted, and I don't blame you. You're in an awkward position here with the doctor. You don't dare leave him. Not voluntarily anyway. If you did, you're afraid he'd report you for entering the country illegally, and you'd be deported back to

Mexico. You can tell me differently, but I know your truth. You've nightmares about being discovered."

Lupe crossed herself. "You have to understand, the doctor saved my life, and for that, I'm forever thankful. You won't hear any different from me, no matter how difficult he can be. But, please, whatever you do, promise me you won't say anything."

"I don't plan to. I'm not interested in anyone but Jared. What I need to know is more about his friends, his rat pack. Who they are and how often they were here."

"I can't really say. Most nights, I leave here about eight p.m. If Jared had friends up to the house, it was after I left. During the day, sometimes I'd see Billy. He was in and out with the bees. And, of course, Raul, Jared's best man. I always thought Raul had a thing for Amy and was looking for an excuse to hang out so he could be around her."

"A thing?"

"You know, a crush. He couldn't keep his eyes off her."

I made a mental note. Raul wouldn't be the first best man guilty of lusting after a groom's fiancée. But I knew there wasn't room for Raul in Amy's heart.

"What about Jared's cousin, Matthew?" I asked. "Did he hang out here as well?"

"Not so much. Sometimes he'd come by with his mother to play tennis. She's here a couple of days a week. Works out with her coach or sometimes just hits balls."

"The doctor play?"

"Not anymore. But from time-to-time, when Madeline's done, she stops by with Matthew, and they visit with the doctor on the veranda, and I'll fix them iced tea."

"She doesn't rush off to work?"

"Work? I doubt the doctor's sister ever had a job."

"She doesn't have anything to do with the company?"

"Other than to represent them at various charity functions? No. I don't think so. She's more of a social butterfly."

I thought back to the Red Tesla I had seen parked in the motor court.

"That her car out front, the Tesla?"

"I wouldn't know. She changes cars like some women change clothes. Always drives a different car."

I laughed. "The rich and famous, huh?"

"They can afford to live differently." Lupe took another sip from her cup, and I raised my glass to her.

"How about Billy? Is he around today?"

"I saw him out back when I was talking with the gardener. He's planning on moving his hives. He said he didn't think he could stay around any longer. He feels awful about Jared and what happened. I think he blames himself."

"Why?"

"You don't know?"

"Know what?" I asked.

"Some psychic you are. The coroner called the doctor this morning. The tests he ran came back positive for bee venom. The doctor told Billy, and now Billy's packing up. Can't say as I blame him."

"I need to talk to Billy," I said. "Hail me if the doctor comes back, will you? I don't think it'd be good for you if he knew you'd let me in."

"You're probably right."

"I'm sure I am," I said.

"So we're good then? You're not going to tell the doctor about the ring—"

"Or bust you with ICE or anybody else," I said.

"Good, then I'll call Roger at the guard shack. We're friends. I'll ask him to let me know when the doctor drives through the gate."

Chapter 14

I left Wilson in the house with his lady friends and asked Lupe if I might borrow the golf cart. My arthritic knees weren't up to hiking the entire estate in search of Billy. Lupe acquiesced, so long as I promised to return the cart in good shape. I assured her it wouldn't be a problem, and with a quick wink to Wilson, added, "I've been told I drive like a little old lady. You'll hardly have to worry."

The golf cart had more spunk than I anticipated. My foot had barely hit the pedal when it took off like a baby bird on its first flight. I held tight to the wheel, and like a drunken sailor, nearly rolled the cart as I turned away from the big house. With the wind in my hair, I zigged and zagged down the path, past the guest house, and onward toward the garage.

Billy was in the drive, loading his truck. When he saw me and realized I wasn't Lupe, he dropped his tool belt into the truck's flatbed and headed for the garage.

"Billy?" I shouted.

He stopped and turned back to me. "Do I know you?"

I parked the cart and shuffled toward the truck. "I'm a friend of Amy's. I thought we should talk."

This was the first time I'd seen Billy close up. Beneath a healthy head of hair, he appeared to be a sweet-faced, gentle-natured young man.

"Amy came to visit me a couple of days ago. My name's Misty Dawn."

I waited to see if there was a response. If perhaps my name might trigger a reaction. I saw none, just a confused look and a sense of angst that buzzed around him with more flurry than the bees in the hives in the yard next to us.

"Lupe told me you're leaving."

"Yeah, what's it to you?" Billy walked back to the garage and returned with a shovel and a rake and tossed them into the truck's bed.

"Seems a little sudden, that's all. Everything okay?"

"No, it's not okay, not at all. The doctor told me this morning the coroner called. He said after the coroner completed the autopsy, he ran some skin tests, and the results had come back from the lab. They found bee venom on Jared's neck and face, a small amount, but enough to trigger a reaction."

"And you're feeling guilty. Thinking maybe you're to blame."

Billy jerked his head back. The realization I had read his mind unsettled him.

"Yeah, well, I was with Jared when it happened, so who else could it be? I got stung that morning. A couple of bees got inside my mask, and I had an open bite on my neck. I cleaned it up, but evidently not enough. Must have been me who exposed him."

I closed my eyes. I could see the scene in my mind's eye: a thin, nearly invisible veil of bee venom on Jared's neck, and his reaction. A physical manifestation I could feel within my own body. A clamminess. A tightness about my chest and throat, followed by a shortness of breath, and itching. Jared's exposure to the bee venom had been so subtle it had killed him without any outward sign of the attack or the attacker. Like death by the Visha Kanya. But I doubted that attacker had been Billy. There may have been bee venom on Jared's neck, but the idea that Billy had accidentally exposed Jared to bee venom from an open sore just didn't fit. Billy would have been too careful in treating the wound, and the likelihood of any bee venom remaining on his neck from that morning would have been highly unusual, if not almost impossible. The venom from a sting would have been internal, not external. Like a magnet that repels, the picture of Billy as Jared's murderer just wouldn't come together. Something was missing.

"You're leaving because Jared died, and you're afraid everyone will blame you?" I asked.

"I don't think the doctor's going to want me around. Kind of a sore reminder, don't you think?"

I could feel Billy's pain. The overwhelming sense of guilt he had done something to cause Jared's sudden death.

"Have you told Amy?"

"What? That I'm leaving?" Billy rested his hands on the rim of the truck bed. "I don't imagine she's thinking about me right now."

"I think you're wrong about that. I'm a psychic. Amy came to me because she was confused. She thought she had lost something, and she wanted me to help her find it. I think you know what it is."

Billy's jaw tightened. "I don't know what you're talking about."

"Amy doesn't know it, at least not consciously, but she was afraid if she married Jared, she'd lose you."

"What are you talking about?"

"She's confused, and she needed to talk to someone. The two of you have a history together, and I don't believe it's finished."

Billy backed away from the truck.

"You still care for her, Billy. It's written all over your face."

"Look, I never did anything to come between Amy and Jared. We've known each other since we were kids, and Amy was happy. So I was happy for her, okay?"

"Are you telling me, or are you telling yourself?"

"Hey, it's not like I could compete. Take a look around. This place is a palace, and Amy was about to be the queen. What have I got? A truck and a couple of angry beehives."

"I think you underestimate Amy. I don't believe she's all that materialistic. The city can be overwhelming, especially for someone who's not familiar with all the trimmings. It's easy to get a little distracted. When she moved here, she'd just lost her mother. It's understandable, don't you think she might feel a little lost?"

"She told you that?"

"Some of it. Some I pull from those I talk to. That is if they're open to being read."

"You trying to pull something from me?"

"Only if you'll allow me to."

"Well, I'm not into that. I don't believe in psychics, and I don't have time to waste." Billy walked back into the garage and returned with a toolbox.

I glanced back at the hives. "What about bees, you going to take them too?"

"I'll come back for them later, but for now, I'm outta here."

Billy tossed the toolbox into the truck bed and turned to open the cab door. As he did, the box flipped open and fell onto its side. He reached back into the truck bed to close it, but before he could, several tools fell out, along with a small, cylinder-shaped tube.

His eyes met mine.

"Is that an EpiPen?" I asked.

"Yeah. So what?" Billy picked up the pen and stuffed it back into the box with the other tools. "The doctor gave it to me a couple of weeks ago. Told me he wanted me to have it, just in case. I guess you would say he had a premonition. Too bad I didn't have it with me the night of Jared's party. Maybe it could have made a difference."

"But Jared had one," I said. "I know because the police spoke with everyone who was at the party."

"Yeah, that's right. The cops spoke to me too and a couple of the other guys as well. We all saw Jared use it, but it didn't work. If it had, he'd probably still be here." Billy picked up the toolbox and put it on the passenger seat inside the truck's cab. "Look, lady, I'm sorry, I need to go."

I backed away from the truck. "If you need to talk to me, Amy's got my number."

"Don't hold your breath." Billy got in the truck and slammed the door.

I returned the golf cart to the house, where Lupe stood outside the back door, anxiously waiting for me. The doctor had come home, but because the Rolls had been parked to the side of the house, he hadn't noticed it. Lupe wasn't taking any chances. She wanted me out and pointed to a gate alongside the house and told me to leave, quickly as possible.

When I got back to the Rolls, Wilson was sitting behind the wheel, playing with a ladybug. The creature had flown through the open window and landed on his hand. Wilson watched it as it gently crawled along his index finger, and then as though the ladybug knew it was time to go, took flight and escaped the car.

For the moment, Wilson appeared lost in thought.

"Are you okay?" I asked.

"Do you think it's really possible to communicate with animals, to get them to do your bidding, like Eli and Christina claim?"

"I assume you're speaking about the gophers and the holes in the doctor's garden?"

Wilson looked over at me as he put the car in gear. "And the bird doo-doo on the doctor's car. Can luminaries really do that?"

"Easily," I said.

I shared with him a story that forever changed my life. Years ago, when I had first come to California, I lived in a hippy commune. At the time, my friends and I were searching for peace, love, and a connectivity between ourselves and the universe. I was committed to finding that connection, and as will happen, where we place our energies, results will follow. For me, it was a news story about a giant sea turtle that had rescued a woman who had been shipwrecked in the Philippines. She had been sailing with friends and washed overboard. Just when she was about to give up hope—fearing the worst was about to happen—this giant turtle appeared from beneath the depths below. She grabbed hold of its shell, and for two days, the turtle towed her on his back. Never once did the turtle dive for food, which would have been its natural instinct. Instead, it swam with her, clinging to his shell, until a ship headed into port, spotted her, and tossed her a life preserver. Only when the woman was safely aboard, did the turtle swim away. From that day on, I felt certain there was a connection between our world and the animal kingdom, and the veil that separates us from this world and the next.

"I don't know what spirit communicated with the turtle and directed it to save her, or why. But I knew if I honed my talents, I might be able to better understand that connectivity between my mortal world and the next. I've made it my mission to do so."

"And have you," Wilson asked, "learned to communicate with animals?"

"It's not as easy for mortals. Even for me. There's a gravity on this side of the veil that holds us from accepting the energy that exists among all living things. Birds. Bees. Even flowers and trees. Everything's connected. Ancient cultures believed it. The early Indians in this country believe it. But today the world is full of skeptics, and there's so much noise, it's hard to tap into. Your lady friends, however, understand it all too well. And while they can't tap into that energy to create anything more than a nuisance, they are able to persuade those creatures with whom they come in contact to do what comes naturally."

"Is it something I could learn?"

"When you're ready, yes. It's the next level for you. It would mean you're advancing, moving onward. But I would hope you'd use it for good and not evil. How you use it would be very decisive for your future."

"You mean instead of selfishly communicating with gophers and requesting they dig holes or instruct pigeons to poop on windshields and Italian leather?"

"Exactly," I said.

Chapter 15

Detective Romero arrived just as I was about to sit down to dinner. Not that I was surprised. I needed to chat with him, especially after I'd seen the EpiPen in Billy's truck. It would have been illegal for me not to call and let Detective Romero know about the EpiPen since I knew they were looking for one. Not that I was convinced Billy was hiding it or that he was responsible for Jared's death. But because if I didn't, I might later be accused of aiding and abetting a potential suspect.

However, I wasn't in any hurry to reach out to the detective. I knew he would call me. I could feel it in my bones. He had news, an update I expected, and a convenient excuse to stop by. So instead of calling him, I busied myself and made a fresh pot of tomato soup with an assortment of heirloom tomatoes from my garden and garnished it with a sprig of wild rosemary. I had just sat down to wait when my front bell rang. Soon as I opened the door and got a whiff of the detective's cologne, I knew I wasn't the sole purpose of his visit.

"On your way to dinner?" I asked.

Romero stepped inside. "How did you know?"

"Really, Detective? You have to ask?" I shut the door behind him and shuffled back to the kitchen with the detective behind me.

For all practical purposes, Romero was a reluctant believer, one I considered to be on the cusp. Content only if I could provide him with the type of evidence he could drag into court before a judge and jury.

"Denise wants to try a new restaurant tonight. A French place,

The Petit Trois, down on the boulevard." Romero went directly to the stove and lifted the top off the soup pot. "I thought I'd stop by on the way to pick her up and say hello."

"Nonsense." I slapped Romero's hand with the back of a wooden spoon. "You're here because you're either concerned about my mysterious visitor in the gray sedan, or you have an update on our case. Which is it, Detective?"

Romero replaced the lid on the pot. "Neither. In fact, I'm not convinced whoever followed you home the other day was someone from Jared's memorial. And forensics didn't find any prints on the rock. It's more likely a disgruntled client or someone in the neighborhood who doesn't like psychics. After all, you are new here." Romero rubbed his hands together. "As for our case, I'm sorry to disappoint you, but there's not much there. The coroner found traces of bee venom on Jared's neck and face, but rather than anything malicious, he's convinced Jared had an allergic reaction from the cologne he used the night of his party. The doctor, however, doesn't think so. He says that's impossible. That the cologne Jared always used was from Conroy's venom-free line. Either way, the coroner doesn't believe Jared's death was a homicide. As a result, close as Dr. Conroy is to the department, LAPD's pulling back. The doctor's not happy about it, but what are you going to do? There's not enough manpower to chase a case just because someone thinks things just don't feel right."

Feel right? I sensed the detective's comment was a jab at me. I sat down and took a sip of my soup, then slammed the soup spoon down on the table.

"I don't suppose you'd be interested in knowing what I've been up to? Or what doesn't *feel right* to me about the case?"

Before Romero could answer, Wilson entered the kitchen with Bossypants behind him. Bossy jumped up on the counter, and Wilson, who was still wounded from the detective's previous comment concerning my—or his—driving like a little old lady, began to bat the copper pots above my head with the flat of his hand. I stifled a laugh, stood up, and grabbed the cat in one hand while I steadied the pans above my head with the other. From the startled look on Romero's face, I could see he was questioning whether the pots had swung as a result of the cat's quick movement or if perhaps I had done something to cause the disruption. Rather than entertain an excuse, I sat back down and smiled innocently.

The detective grunted. "All right then, Misty, tell me, what have you been up to that makes you think—excuse me, feel—that Jared's death was anything more than accidental? And don't tell me it's because you've summoned his spirit and spoken to him."

Wilson softly tapped one of the pots again. The hollow sound, barely audible, like that of a wood chime. Romero's eyes flashed quickly back to the pots overhead then snapped back at me. *Was I playing games?*

I shook my head. Sometimes Wilson could make things so difficult.

"You don't need to worry. You'll be happy to know Jared's been unavailable to me. He has no intention of making contact with those he's left behind. All the same, I have spoken to several of his mortal friends. Persons more to your liking. In fact, Carlene Muller, Amy's best friend, came by to visit me Sunday morning."

"Carlene Muller?" Romero's brow wrinkled. "I don't recall anyone with that name on the list of Jared's friends the police talked to."

"I'm not surprised. Carlene was more of a secret friend. She was the one who introduced Amy to Jared. Neither she nor Jared or Amy, for that matter, wanted anyone within the Conroy clan to know about their relationship." I put Bossy on the floor and turned my attention back to my soup.

"Because?" Romero pulled up a chair opposite me and sat down.

Information, like hot soup, is best dished out slowly. I took a sip of my soup and smacked my lips. "Umm. Not quite right, needs a little more salt."

"Oh, for heaven's sake, Misty, tell the man." Wilson stood behind us, his hand back on the frypan.

I narrowed my eyes.

"Because her real name isn't Carlene Muller at all. It's Carlita Munoz. She's Dr. Conroy's illegitimate daughter. And yes, before you ask, she has the DNA testing to prove it. Her mother was Conroy's housekeeper, and Carlene, or Carlita as she was known back then, grew up on the Conroy estate. It was all very hush-hush. After Carlita went off to college, her mother died, and Dr. Conroy refused to let her return to the estate. He made it very clear he didn't want the girl around or to have any connection to the family."

Romero set his elbows on the table and tented his hands. "And yet, if what you tell me is true, she did."

"Carlene ran into Jared shortly after he returned from Europe. It was an accidental meeting." I explained how, after Carlita graduated from college, she had changed her name, thinking it would be better for business. "She was working as a party planner when she ran into Jared at a smoke shop in Beverly Hills. The two talked, and Jared told Carlene he was working for his father and not at all happy about it."

"Did she tell Jared about their connection? That the doctor was her father too?"

"Not right away. But when Jared started to talk about his father and how anxious he was to collect this inheritance and move on with his life, things came out. They bonded over their genetics as much as they did their dislike for the doctor."

"Are you saying they came up with a plan to defraud the doctor?"

"Not exactly. At least I don't think you would call it fraud. Jared made it very clear to Carlene he had no intention of remaining with his father's company. He wanted to separate himself from the doctor and the business as soon as possible. He just needed his inheritance to do so."

"So the two of them cooked up a scheme to secure Jared's trust."

"All Jared needed to do was prove to his father he was sober, that he had changed his lifestyle, given up drugs and alcohol, and wait for his thirty-first birthday. Carlene suggested she could improve upon that plan a little by bringing around a nice girl who might help to convince Jared's father of his son's newfound ways. And if romance followed, so be it. Either way, Jared could pay Carlene a finder's fee, something that might provide her with a small stipend to make up for the fact the doctor had written her off."

"How much of a stipend?"

"Fifty thousand dollars."

"Nice fee. But it's not a crime. Not between two consenting parties."

"Maybe not, but certainly something to think about. You see, when Carlene left here Sunday morning, the last thing she told me was that she was worried about Amy. She's concerned the doctor was overstepping his bounds with Amy and the baby by insisting she stay with him."

"Still not a crime, and understandable. The man's just lost his son, and the girl Jared was planning to marry is carrying the doctor's only grandbaby. Nothing wrong with that."

"Yes, but what if it's more than that? What if the doctor found out about Carlene and Jared's agreement? What if he's involved?"

"With Jared's death?" Romero wrinkled his face. "Misty, the doctor's driving the investigation, why would he do that if he were involved?"

"Exactly," I said.

"You really think he'd kill his own son?"

"There are those who believe he killed his wife."

"Rumors," Romero said. "Nothing more than tabloid gossip. The District Attorney never brought charges. The woman was depressed and had a history of mental breakdowns, and the coroner ruled her death a suicide."

I decided for the time being to let the rumor lie and moved on. After all, I had no physical evidence, and Romero certainly wasn't going to accept that I'd been chatting with the doctor's late wife.

"What if I were to tell you Amy came by to see me yesterday?"

"What for?"

"To get her ring, and—"

"Her ring?" Romero jerked his head.

"Yes. It's why she came to see me in the first place. She had lost her engagement ring and—"

"She expected you to find it?"

"I'd told her she had probably misplaced it, and I didn't really think I'd see her again. At least not about that, but then she came back after Jared died. She was concerned something wasn't right, and she didn't know what to do."

"And that's when you called me and then later decided to take matters into your own hands."

I shrugged. Romero already knew about my visit to the Conroy Mansion.

"When I was at the mansion, I met Lupe, Conroy's housekeeper. Lupe told me she had found Amy's ring in the guest house and had given it back to Jared for safekeeping. Of course, it was exactly as I'd told Amy it would be. She had simply misplaced it, taken it off, and forgotten where she left it. Lupe said Jared put the ring in the pocket of his wedding tux and planned to surprise her with it when the minister asked him to place the ring on her finger."

"Kind of romantic," Romero said. "But it doesn't explain why you had the ring."

"Yes, well, it's really quite simple. Lupe gave me the tux, thinking I was from the mortuary—which I know you think was wrong—and after she handed it to me, she remembered Jared had put the ring in the pocket. That's when she showed it to me."

"And you took it. Because you thought she'd steal it." Romero folded his hands and twiddled his thumbs.

"See, Detective, intuition isn't all that hard. Although I'd prefer to say I borrowed it. I gave the ring back to Amy this afternoon."

Romero put his hand to his head and looked at me from beneath his bushy brows. "Why do I get the feeling this isn't the end of the story?"

"Perhaps because it's not. In fact, I think it's just the beginning."

"Go on. Tell me everything."

"The day of Jared's memorial, Lupe spotted me. I really thought she wouldn't recognize me. I had done such a good job trying to disguise myself after visiting the mansion. I had on this hat with a little brim to it, with my hair tucked under and a long duster jacket—"

"Spare me the details of what you were wearing. What happened?" Romero's thumbs twiddled faster.

"Well, she came after me like some psycho, with her arms flailing, and grabbed me by the wrists. She accused me of stealing Amy's ring. But then I convinced her I was working undercover with LAPD, and—"

"You what?" Romero sat back and slapped his hands on the table.

"Relax, Detective. She knows better now, but when I went back to the mansion—"

"Wait a minute. You went *back* to the mansion?"

"Why, yes. I had to. Lupe insisted, she wanted to see me. Anyway, my point is, when I was there—"

"When?" Romero raised his voice.

"This afternoon." I paused and swept my spoon slowly across my soup. Romero's news that the police were ready to dismiss the case had come as no surprise to me. However, the next words out of my mouth would be a big surprise to him. "I talked to Billy, the beekeeper. Did you know the doctor keeps bees on the property? Oh, probably not. I'm sure your detectives were busy checking the guest house and talking to the guests. Surely they knew, but even if they had seen the hives, what were they going to do, arrest a bee?" I chuckled. If the police had spoken to Billy, they had no doubt dismissed him as a suspect in light of the coroner's report believing Jared's death to be accidental. "Anyway, Lupe told me Billy was planning on leaving, and I decided I should have a talk with him."

"The beekeeper?" Romero repeated the word like it was the first time he had heard of such a person. Clearly, the detectives who had visited the mansion the night of Jared's death hadn't mentioned anything to him.

"Yes, the beekeeper. He and Amy were an item once. High school sweethearts. She broke up with him when she moved to LA. Anyway, to make a long story short," which I was enjoying immensely, "I was standing there, chatting with him, when he threw his toolbox into the back of the truck. And guess what?"

"What?"

"It fell open."

"And?"

"And an EpiPen fell out."

"A what?" Romero's jaw dropped open.

"An EpiPen. You know the type Jared used for allergic reactions. I asked Billy about it. I mean, who wouldn't? He told me the doctor had given it to him. Interesting, don't you think?"

Romero reached into his pocket for his cell phone. "And you didn't think you should start out this conversation with that little piece of information?"

I shrugged and took another sip of my soup.

"I'm afraid I just wasn't *feeling it,* Detective. Besides, Billy blames himself for everything that happened. He told me he had been stung the morning of the party, and he's convinced he's the one who exposed Jared. But I hardly think he's your suspect. He's no Visha Kanya if you will. I'm just not getting that assassin vibe off the boy."

"Maybe not, but I need to call LAPD and put out a BOLO alert. We've been missing an EpiPen, and if Billy's got one hidden in his toolbox, I'd like to see it."

I looked back down at my bowl. My soup was growing cold. "I suppose that means you and Denise won't be going to dinner together tonight."

Romero shook his head. "You knew that when I came in, didn't you?"

I smiled.

Chapter 16

How Bossypants got outside, I may never know. She may have snuck out when Romero left the night before. Bossy's an escape artist, an indoor-outdoor mouser well into her seventh or eighth life. I'm not sure which. She came to me, as spirits do, embodied as a mature feline, set in her ways and in need of little more than food and shelter. We had an understanding. I supplied her with her creature comforts, and she supplied me with the occasional leg rub, brushing up against my tired calves, or whatever seemed to please her. I always felt her spirit was that of a former working girl, who, for whatever reason, the universe had returned, which explained her need to cat-about late at night and to drag home the oddest of creatures.

Which she did, the very next morning.

I was in the kitchen, prepping my tea when I heard a knock on the door. Not the kind of soft knock a client might use early in the morning, but a heavy banging, like a jackhammer. A pounding so strong it shook the entire house. Whoever it was wanted my attention, and they wanted it now.

I shuffled to the door, and Wilson poked his head out from the study. "What's up?"

I shrugged. I had no idea. Only that as the pounding continued, my caller sounded ever more insistent.

Wilson fell in behind me. I opened the door, the screen between myself and a beastly looking man who held my cat in his arms. Bossy struggled to escape. The man was short, square bodied, and dressed unseasonably in a gray raincoat with gloves and a scarf about his neck that covered his mouth and nose. On his head, he wore a low-fitting baseball cap, which made his face and eyes hard to see.

"This your cat?" The man's voice matched his husky appearance.

I opened the screen. "Yes, it is."

Bossypants sprang from the man's hands and scurried inside like she'd been shot from a cannon. It didn't take being psychic to know this was no Good Samaritan returning my cat. The hat, the heavy raincoat, and the gloves hadn't been so much to hide the man's appearance, as it was to assure Bossy wouldn't claw him.

I pulled the screen door shut, a thin barrier between us. "Who are you?"

"Just a messenger, ma'am. Here to tell you to keep an eye on what's yours and leave alone what doesn't concern you."

"What's that supposed to mean?" I pushed the latch on the screen to the locked position and put my hands on my hips. I'd been threatened before and wasn't about to let this derelict get the best of me.

"I think you know damn well what it means, and if you know what's good for you, you'll leave the girl alone. I'd hate to have to come back and finish the job. Have a good day, Ms. Dawn."

I slammed the door, something I seldom do. I hoped the sound of it returned a message to this heartless middleman that I wasn't scared, and that I wasn't about to abandon my mission to help Amy.

I joined Wilson in the study. He sat on the window seat next to Bossypants and stroked her, while she purred like a broken muffler.

"How is she?" I knew better than to be deceived by the sound of Bossy's purr. A cat's purr can be as much of a sign of distress as it can happiness, and I sensed Bossypants was far from content.

"Frightened." Wilson placed his hand gently on her back and closed his eyes.

"You're reading her," I said, "or attempting to."

"You might say that, but I can do much better. Watch this."

Wilson stood up in front of the cat and assumed a ninja pose. I had never seen him do anything like this before and was uncertain what he had in mind. With one leg raised, his knee bent at a forty-five-degree angle, and one hand above his head, he twisted his wrist and pointed three outstretched fingers in the direction of the cat. I felt a wave of energy pass between the two, then Bossy stood, arched her back, and hissed.

"Stop!" I grabbed Bossy off the window seat and hugged her to me. "Is this what your lady friends have been teaching you?"

The idea Wilson had sought their advice and had learned how to communicate with the souls of animals didn't rest well with me. It was silly, I knew. Wilson had grown and was free to experiment and learn that beyond what I could teach him. But it worried me. I had felt a growing kinship to Wilson. The idea his lady friends might steal him from me, tarnish his soul with no concern for his future, and send him on at the mercy of the universe, sent a sharp pain through my chest. Tears began to form behind my eyes. Nothing I dared let Wilson see. I turned my back, snuggled Bossypants to my chest, and looked up at the ceiling.

Wilson put his hand on my shoulder. "You're not worried about losing me to a couple of luminaries, are you, Old Gal?"

I blinked back the tears. "You give yourself too much credit, Wilson. If you think I'd be worried about such a thing, you're wrong. You're perfectly free to come and go as you please—fraternize with whomever you like, but remember, luminaries, aren't about freely sharing their energy, not without getting something in return."

"You don't think I know that?"

"I don't know what you know. Only that I worry you're being foolish." I brushed Wilson's hand from my shoulder.

"Maybe so, but there's only room for one spirit guide in my life, and like it or not, I appear to be stuck with you. However, the fact of the matter is my lady friends do appear to have mastered the ability to communicate with the wilds around them. And as you've so wisely pointed out, I best learn what I can do to improve my lot with the universe with what little time I have. So I've been practicing." Wilson kissed me on the forehead.

I caught my breath and was surprised by my own reaction. Like many professional relationships, I'd grown fond of Wilson. He was as irritating as he was entertaining and had grown to be a delight. I assured myself my feelings were nothing I needed to give any deep thought to. Wilson was my spirit guide—my connection to the other side of the veil—and I was his friend. How could I possibly think the two of us, each of us so opposite from the other, could possibly feel anything else? And yet, he was the energy in the room, like the sunshine on my back and the gentle breeze on my face. And most importantly, I reminded myself, a temporary distraction, and one in which I dare not lose myself. I turned my attention back to my cat and held her up to my face so that we were nose to nose.

"And just what does Miss Bossypants have to say for herself?"

Wilson put his hand on her head. "She says the man who kidnapped her tried to poison her."

I pulled Bossy back to my chest, cupped one hand on her head, and whispered in her ear. "How?"

Wilson started to answer.

"No. Not you, Wilson. Bossy needs to tell me herself. I need to see what she saw."

Animals speak in pictures. They relay symbols and signs in the form of mental images, and Bossypants and I had a large vocabulary of such graphics. I bent my head close to her face and closed my eyes until I could see in my mind's eye the very images she wanted to share.

I translated for Wilson.

"Bossy believes our kidnapper lay in wait for her last night— she must have gotten out when I didn't see. He grabbed her, stuffed her in a cat crate, and took her back to his place." I stroked Bossy's back. I could feel her resist her napper's cruel hands as the muscles on her back tightened. "It's not far from here. It doesn't feel like a house, more like an apartment. When they got there, he took something from the trunk of his car." I pinched my eyes shut tighter and tried to concentrate on what it might be. I pictured a gallon bottle of something dark brown. I couldn't make it out, but I did have a clear image of a heavyset man carrying Bossy up the stairs with the crate in one hand and a gallon bottle in the other. Then another picture. The man took a piece of salmon from the refrigerator and poured liquid from the gallon jug over it, then stuffed the fish inside Bossy's crate. "He tried to poison her. He left the fish in the crate with her, and when he came back to check on her this morning and found she hadn't eaten it, she tried to scratch him."

Wilson stepped to the window and peeked out to the porch. "He intended to kill her. A little Godfather-ish, don't you think?"

"Very," I said. "But when he found Bossypants alive, he decided to bring her back and threaten me directly."

"What do we do now?"

"We," I said, "aren't going to do anything. You, on the other hand, are going to stay here with Bossypants and make sure she's okay. I'm going to call Detective Romero. I'm convinced whoever followed us home from Jared's memorial is the same person who tossed the rock through the window in an attempt to frighten me. And when that didn't work, he kidnapped Bossypants. I've had enough. The detective needs to understand this isn't just some disgruntled client or unhappy neighbor. This has to do with Amy, and I intend to prove it."

Chapter 17

I called Romero, and we agreed to meet at Jerry's Deli in the valley, a popular lunch spot for the Hollywood set, and a favorite of the detective's. When I arrived, I found him sitting in the back of the restaurant in a red vinyl booth, facing the door. Cops always sit facing the door. Mostly so they can see if trouble comes in, but in Romero's case, I knew it was more about star sightings so that he might brag to Denise about whom he had seen that day.

When he spotted me, Romero stood, wiped his face with his napkin, and waved for me to join him. He had ordered one of Jerry's specialties: pastrami on rye with a giant green pickle on the side and a diet cream soda. Seated next to him, with plates piled equally as high with deli-specials, were two other men—detectives, one of whom I recognized.

"Misty Dawn." Detective Smiley, the elder of the two, extended his hand. "We met a couple of years back. You were called in to help us find that missing college girl."

"My celebrity case," I said. Years ago, I had helped LAPD locate the body of a missing college coed. She'd fallen into one of the piling holes contractors had dug for the building of a new dorm, and despite the use of police dogs, her body could not be found. The case had brought a renewed interest in my ability as a psychic and the respect of LAPD.

"Big fan of yours. Have to say, you made me a believer." Smiley elbowed the detective sitting next to him. "She found that girl despite the fact contractors had already filled the piling in with cement. Dogs never had a chance."

Romero offered me the seat next to him and introduced the second, younger detective.

Williams put his sandwich down and wiped his mouth.

Romero made introductions. "Detective Williams—meet Misty Dawn."

Williams, Romero explained, despite his youth, was the lead investigator on the Conroy investigation. He was new to the unit and had taken the chief's call the night the doctor called in and requested the police look into the matter.

Williams shook my hand.

I sensed the young detective was anxious to make points with the chief and was not a believer.

"Misty here's been keeping me busy. She's convinced Jared Conroy didn't die accidentally. She's the one who gave me the lead on Billy Martin yesterday." Romero looked at me, "The reason Detectives Smiley and Williams are here with me is because I thought you should know that we picked up Billy last night. He had an EpiPen with him, just like you said, and he was planning to move back to Carpinteria."

"He's not your man." I pulled a menu from the center of the table. I wasn't in the mood for much, but I had never been able to pass up a slice of one of Jerry's pies. I signaled the waiter and ordered a deep-dish apple a la mode.

"You don't think so?" Smiley put his sandwich down and leaned back against the booth.

"No, not at all," I said. "He's broken up over Jared's death, but he's too gentle-natured to have murdered anyone. Doesn't have it in him."

Williams scoffed, then bit into one of the green pickles in the center of the table. "I've arrested a lot of murderers whose mothers would have said the same, but the courts didn't agree, and I don't either. Romero tells me Amy confessed to you that she and Billy were involved. I wouldn't be at all surprised to find your client's got something to do with all this. Jealousy can cause a man to do things he might not otherwise."

My pie arrived, and I pushed it aside.

"Jealousy? That's your proof? That Amy and Billy were involved in high school?" If the investigation stopped there and the police charged Billy with Jared's murder, I'd be hard-pressed to suggest any other suspects without some type of physical proof. And nobody, particularly this young detective, was going to believe my conversation with a couple of vengeful luminaries.

"It's more than that, Misty." Romero crumpled his napkin. "Late yesterday, the coroner got the results back from Jared's blood tests. There were no signs of epinephrine in his system. The coroner said that didn't make sense. There should have been something. Instead, there were traces of bee venom found in the tissue around the injection site. The coroner thinks instead of epinephrine that Jared shot himself with an EpiPen full of bee venom."

"Bee venom?" I shut my eyes and had a vision of Billy's hives behind the garage and the sound of swarming bees in my head. "What are you saying?"

"We think someone may have messed with Jared's EpiPen and replaced the epinephrine with bee venom. It certainly explains why the EpiPen went missing, and neither the paramedics nor the detectives could find it."

Right away, I could think of three people who might possibly have known how to alter the pen, and they all had connections to Conroy Cosmetics: the doctor, his sister-in-law Madeline, and her son Matthew Conroy. All would have had easy access to the venom through the company. As for Billy, I doubted Billy, a simple beekeeper, would have the knowledge of how to harvest bee venom without killing the bees. Something Billy certainly wouldn't do. And yet, he had been found with an EpiPen.

"Are the police convinced the pen they found with Billy is the same pen Jared used the night he died?"

Romero answered. "Not yet, but we'll know shortly. Forensics is running tests now."

"I assume you asked Billy where he got the pen. He told me the doctor had given it to him."

"The doc denies it," Smiley said. "He says he can't believe Billy had anything to do with Jared's murder. He thinks maybe Billy's confused, that maybe Jared gave Billy the pen, just in case."

I looked at Romero. "So you're waiting to see if the pen you found is the same one Jared used the night he died. And once the results from the tests come back, if it's positive for bee venom, you'll arrest Billy, and until then, you'll hold him. Is that right?"

Williams answered. "We can hold him for up to forty-eight hours. Right now we've had him less than twenty-four."

"Well, Detectives, I think you'll be surprised." I explained Billy believed he was to blame for Jared's allergic reaction at the party. That Billy had been stung that morning and had several open wounds on his face. Without thinking about it, he had hugged Jared at the party and exposed him to the venom. "Billy feels guilty about what's happened, and I also think he's still in love with Amy. But I don't for a second think Billy killed Jared."

"You're sure of that?" Williams asked.

"Certain enough for me to suggest you keep looking." I knew they wouldn't believe me if I told them I was beginning to think the doctor was a possible suspect. I had no proof. Just because the luminaries had accused the doctor in their own deaths didn't mean Conroy had killed his son. And with the doctor's close ties to the police commission and his insistence the police investigate, I would be pushing an idea they thought ludicrous. As for Madeline, I could understand a mother's ambition for her son's success. Her desire to see him as Conroy's new VP. Matthew certainly would have had no problem with his new role. But beyond my suspicions about either Matthew or his mother, I had nothing concrete. However, there was one other possibility.

"Have you given any thought to the man in the gray sedan?" I asked. "The one who followed me home from Jared's memorial, and later came back and tossed that rock through my window."

"You've seen him again?" Romero wrinkled his brow.

"Not just seen, but spoken to. In fact, it's why I wanted to see you this morning. He was on my doorstep less than an hour ago with my cat. He tried to kill her."

Romero briefed Williams and Smiley on the gray sedan that had followed me home, and the two exchanged a look. The type of look one gives a young child who makes up stories or an elderly indigent no longer in touch with reality.

I didn't wait for them to fantasize further about my situation. I blurted, "He told me to leave the girl alone. And he was wearing a mask."

"A mask?" Williams asked.

"More like a black bandana. He had it wrapped around his face so I couldn't see him. And he had a raincoat on, and gloves too. Odd for this time of year, don't you think? My guess was so Bossypants couldn't scratch him, but I'm sure she did. If you tried, we could get scrapings from under her nails, and—"

"What? Do a DNA test? On a cat?" Williams dropped his head. "You're not serious?"

Romero interrupted. "Hold on a minute, I'd like to hear what Misty has to say about what this masked man told her."

"He said he was a messenger, and that if I knew what was good for me, I'd leave the girl alone."

"The girl?" Smiley asked. "He didn't use Amy's name?"

I shook my head. "No, but—"

"And you think this man in the gray sedan meant Amy?" Williams' eyes bore through me.

"Of course he meant Amy. Who else could it be?" I stabbed at the pie in front of me. My ice cream was melting, along with my hopes anyone would take me seriously.

"No disrespect, ma'am, but do you have any clients who might also want to send you the same message?" Williams looked at Romero. "I mean he just said leave the girl alone, he didn't use Amy's name."

I put my fork down. "I don't have unhappy clients, Detective Williams. Not like that, I don't."

"You'll excuse me if I say I don't have a lot of respect for what you do." Williams wiped his hands on his pants. "I get that you found that college girl and all, but for all I know, it was a lucky guess. You and everybody who read the paper knew about the construction going on at the university. You probably figured the girl went out for a walk after dinner. Isn't that what her roommate said? Hey, it was getting dark. She was new to the campus. You told reporters you thought maybe she took a short cut back to the dorm and fell into one of the piling holes. How many pilings did you point to? Two? Three? Come on. It didn't take much to figure out. Construction guys dig up a couple, and suddenly you're taking credit for finding her."

"If only it were that easy," I said.

Even those who believed in psychics thought information just suddenly appeared out of the ether. That it's a painless journey when so often it's wrought with raw emotion and the knowledge that the news I would deliver would cause pain to those seeking the truth they hoped to avoid. Frequently, it's a battle of the senses, weighing the truth as I knew it to be, versus as I would like it to be.

"Look," Williams threw his napkin on the table. "I've dealt with a few of your kind before. Not that you're the same, but fortune tellers aren't exactly high on my list of credible witnesses."

I pushed back from the table. I didn't appreciate the comparison.

"How dare you, Detective Williams. I'm not a fortune teller. I don't use crystal balls or cards, and if I were you, I wouldn't be so quick to judge."

"Psychic then. Whatever you want to call it, doesn't matter to me. I don't believe any of it."

"Why? Because you were burned?" I asked.

"Nice guess. Only it wasn't me. It was my mother. Psychic took her for ten-thousand dollars. Ten-thousand dollars we didn't have. Told her she had a curse on her, and only she could remove it. Believe me, if I thought I could have gotten the money back, I might have done the same thing as your masked man—shown up on your doorstep and threatened you."

Romero cleared his throat and pinned his eyes to Williams, a clear message for the young detective to dial it back.

"I think we're all interested in what you have to say, Misty. You'll have to excuse Detective Williams. He's new to the idea of working with someone like yourself. Speaking for me, it takes some getting used to, but I've found leads come from people and places you may least suspect, and it's best to keep judgment to yourself and your eyes and ears open."

"Thank you, Detective Romero." I flashed a smug, if not overly confident, smile at Williams and proceeded to explain how I felt the masked man on my porch was a hired hitman. "I don't believe he's Jared's killer, but I do feel as though if you could find him, he'd lead you to whoever killed Jared. In fact, I'm quite confident about it."

Romero responded. "Unfortunately, you didn't get a plate number, and without it, it's just not possible for the police to track every gray sedan in the city."

I expected such a response and explained he might not have to. "You see, my cat told me the man who kidnapped him—or in this case, catnapped—lives in an apartment. A walkup, somewhere on the west side, I believe. She described it as an older unit. I'm sure if you put your detective skills to work, you could cross-reference apartment dwellers with owners of a gray sedan or whatever it is you do to track down criminals these days."

Williams put his hand to his head and laughed out loud. "Your cat told you that?"

Smiley took his napkin from his lap and put it on the table. If he was about to come to my aid, I didn't care. I had had enough of this smug, young detective, and was about to slap his hand when Romero interrupted.

"I think we've got everything we need here, Misty. You need a lift home?"

I nodded. I had taken an Uber to the restaurant. I could have driven my old VW van, but I didn't trust it on the road. And Wilson's cars? Well, by now, I'd gotten used to a driver.

"Then how about I drive you home and take a look around your property? See if I see anything, and Detective Williams here can order up a car to increase patrols in your area. That fine with you, Detective?" Williams nodded. "If this masked man of yours has anything to do with Jared's murder, we'll find him. I promise you that. Meanwhile, batten down the hatches and stay close to home. Okay?"

Chapter 18

The following morning the universe was abuzz with news of Billy Martin's arrest. On both sides of the veil, news traveled like a hoard of bees, across telephone lines among mortals, and on the backs of light waves in the spirit world.

After hours of interrogation—even while the results from the forensics lab on the EpiPen found in Billy's truck still weren't back—Billy rolled over and confessed. In addition to the EpiPen, the police had recovered a note stuffed into the glove box of Billy's truck. A single page apology Billy had written to Amy and planned to post before he left town. Unfortunately, the police pulled Billy over before he had a chance, and the note's contents read like a confession. Billy penned he was too distraught over Jared's death to stay behind, and he was sorry for the pain he had caused everybody. He hoped Amy would be able to forgive him. He'd never forgive himself.

Per the law, Billy was given one call. He made that call to Amy, told her he had been arrested, and asked if she'd call him a lawyer. Amy, shocked at the news, came unglued. The doctor found her in the kitchen with the phone in her hand, slumped against the counter, crying hysterically.

Dr. Conroy insisted Amy lie down and promised her he would look into Billy's arrest. She shouldn't worry herself. Bed rest was what the doctor ordered. While Amy was returned to bed, Eli and Christina reached out to Wilson, who through their cosmic ability to communicate on the back of light waves, shared with Wilson the news of Billy's arrest, and the happenings inside the House that

Vanity Built.

Meanwhile, from her bed, riddled with guilt and shame, Amy called Carlene and poured her heart out to her friend about Billy. No sooner had Amy hung up then Carlene called me.

Hence, news of Billy's arrest reached me two-fold: via Carlene and via Wilson, who at the exact same moment as my phone rang, appeared from the study.

"Billy's been arrested!" Carlene gave voice to the very words Wilson mouthed to me.

I wasn't surprised. When I woke that morning, I had a sense of dread and a vision of Billy, sweet-faced young Billy, in my head. After visiting with Detective Romero yesterday, I knew it would only be a matter of time before the police charged Billy with Jared's murder. And here it was, less than twenty-four hours later, a false narrative I was going to have to deal with.

"How's Amy?" I asked.

"Not good." I could feel Carlene's heart beating through the phone. "I'm worried about her. The doctor gave her something to calm her down. She didn't sound like herself. I can't be sure, but I think maybe the doctor asked her who she was talking to. I'm afraid she may have told him an old friend of Jared's. If she did, and if he puts two and two together and thinks it's me, I'm screwed. He'll kill me, I know it."

I wanted to tell Carlene her fears were irrational, but I knew better. I could feel a dark presence, like storm clouds, about to engulf her. She had every right to be worried. Lies, like those Carlene had told Amy, seldom stay hidden. Whether the doctor knew about Carlene's friendship with Amy or not, it was only a matter of time before he did.

"Do me a favor," I said. "Change your greeting on your phone. Use the generic message and erase your own. And if Amy calls again, don't pick up." I was afraid, if the doctor got Amy's phone and hit redial on her last call, he'd get Carlene's voicemail, and the last thing she needed right now was to have the doctor knowing how to get hold of her. "I'll take care of Amy. You take care of yourself. I'll be in touch."

I hung up the phone and looked at Wilson. "Carlene's concerned about Amy."

"As are my lady friends." Wilson went to the fireplace and adjusted the candlestick on the mantel. "The doctor's acting strangely. They want to see you right away."

"Me?" I sat down on the sofa and held the phone against my chest.

"Yes, you. I could go, but they requested I bring *the old lady*."

I scowled. Enough with the old lady remarks.

"For whatever reason, they want to talk with you." Wilson shrugged like he couldn't imagine why.

It's not often a spirit will request the audience of a psychic. Usually, it's the other way around. The abnormality of the situation alarmed me. I felt myself growing warm, and my heart began to race. At least I thought it was my heart. That was until I realized it was the phone buzzing against my chest.

I glanced down at the face of my cell.

"Misty." Lupe's voice was strained. "Something terrible has happened. I need to see you right away. The doctor's out with Amy. I don't know for how long, but you need to get here. I'll tell the guard to let you through."

When Wilson and I arrived at the mansion, I was surprised to find a yellow Ferrari convertible with personalized plates that read BUZZED parked in the courtyard. I hadn't expected to see any other guests at the house, not after Lupe's distressed call and urgent request for me to come immediately. I had thought the house—not counting the help—would be empty or as near-empty as a mansion haunted by its former first lady and husband's paramour could possibly be.

Nonetheless, there was Lupe in the motor court, talking casually with a young man I recognized from Jared's memorial. She introduced him as Raul, Jared's best friend. Soon as she said his name, I rushed to introduce myself and took his hand.

"I'm Anne," I said, "an old friend of the family." I was most anxious Lupe not use my real name, should Raul later make mention of my visit to the doctor. "What a handsome ride. I'm a car person myself." I nodded to the Jag. Raul's hand still in mine. "Of course mine's much older—like me—vintage. Mind if I ask where you got it?"

"Ventura County." Raul dropped my hand, too quick for me to get a read on anything but the young man's angst, and headed back to the car.

I wasn't about to let him get away. Not with him being one of my possible suspects. I staggered behind him.

"You from there?" I asked.

"Not really." Raul started to open the car door. I noticed a small, brown paper sack in his free hand. The type one might use to hide a bottle of booze.

"I suppose you stopped by to visit with Amy. Dropping off a gift, maybe?" I nodded to the bag.

Raul's eyes darted from me to Lupe, then back to the courtyard's entrance. He was obviously pressed for time. "Amy called me this morning. She sounded down, and I thought I'd come by and say hi. But she and the doctor are out. I guess I just missed her."

Raul's hand tightened around the neck of the sack. Was he hiding something? I took a step closer to his car, blocking any chance of his getting in.

"Surprising news about Billy this morning. I suppose you heard?"

Raul took a step back. "It was on the news."

"You two friends?" I put my hand casually on the car's window frame to steady myself.

"Not really. Why do you ask?"

"Just curious. You being from Ventura and all. That's where's Billy's from. Carpinteria actually, and Amy too."

"Sorry. Can't help you." Raul put his hand back on the car

door, inches from my own hand.

I sensed his connection to Billy had begun far earlier than he let on.

"But you do know him, right?" I gripped the car door tighter. "I mean, he was part of your group."

"Yeah, so what? Billy and his folks, they lived on some land my family owns in Carp."

The fact Raul had referred to Carpinteria by its shortened name convinced me he was far more familiar with the area and closer to Billy than he let on.

"Citrus or vineyards?" I asked. Nearly every farm up there was one or the other.

"Both." Raul nodded to the Ferrari's personalized plates.

"Buzzed?" I knit my brows curiously.

"Wine and bees," Raul said. "My family's been in the business for years."

"Clever," I said.

"Yeah, I guess. Anyway, you're right. Billy and I knew each other, or of each other anyway. It wasn't exactly like we grew up together and hung out. Amy brought Billy into our group, and I ended up vouching for him. Like I said, we really didn't know each other well, but Jared was cool with it, so why not?"

"You must have been surprised then to hear about the arrest?"

"I suppose. You never really know people, right?" Raul pulled open the car door and slid behind the wheel. "Sorry, but I have to get going." The Ferrari roared to life, and Raul hollered back to Lupe. "When Amy gets back, tell her I got her message and came by." Then raising the sack above his head, added, "And thanks for this, Lupe. I owe you."

I waited until Raul had driven away. "What was in the bag?"

"What do you think?" Lupe said. "You're the psychic."

"The flask," I said. "The one you found in the guest house."

Lupe began to walk back toward the house. "Raul gave the flask to Jared as a gift some time ago. It's engraved. To Jared from Raul. He's afraid if the doctor finds the flask, he'll blame Raul for

Jared's drinking, and if the cops don't pin Jared's death on Billy, he's worried the doctor will come after him."

That explained why Raul wanted to distance himself from Billy, and while Raul may have felt picking up the flask had been enough to throw the doctor off the track, I wasn't so easily convinced. As far as I was concerned, Raul's need to pick up the flask and his connection to a bee farm, made him all the more a person of interest.

Wilson and I followed Lupe and got as far the front door when her cell rang. She glanced at her phone. "Not again. You'll have to excuse me. It appears our gophers have got the best of our handyman." Wilson poked me in the ribs. The mansion's resident luminaries were hard at work. "Go on inside," she said. "I'll meet you in the kitchen."

Chapter 19

I felt a tingling down my spine as Wilson and I entered the sunroom. Eli and Christina were seated as they had been before, in front of the window with their hair perfectly coiffed and faces painted like porcelain dolls. I reminded myself that while they had requested I come to them, these were luminaries, anything and everything they said and did would be for their own self-interests. Not Amy's, and certainly not mine.

"Misty, dear, what a shame you missed all the excitement this morning." Eli's sing-song voice belied her sincerity. "A real row, if you will. When Amy heard the police had arrested Billy, she fell apart, right there on the kitchen floor. Like a rag doll." Eli pointed a long, manicured finger in the direction of the kitchen counter. "And when the doctor found her, he tried to give her some pills, but she threw them in the sink and started screaming it was all her fault."

Christina leaned forward. "And then, Dr. Conroy went berserk. Something snapped inside him, and he started to yell back." Christina touched her head like the memory was too much for her. "Ugh. The things he said to that poor girl. He accused her of conspiring with Billy to kill Jared."

Eli explained that Amy ran from the room, and the doctor chased after her. "It was such a racket. She slammed the door to the guest bedroom, and it echoed throughout the whole house. Heard it all the way down here. The doctor pounded on the door like a madman, begged her to let him in. When she wouldn't answer, he started to sob like a child." Eli clapped her hands together, the glee of the doctor's tantrum written all over her rouged face.

"He told her he knew she was friends with Carlita." Christina's eyes widened and met mine. For a second, I could see Carlene in her mother's expression. Her dark eyes and high-brow; the mother-daughter connection was undeniable.

"Which is true, isn't it? Matthew told him. I heard him tell the doctor he saw Carlita with Amy at the Starbucks where Amy worked."

My jaw dropped. Luminaries were usually so caught up with their own missions that they seldom concerned themselves with things that have happened since their passing. As a result, I didn't think Christina had a clue about her daughter since she had left for college or even cared.

"Didn't think I knew, did you?" Christina smiled. "Oh, come now, don't deny it. I know you know Carlene's my daughter, and that she changed her name and used to live here. I can read your mind."

I should have known. Spirits have an advantage over mortals. They can read our minds, while we, on the other side of the veil, even psychics like myself, can't begin to guess what they're thinking.

I took a deep breath. "What about the doctor's mind, have you read him as well?"

Eli rested her elbow on her knee and put her hand beneath her chin. "We could if the man was sound, but the doctor's not a well man. His mind's too addled for either of us to read. I suspect dementia."

"Or perhaps he's just riddled with guilt," Christina giggled.

"Whatever." Eli unfolded her arms and brushed her long fingers across her skirt. "He was once such a brilliant mind. Top of his field. Although, I suspect the cost of getting there was a little self-experimentation. Some of which might have caused his madness. However, he never was particularly well balanced to start with, but then I suppose most geniuses aren't."

Eli's words were of no comfort to me. If she couldn't read the doctor, there was no way I would be able to. Even if the doctor were to allow me to, it's not possible for a psychic to read someone who was mentally unbalanced or suffering from dementia. Any hope I had of learning anything more about the doctor's relationship with his son or about Jared's murder wasn't going to come from the doctor. I would have to find it on my own.

"However," Eli said, "what you may find of interest, and one of the reasons we wanted to see you today, is that the doctor revised his will. Which, in the end, could be a very good thing."

"For Amy?" I asked.

"For us all," Eli said. "The doctor's made special arrangements to transfer Jared's trust and future inheritance to the baby, naming himself as the executor should anything unfortunate happen to Amy."

I blinked, had I heard her correctly? *Should anything unfortunate happen to Amy?* Suddenly, Carlene's fears, which up until now had felt more like paranoia, were starting to feel very real to me.

"Certainly, you're not suggesting the doctor would do anything to hurt her?"

"More likely he intends to claim she would be an unfit mother," Christina said. "That way he can leave whatever needs to be done to the courts. No reason for him to get his hands dirty."

"That's ridiculous," I said. "What proof would he have?"

"He wouldn't need any if he could convince the court Amy had something to do with Jared's death," Eli added.

"But why would Amy murder Jared? She was about to be his wife. If she waited until after the wedding, she'd inherit everything."

"Ahh, that's where you're wrong," Eli said. "Jared had a trust, and as long as Amy was married to Jared, she was entitled to the proceeds of the trust, but nothing more. If she divorced Jared or he died, she'd get nothing."

"And you think the doctor, in his very addled state, actually believes Amy might have killed his son?"

"Who knows what that man believes, he's mental." Christina

took a nail file from within her robe and began to file her nails. "Knowing the doctor, he'll try to convince the police Amy and Billy colluded—perhaps with Carlene—to have Amy marry Jared, and then cash in on Jared's trust fund. But that at some point, Jared found out what they were up to and threatened to expose them. No doubt they killed Jared to shut him up and settled for the price of what that lovely engagement ring Jared gave Amy would bring." Christina stopped filing her nails. "Whether it's the truth or some variation of it, it feels close enough, don't you think?"

I had to admit it was a story the doctor could easily spin to the police. While the facts were twisted, it was a little too close to the story Carlene had originally shared with me, and what I knew to be the truth.

Eli continued. "The reason we wanted to see you is we believe the doctor's planning to take Amy's baby and start over again. It's all he's been talking about ever since he learned Amy was pregnant. And now, with Jared out of the picture and Matthew as VP of Conroy Cosmetics, Elliott has both the time and the opportunity to do just that. Start over."

"With Amy's baby?" The idea that an old man, particularly an old man like the doctor, might think he could begin again was incredulous. Not only was he old and frail, he was insane.

"All he has to do is convince the police that the story I just told you is true," Christina dropped her wrist and pointed the nail file at me.

"And he's very good at convincing people," Eli added.

I worried she was right.

"Where are Amy and the doctor now?" I asked.

"They've gone to visit Amy's OB/GYN," Eli said.

I jerked my head. I hadn't expected that bit of news.

"What, did they kiss and makeup?"

"One might think so," Eli said. "When the doctor collapsed outside Amy's door, he changed his tune and pleaded with her to talk to him. He said that losing Jared had destroyed him, and he was a broken man. And Amy, being the sweet naïve young thing she is, opened the door and tried to comfort him."

"Which is more than I would have done." Christina started to file her nails again. "Stupid girl. She cuddled him in her arms and told him it would be all right. That she understood what he was going through. That they were both going through it."

I could visualize the scene. Amy was a soft touch, no match for someone as sophisticated and duplicitous as the doctor.

"She asked if the doctor wanted to come with her to her OB appointment. Can you imagine? Amy comforting him, after what she's been through? She told him she had called her OB after Jared died, and her OB told her to come by to do an ultrasound. She thought the doctor might like to go with her to hear the heartbeat."

I glanced about the room. I could still feel the static energy from their argument that morning. It layered the air like the smell of something burnt, and with it, the subtle flow of dark energy. The luminaries were trying to telegraph me an idea.

"And what is it you want me to do?" I asked.

"What do you think?" With one hand, Eli circled her thin fingers in front of her, as though she might mix the air with her thoughts. "Certainly you must have some ideas of your own? Something that might, shall we say, save Amy from a fate worse than death?"

The luminaries chuckled.

I knew what Eli wanted. She had planted the thought in my head, and I couldn't believe the words about to come out of my mouth.

"You want me to kill the doctor?"

Christina shrugged. "If not you, then I suppose we could ask Wilson."

"No." I stretched my arm out in front of Wilson, like a mother driving a car who had stopped too fast at a light. He wasn't going anywhere, and he wasn't going to kill the doctor. If Wilson were engaged in such an act, his fate would be sealed, and all my work to help convince the powers of the universe that he was more than just a lost soul would be for naught.

"You have to understand, Amy and the idea of the baby have become too much of a distraction." Eli looked to Christina for verification, and her husband's former paramour nodded dutifully. "Oh, it was fine before Jared passed. Amy wasn't here, not in this house anyway, and certainly not full time. But now that the doctor's insisted she move in, her presence is interfering with our plans."

"I can't believe you would ask such a thing. You've no idea who killed Jared, and you've no proof it was the doctor. None at all. What if it's not?"

"Oh, please. Does it really matter?" Eli asked. "If Jared had been killed here, we'd know who killed him. But he wasn't. As luminaries, our knowledge of the world is sealed to the confines of this house, and since we're unable to leave until we've completed our mission here, we may never know. But the fact of the matter is, if the doctor did kill Jared, it wouldn't be his first."

Christina waved her hand. "Not at all. Believe me, I never accidentally fell off a ladder while stringing Christmas lights."

"And I never overdosed on sleeping pills. Elliott mixed up my medications with a little something he said would help with my beauty sleep. Little did I know it was a sleep I'd never wake up from. So you see, if the doctor were to die now, it would all be very justifiable. Best of all, the will the doctor signed would transfer the house and everything in it to the baby with Amy as the baby's executrix. We'd be gone with the doctor, and the house would be Amy's. As a result, Amy and the baby would be taken care of as beneficiaries of the company for the rest of their lives. Kind of what people today call a win-win." Eli smiled. "But if you wait—"

"I'm sorry." I backed away, my hands in front of my face. "I can't murder the doctor. It's not what I do."

"If it's because you think you might be caught, there's no reason anyone ever need to know. You could call the doctor, and suggest he come by for tea and a casual conversation about Amy. I happen to know he likes tea almost as much as you do." Christina giggled, the idea of the doctor and me sitting down to tea appeared to tickle her.

"What Christina's trying to say is, the doctor has a heart problem. You could slip a little something into his tea. There's a prescription bottle of digitalis in his bathroom cabinet."

"Or," Christina volunteered, "if you're into something a little more organic, the doctor grows foxglove out behind the garage. It's a natural form of digitalis. Quite deadly and very difficult to detect. In fact, I believe it's what the doctor may have given me."

"No!" I said.

Chapter 20

"Are you talking to yourself again?" Lupe entered the kitchen and shut the door behind her. I noticed her shoes were covered with mud from the backyard.

"Muttering," I said.

"Well, stop it, will you? I need you to take a ride with me. I want to talk, and I'd prefer it not to be here. Lately, I feel as though the house has ears."

I glanced back at Wilson with his lady friends. The three of them smiled at me, and Wilson waved for me to go on. I followed Lupe out the door to the golf cart.

"What's going on?" I asked.

Lupe didn't answer. Instead, she put the cart in gear, and we swept down the hillside, toward the guest house, with me hanging white-knuckled onto the handrail.

When we got to the guest house, Lupe stopped the cart, reached into her pocket, and took out three small oatmeal-colored capsules.

"It's these. Dr. Conroy's been giving them to Amy. At first, I didn't think anything of it—his being a doctor and all—but this morning, there was an argument. Amy got a call from Billy, and when he told her he had been arrested, she collapsed. It was awful. The doctor tried to give her some pills, but Amy threw them in the sink. I don't know what to think anymore, but I'm beginning to wonder if maybe Jared's death has caused the doctor to really lose it. He's always been a little strange, but nothing like this. Lately he's been coming downstairs in his bathrobe. The man never used to do that. He always dressed for breakfast. And these last couple of days, he's been talking to himself more than usual. I can't imagine he'd do anything to harm Amy or the baby, but something about it doesn't feel right. I thought maybe you might know what to do or what these are." Lupe put the pills in my hand. "I certainly can't call the police, and I'm not about to ask the doctor."

I stared at the capsules filled with a cream-colored powder. I placed two on my lap and emptied the third into the palm of my hand. No smell. No bitter taste. They could be anything.

"How long has she been taking these?" I asked.

"I don't know. Since Jared died, I think. I heard the doctor tell her they'd help her sleep. I'm sure he wouldn't give her anything that might harm the baby. But right now, I just don't know."

A chill ran down my back. Had the doctor given her pills like he had his late wife? I couldn't imagine the doctor would give Amy anything that might harm the baby. All the same, I wrapped the pills in a tissue and put them in my bag for later analysis.

"The thing is," Lupe said, "I know the police arrested Billy, and maybe they have their reasons, but I don't think that boy's the killer. You ask me the police have the wrong man. He's too mild-mannered."

I wondered if Lupe had her own list of suspects, some of whom I sensed might my match my own. I hesitated to put words in her mouth. I needed her to tell me.

"Then who else?" I asked.

"I don't know." Lupe grabbed a stack of towels from the back of the golf cart and headed for the guest house. I followed her inside.

I sensed she was mentally blocking any name she might not want to think was connected to Jared's murder.

"You must have some idea. The coroner found bee venom in Jared's system, and the police believe someone close to Jared replaced his EpiPen with one loaded with enough venom to trigger the reaction that killed him."

Lupe crushed the towels to her chest.

I could feel her angst. The thought someone close to her had killed Jared was breaking her heart.

I pushed a little harder. "Think, Lupe."

"I don't know. For a while, I thought it might be Raul. I know he was worried the doctor would find out he had given the flask to Jared, and—"

"And what?" I asked.

"He had a thing for Amy."

"A thing?"

"I don't think he wanted Amy to marry Jared, but I just don't see him murdering his best friend to stop her."

I didn't feel so either. But if the police did charge Raul, I'd need whatever evidence I could find to rule him out.

"No," I said. "I agree. The boy strikes me as more a lover than a fighter. Am I right?"

"Raul was all about having a good time. Jared used to tease him that in college there wasn't a bar in town that didn't know Raul. He said Raul majored in Partying 101. I doubt he ever saw the inside of a science class, much less knew how to get venom from a bee into a syringe."

"However," I said, "his family does own the land where Billy grew up, and if what he says is true, he had access to his father's orchards and the hives."

"Owned is the operative word." Lupe raised a brow. "Have you seen Raul's hands? No calluses. I doubt the boy ever labored a day in his life, much less on his father's land."

I had to agree. Despite Raul's early morning call to the mansion to retrieve the flask, he struck me as more of a playboy than a premeditated killer. He may have known Billy growing up and had access to the family farm, but it would take someone with more than a casual knowledge of bees to know how to harvest the bees' venom. It had to be someone who understood the science behind the extraction, and how not to harm the bees. In my mind, that also meant it couldn't possibly be Billy. Billy would never have experimented on his precious bees. They were not only a means by which he earned his living, but their very being an extension of his organically sweet nature. The boy didn't have it in him. No, the venom more likely came from someone who worked in the bee-tox program for Conroy Cosmetics.

"What about Jared's cousin Matthew?" I asked. "I noticed he wasn't sitting with Jared's friends at the memorial, and yet, according to the police report, he was at Jared's bachelor party."

Lupe bundled the towels in her arms and walked past me into the master suite.

"I'm afraid I didn't pay much attention. In fact, I didn't even know Matthew was here until Roger from the guard shack called and said he had just let Matthew through the gate with a party bus. When I told the doctor, he didn't appear at all surprised."

"Had the doctor ordered it?"

"I guess. I didn't ask."

"Do you think Dr. Conroy suspected Jared might have been drinking?"

"I don't know. At the time, I just thought it was a nice gesture. A way to make sure everyone arrived at the party safely. When Matthew came in, Madeline was with him—"

"The doctor's sister-in-law?" I wanted to make sure I understood who was at the house that night.

"Yes, the two of them went into the doctor's office, and Matthew went on down to the guest house."

"You didn't think that odd? That the two of them were alone?"

"Not really. I just assumed they had business to discuss."

"She wasn't there to go to the party?"

"Hardly. She looked terrible. She'd done something to her face. Shots, I think. It was all swollen. I suspected that's why she'd come by to see the doctor. She was always experimenting with some new chemical something or other, and the doctor would have to help her."

I tabled the thought of Madeline's visit to the doctor and thought more about Matthew's arrival with a party bus. It might have explained why his name hadn't been on the guest list, and why he was there.

"And then you went down to the guest house," I said.

"Just like I always did, right before I went home."

"When you got there, what was going on?"

"It was a party. Jared and his friends, they were in the living room, drinking and laughing. It looked like they were having a good time. I tried not to interfere and went to hang the towels in the master bath, and that's when I saw Matthew."

"He was in the bedroom?"

"Yes."

"What was he doing?"

"Nothing really. He was just standing there by Jared's dresser, staring at a photo of Amy and Jared." Lupe pointed to a picture on Jared's dresser of the engaged couple in front of the Arc de Triomphe in Paris. One of the many trips Amy said they had taken during their whirlwind romance.

"Then what happened?"

"I heard Dr. Conroy come in. He had come down to say goodnight to Jared. By then, I was in the bathroom, and when I heard the doctor and Jared come into the bedroom, I busied myself and straightened the towels."

"Anything else?"

"I heard Matthew say something about how lucky Jared was to have found a nice girl like Amy, and then he left."

"And that's it?"

"No. Jared went to get his coat out of the closet, and the doctor stopped him."

"Why?" I asked.

"I don't know, a tender moment maybe? At least it looked like it. Jared had just put on some cologne and then—" Lupe looked at the dresser and not seeing the cologne paused. "That's odd."

"What?" I asked.

"The cologne's missing. It was here the other day. I wonder what happened to it?"

I knew exactly where the bottle of cologne was. Courtesy of

Wilson's inability to leave a crime scene without a souvenir, he had taken it home with him.

"Perhaps the police picked it up when they investigated," I said.

"Humph." Lupe wrinkled her brow. "Anyway, after Jared splashed himself with the cologne, the doctor asked him if he had forgotten anything. Jared checked his pockets. I think he was looking for his EpiPen. The doctor seemed to know what he was looking for and went to the dresser and took the pen from the top drawer where Jared always kept it."

"From the dresser, where Matthew had been standing?"

Lupe nodded.

"Do you think Matthew might have done something? Maybe switched out the EpiPens while he was in the room?"

"I don't know. I certainly didn't think about it at the time," Lupe said, "but maybe."

"And you're sure it was the doctor who put the pen in Jared's pocket?" I needed to verify in my own head that the doctor was the last to touch the pen.

"Yes, and then the doctor put his hand on Jared's shoulder, and the two of them just stood there and stared at their reflection in the mirror." Lupe pointed to the armoire's mirror, and for the moment, I could imagine the father and son standing there.

Lupe dabbed away a tear. I took her hand and reassured her. "You did the right thing calling me. I'll check out the pills. They're probably nothing. I'm sure the doctor wouldn't give Amy anything that would harm the baby."

"Do you think maybe Matthew had something to do with the EpiPen?" Lupe asked.

"I don't know, and I don't think we'll have any firm answers until we find the pen Jared used that night."

"I can't believe anyone close to Jared would have done something deliberate. His friends loved him. In my opinion, it's some outsider, maybe one of the doctor's competitors. I can't tell you the number of times I heard the doctor arguing on the phone about trade secrets, and how he thought someone was always trying to steal from him. Believe me, there's nothing pretty about the beauty business. The doctor has a lot of enemies. If anyone wanted to hurt the doctor, it'd be through Jared. He loved that boy."

I wasn't so certain.

Chapter 21

Back in the car, Wilson and I compared notes about our meeting with his lady friends and my visit to the guest house with Lupe. After a brief recap about what Lupe had shared with me concerning the pills Dr. Conroy had given Amy, Jared's last appearance in the guest house with his rat pack, and Matthew's arrival with his mother and the party bus, I circled back to the more pressing matter, concerning our discussion with Eli and Christina. Their absurd suggestion that I was in the position to poison the doctor and that my services were necessary, was—to say the least—mind-blowing.

"And not because they think the doctor killed Jared," I said. "But because they're upset about Amy moving in and her interfering with their hauntings."

Wilson glanced over at me. He was driving slower than usual. "Everybody's upset about Amy."

"Maybe so, but nobody else is suggesting I kill the doctor." I crossed my arms and leaned against the passenger door. "The idea is totally preposterous."

"Although, not that I'm proposing you do so, but...how did Eli put it? It'd be a win-win for everyone. Amy might be better off."

"Murder is never a win-win, Wilson."

He drove on in silence. I wasn't sure if he was weighing the advantages of the luminaries' suggestion or concerned how upset I was over the idea.

"Besides," I said, "Lupe's not convinced Dr. Conroy killed Jared. She thinks he's innocent, overwrought with grief, and acting irrationally as a result of losing his son. Which under the circumstances, could very well be."

Wilson's eyes slid from the road to mine. "You really think that? Because you mustn't forget, Lupe doesn't believe the rumors about the doctor killing his wife or his paramour either." Wilson took one hand from the steering wheel and patted his heart mockingly. "She thinks he's simply haunted by his loss. Bereft and deranged by their deaths, but if what Eli and Christina say is true—"

"Which considering the source, may or may not be. Don't forget, Wilson, luminaries lie."

"Perhaps, but in this case, I believe what they're telling us is true."

"And hard to prove." I couldn't imagine how I'd explain to Detective Romero I had come to such a conclusion. The cases had been closed long ago. The coroner had confirmed the causes of the deaths as accidental and suicide. It was only tabloid gossip that kept them alive.

As we approached the guard gate, neither of us spoke. I glanced back in the direction of the House that Vanity Built. A superstructure of monolithic proportion surrounded by marble statues of youthful gods. I wondered how many secrets the house kept and the price the doctor had paid for such fame.

Finally, it was Wilson who broke the silence. "So, that leaves Matthew."

"And his mother," I said. "She had motive. She had connections inside the company, which would have given her access to bee venom. And what mother doesn't want to see her son advance?"

"Agreed," Wilson said. "Who do you want to start with?"

"Matthew," I said.

I glanced at my watch. It was exactly four fifteen p.m. By now I figured Madeline to be either prone on some suntan bed in Beverly Hills or bending her elbow at a private club with some gentleman she probably wouldn't want her husband to know about. But Matthew, I was more certain about.

"If I'm right, we can catch Conroy's new VP just as he's leaving his office. Think you can get us there?"

"Conroy's Cosmetics? Fasten your seatbelt, Old Gal."

Conroy Cosmetics was a good hour's drive in rush hour traffic, but if Wilson took Mulholland and we zigzagged through the residential mountain areas, there was a good chance we could cut off fifteen to twenty minutes and make it in time to catch Matthew exit the building. I knew exactly how I planned to coax Matthew into a conversation. Never underestimate the powers of an innocent-looking old lady stranded by the roadside with a little white hankie in her hand.

At exactly four fifty-five, we pulled up in front of the headquarters for Conroy Cosmetics. A handsome looking building that had once housed the business offices for a large movie studio. Wilson found a parking space on the street across from the building's main entrance. I took the keys from the ignition, got out of the car, and with my bag under my arm, promptly dropped the keys on the pavement.

Wilson hollered from the car. "What are you doing?"

"You have to ask?" I waved my hankie in his direction and teased the bottom of my skirt. It fluttered just so, and I twisted my ankle coquettishly.

Wilson put his hand to his head. "Don't tell me. Claudette Colbert. *It Happened One Night.* "

I grinned.

I may have been fifty years older than Claudette Colbert, who played Ellie Andrews, a young, spoiled heiress in the movie with Clark Gable, and was well known for the classic scene where they had broken down on the side of the road and appeared to be stuck. It was Ellie who came to their rescue and managed to flag down a passing motorist, hiking her skirt and causing the driver to come to a skidded stop. Despite the fact my ankles weren't up to Colbert's, I could be just as sassy, and when it came to men and cars, I was one up on her. Age has its advantage; wisdom is seldom wasted on the young.

"You really think he's going to stop for you?"

"Sit back and watch. You might be surprised."

Moments later, Matthew appeared from the building. I recognized him from Jared's memorial. Unlike his handsome cousin, Matthew Conroy was geeky-looking with thick black glasses and a mop of unruly dark hair he had pulled back into a man-bun in an attempt to look hip. His brand new Bentley convertible, similar to the doctor's, was parked in an area reserved exclusively for the company's new VP.

I waited for him to get into the car and steer toward the lot's exit, then stepped out into the street, raised my hand, and waved the hankie in a very desperate manner.

Just as I had predicted, Matthew was easy pickings. If not for the well-being of a little old lady standing alone on the side of a busy street, then because Wilson's vintage Jaguar at my side had caught his eye.

Matthew pulled slowly up beside me, gave me a quick once over, then looked closely at the car's classic lines.

"Please, sir, could you help me?" I hobbled forward, put my hand on the Bentley's door frame, and with my shoulders slumped and mouth half-open, mustered my most woeful look. "I'm afraid I'm stuck."

I gestured helplessly toward the Jag.

Matthew made a quick evaluation, and with a jut of his chin, told me to step back, and pulled the Bentley up in front of the Jag.

I sensed he thought the Jag and I were an impossible match. What was a doddering old fool like me driving around in such a cool car in the middle of rush hour traffic?

"This your car?"

"It was my late husband's. I thought I'd take it out for a spin and do a little shopping. Lady's got to have her moisturizer, you know." I pointed to the building that housed Conroy's huge showroom full of cosmetics and merchandise on the ground floor.

"When I came back out, I couldn't find my keys."

Matthew glanced back at the Jag. Despite his impatience to move on, the Jag was worth his time.

"Nice car." Matthew walked around the Jag and ran the tips of his fingers along the car's sleek frame, then stopped and with his hands against the blackened driver's window, tried to peer inside.

I held my breath. Under the best of circumstances, Wilson was unpredictable, but I knew putting up with someone manhandling his precious Jag would be problematic. If Matthew were to kick the tires or try to spit-shine some nonexistent water spot on the hood, I feared Wilson would lose it. I didn't dare risk an altercation.

I looked down at my feet and kicked the keys.

"Oh, for goodness sakes," I said. "I must have dropped them."

Matthew looked down at my feet, then bent down and picked up the keys.

"Well, then, here you go." He dropped them into my hand and just as quickly turned to leave.

I grabbed his arm. I wasn't about to let him go.

"Please, sir, let me thank you."

Matthew must have thought I meant to give him money, and took my hand and tried to pull away.

"There's no need," he said. "I didn't do anything."

"But you stopped." I squeezed his arm tighter. "I left my cell phone in the car, and with no one at home to call anymore, I might have been here hours had you not come along and been so kind. Please let me pay you."

"Nonsense. It's fine, really." Matthew tried again to remove my hand from his arm, but I held tight.

"No, I insist. I can see you don't need money," I nodded to the Bentley, "but I'm a psychic. The least I can do is offer you a reading."

"A fortune-teller?" Matthew chuckled.

"I prefer to think of myself as an intuitive, but if fortune-teller makes you happy, so be it. Please." I pulled him closer, my eyes searching his to see if by some small chance he might have recognized me from Jared's memorial. Seeing none, I continued. "The universe seldom makes mistakes. I feel as though we were destined to meet, and that I might have something important to tell you."

Matthew relaxed his shoulders. "Okay, but it can't take long. I'm in a hurry."

I continued to hold his arm. I dared not let go. Psychics can only read those willing, and since Matthew had consented, I wanted to accelerate that read as quickly as possible before he suddenly changed his mind.

"You've recently experienced some big changes in your life." I glanced back at the Bentley.

Matthew smiled. "Dealer plates give that away, did they?"

"Ahh, but it's more than that. A new job, I think. Something you've been groomed for. But it's come at a cost." I closed my eyes and bowed my head, my hand gripping tighter to his wrist. "An unexpected loss. A death of someone you were frequently compared to, and with whom you have or had a complicated relationship." I felt a tightening in Matthew's arm. "In fact, I feel as though the police think his death may have been more an act of foul play than an accident, and that has people close to you are perhaps suspect."

Matthew shook my hand from his wrist and stepped back. "Who are you?"

"I told you, I'm a psychic."

"No, you're not. You're a cop or a private investigator, or maybe even a reporter. Whoever you are, I don't want to talk to you." Matthew jerked his arm away from me. "If you want to talk to me, you'll have to talk to my attorney."

Matthew stomped back to his car and slammed the door.

I got back in the Jag and watched as the Bentley peeled away.

Wilson cocked his head. "Pretty good there, Old Gal. Maybe not quite Colbert, but not bad. Did you get what you were looking for?"

"Not enough, but I did hit a nerve. He knows Jared's death was no accident. Either he killed Jared or knows who did. Either way, he's riddled with guilt."

"What's next?" Wilson put the key into the ignition. "We go to the police?"

"Not yet. We have no physical proof, and I can't count on Lupe to back me up with the story about Matthew being in Jared's bedroom the night of his bachelor party. If the police questioned her, she'd fold. She's not going to say anything against the doctor's nephew or the doctor for that matter. But I do have another idea, one that may work even better."

"What's that?"

"Your sister."

Chapter 22

"My sister!" Wilson nearly drove off the road.

He wasn't at all happy that I wanted to call Denise and invite her to come by the house. But when I explained the purpose of my request was because of him, and the small bottle of cologne he had smuggled home as a souvenir from the Conroy Estate, he hushed up.

A little guilt can go a long way when working with a shade.

"You think the cologne is related to the case?" Wilson asked.

"More than that. I think, in addition to Matthew planting the EpiPen in Jared's dresser, that he switched out bottles of cologne and replaced it with a much more potent variety. One with actual bee venom in it, and if I'm right, Denise may be able to help me prove it."

"How?"

"Denise spritzed herself with the cologne when she was at the house."

"So? I did, too."

"Yes, but you're dead—your sister's not."

"Need you remind me?"

"I'm simply saying that you are not your sister. If I'm right, the allergic reaction she had later that night that prevented her from wearing her flouncy, pink party dress to Jared's memorial was less a result of the chrysanthemums she'd dropped off with me or anything she had eaten that night, but because of the cologne she sampled at my house."

"You think she's allergic?"

"I'm certain of it."

"Fine. Call her if you must, but in my opinion, you should get her to spritz herself again with the cologne, just in case. After all, we do need positive proof."

I rolled my eyes. I wasn't about to be a party to Wilson's sibling foolishness. I had no intention of doing anything to cause Denise any discomfort. My hope was that she had gotten the test results back from her allergist and would know if she was allergic to bee venom. If she were, it would be enough for me to suggest to Detective Romero that he test the contents of the bottle for the presence of bee venom, and the bottle itself for Matthew's fingerprints and perhaps those of his mother. If both tested positive, I believed we were one step closer to catching a killer.

Denise was waiting on my doorstep when Wilson and I arrived home. Dressed in a short summer frock and boots, despite the summer heat, she stood impatiently, tapping her foot. I sensed with the news of Billy's arrest she had second-guessed the purpose of my call and couldn't wait to learn what I knew. Patience, unfortunately, had never been one of Denise's better qualities.

"Tell me this concerns Jared Conroy," she said. "I haven't been able to think of anything else ever since I heard the news about an arrest. Cesar didn't think it was possible, but you were right, Misty. Someone murdered that boy. Do you think it's the beekeeper?"

"No." I opened the front door and pointed to the couch in the living room. "But I do think you may be able to help."

"Me?" Denise fisted her hands in excitement as she entered. She was delighted to be included in my investigation. Wilson slipped in behind her and mockingly mirrored her hand fisting about his head.

"Yes," I said. "You."

With Denise settled on the couch, I picked up the bottle of Naked Nectar, Conroy's Bee-Natural Cologne for men that Wilson had left on the coffee table.

"I have a question for you concerning this bottle." I pointed at the label. "I know it says it's venom free, safe for those allergic to bees, but I think it may have been mislabeled and that you may have reason to know that."

"You think?" Denise took the bottle from my hand and stared at the label. "If I had a penny for every bump and scratch this stuff gave me, I'd be rich. Of course, it's mislabeled."

"You're convinced?"

"I should be. After all the tests I've been through." Denise held out her arm and pointed to a light rash on the inside of her elbows. "Turns out I'm not allergic to the chrysanthemums I gave you or the shellfish Cesar and I had for dinner that night. I'm allergic to bee venom. It's the only thing, other than ragweed, the allergist found I tested positive for."

I took the bottle back from Denise. I didn't need another set of fingerprints to smudge the ones I hoped were there.

"Wait a minute, are you asking because you think the cologne's related to the case?" Denise's mouth dropped.

"I do now. This bottle was on Jared's dresser the day I picked up his suit for the memorial. I've reason to believe it's the same bottle Jared used the night he died."

"Wow!" Denise leaned back on the couch. "You think whatever's in this bottle triggered the allergic reaction that killed Jared Conroy?"

"Partly," I said. "But not entirely. Even though the bottle is labeled venom free, I believe there's enough bee venom inside to have caused a reaction, but not instantaneously. Perhaps because it's topical, it caused more of a delayed reaction. Which, in my opinion, may explain why both you and Jared didn't react right away."

"Have you talked with Cesar about this?" Denise asked.

"Not yet. I needed proof, and as I suspected, your lab results, along with the remains of that nasty rash on your arms, is exactly what I needed to convince the detective."

Wilson walked out from behind the couch. "You're certain she shouldn't try it one more time? Might be more convincing if the rash were fresh."

I cleared the air with my hand above my head, a signal to Wilson to stifle, then turned my attention back to Denise. "How about we call Detective Romero?"

Romero didn't just return my call, he showed up within the hour with Detectives Smiley and Williams. Common sense told me it didn't take three detectives to pick up a bottle of cologne that may or may not prove to be evidence in an open investigation. Rather, I sensed, since Jared's death had been officially ruled a homicide and Romero had credited me with suspecting something was wrong from the start, that both Williams and Smiley had a renewed interest in me and hadn't just come along for the ride.

Denise was first to the door and greeted Romero with a welcome kiss on the cheek and a polite handshake for the detectives.

I followed two steps behind and invited them in as far as the entry.

Noting their curiosity about the house, and sensing neither had ever visited a real psychic before, I pointed out the obvious. The old grandfather clock from a Broadway production of *Arsenic and Old Lace*. The living room set from *Sunset Boulevard*. The candlesticks on the dining table from *The Addams Family* TV series. Then went on to explain that the home's original owner was Denise's brother, none other than the award-winning set designer, Wilson Thorne.

"If you expected globes and tarot cards, you won't find any. However, if you like, I have candles in the closet, but I really don't need them."

Romero cocked his head in the direction of the two detectives with an I-told-you-so expression on his face. "Nobody asked, Misty."

"No, but Williams here is wondering. I can tell." I pointed at the young detective. With what he had told me about his mother's experience, he may not have been a believer, but I could feel his wandering eyes, probing the bookshelves and the narrow cranny beneath the stairs where Bossypants liked to hide.

"She's right, Williams, you can look all you want, but you won't find any of that stuff here. Teapot, maybe, but that's about it." Romero stepped into the living room and spotted the cologne bottle on the coffee table. "This it?"

"Yes, and if you have your people test it for prints, I believe, in addition to Jared's prints, you'll find those of Matthew Conroy and maybe his mother's." I wiped my hands on my skirt. I wasn't worried about Wilson's prints because shades, like ghosts, didn't leave prints. My own and Denise's were easy enough to explain.

I walked over to the table and was about to pick up the bottle and hand it to Romero when Williams stepped in front of me.

"I'm sorry, but you don't really think we can use that? Not after you've removed it from a crime scene and you, and who knows who else, has handled it?"

I didn't care for Williams' authoritative tone.

"Of course you can use it. I found it. It's evidence. Why else would I have called Detective Romero? If you don't want to test it for prints, fine. Test the contents. The bottle may be marked venom free, but I believe if your forensics experts test it, they'll find it contains a high concentrate of bee venom. Possibly higher than that in other Conroy products."

Smiley put his hand on my shoulder. I sensed a sympathetic ally, but still a loyalist to the department.

"What Detective Williams is trying to tell you is that you finding the bottle and having it here like it is now, well...it's not good. There's no chain of custody. No documentation recording where this came from, who found it, or when."

Wilson threw up his hands and walked back to the study. "Don't blame me. If I hadn't picked up the bottle and brought it back, Denise never would have tested it, and you would never have known it was laced with bee venom in the first place."

"Don't be so sure of yourself," I said.

"Excuse me?" Williams looked around the room uneasily. "Are you talking to Detective Romero?"

I glared at Wilson. If he had only left Jared's cologne on the dresser, the police wouldn't be talking to me like a child who had been caught shoplifting.

"More to myself," I said.

"You do that often?" Williams glanced back at Romero.

"Only as often as I need to," I said.

"Well, for now," Williams said, "I need you to focus. You mind telling me how it is you came to have this bottle?"

"Not at all. I took it from the guest house at the Conroy estate where Jared was living, right *after* your detectives completed their investigation."

"And exactly why did you go up to the Conroy Estate?" Williams glanced smugly at Romero.

"Because my client, Amy, asked me to. After she learned her fiancé had died, she was concerned the doctor wasn't thinking straight. According to her, he was acting irrationally and lashing out at people. She was afraid the police might think she was involved. I wanted to assure her she had nothing to worry about."

"And did you?" Williams asked. "Assure her?"

"Not quite. When I visited the estate, I could feel the presence of evil in the house. And that feeling got stronger when I went from the main house to the guest house, where Jared had lived. Whatever happened to Jared started there—in the guest house— and I felt the need to investigate."

"So, you were running an unauthorized investigation on your own?"

I didn't care for William's tone.

"Yes, I knew the police weren't going to find anything. You can call that a hunch or anything you like, but let's face it, the police decided early on Jared's death was accidental. You all knew the doctor was grief-stricken, and no doubt didn't think he was making much sense. If it weren't for the doctor, and his connections with the department, your people wouldn't have given it so much as a look-see. And quite frankly, since the police had already been there, I didn't see the problem if I did a little poking around."

"Well, it is a problem," Williams said. "You've interfered with an active investigation, and whether this bottle of cologne was ever important or not, it won't be now. We've no way of proving where it came from or when."

I realized I was the only one sitting. Denise, Romero, and his two sidekick detectives, who I was growing less and less fond of, were all standing over me, looking down at me like I was some pathetic, deranged little old lady.

"Go ahead, Detective, tell me. I'm fired, right?"

Romero picked up the bottle. "Misty you were never—"

"What? Hired? I'm well aware of that. It was me who called you in the first place, remember?"

"Look," Romero said, "if it makes you feel any better, I'll have Williams take the bottle by our forensics guys and run some tests, but, really it's—"

"Wait. There's something else." I reached into my skirt pocket and took the pills Lupe had given me. "As long as you're doing that, take these as well. The doctor made them up for Amy. I'd be curious to know what's in them."

Williams stepped forward. "How did you—"

"Never mind," I said, "just have them tested."

"Detective." Williams sounded frustrated. "Tell her she can't be using LAPD as her own private testing facility."

Romero took the pills from my hand. "I'm sorry, but Detective Williams is right, we—"

"Save it, Detective. I understand what you and your team think. I've gotten in your way, and you'd prefer I step aside and let the police handle it."

Chapter 23

In my younger days, being asked to step aside would have kept me awake all night. I would have spent the night fitfully shadow boxing the detectives' comments about my actions with retorts of my own about the department's ability to be misled by people like the doctor with his generous donations to the Police Protective League. As it was, I didn't sleep a wink. Not because Romero had made it very clear LAPD didn't need my help, but because I felt Billy did. And if what Eli and Christina had told me about the doctor's will was true, then Amy and the baby were in trouble. And Amy had no idea.

My first thought the following morning was to call Lupe and find a way for her to remove Amy from the house. Maybe take her back to Lupe's own small apartment, where she might stay until I had a chance to clear her name and find whoever was behind Jared's death. But the longer I thought about it, the more I knew the answer wasn't that simple. While Dr. Conroy may not have known where Lupe lived or ever been to her apartment, he did know that Amy was friendly with the housekeeper. The moment the doctor couldn't find Amy, he would question Lupe about the girl's whereabouts. And Lupe would fold, as might my investigation if the doctor were to have any idea what I was really up to.

My second thought was that I had no proof or clear idea who had killed Jared. My brief encounter with Matthew had left me with as many questions as it did answers. Yes, the boy felt guilty. It radiated off him. But was it because he was involved or just suspicious about his cousin's death? As for Lupe's eyewitness report of Matthew standing in front of Jared's dresser, that too wasn't enough to prove he had replaced Jared's pollen-free cologne with one more potent or that he had messed with Jared's EpiPen. Nor was the fact Madeline had shown up at the mansion with her son and the party bus prior to Jared's party. All of it suspicious, but evidence? As the detective would say, "None of it enough to drag into a court of law." On the other hand, the doctor was clearly bipolar, but even in a darkened state, would he have been crazy enough to kill his own son? It was hard to imagine. My thoughts swelled with possibilities.

It's times like these that I've learned to let go and let the universe take over. As a respite, I returned to my garden and tended to my herbs. There's something about planting, pruning, getting my hands dirty that does wonders for my mind. I knew it wouldn't be long before something would break, and when it did, I'd be back in the game again. Invited by LAPD or otherwise.

I couldn't have been in the yard longer than an hour before my cell rang. I put my trowel down, and as I pulled my phone from my apron, my hand tingled. Like a small electrical charge, it ran from the tips of my fingers to my heart. I had felt the sensation before, always with clients with whom I was close and always in situations of great stress. I knew without looking the call was from Carlene.

Her voice was shaking. "The doctor tried to kill me!"

"What?" With one hand on my thigh, I pushed myself to my feet. Getting up and down wasn't as easy as it once had been. "Where are you? What happened?"

"I had an accident. I nearly drove off a cliff last night in Malibu. The police arrested me, and I spent the night in jail. I called an Uber this morning to pick me up. I was going to call Amy, but I didn't dare."

I closed my eyes and had a mental picture of Carlene huddled in the back seat of a car with the phone beneath her chin.

"How are you doing?" I asked.

"I'll be okay, but my car's totaled. It's a miracle I'm alive. Someone must have tampered with the brakes. I just had the car in for service."

"Where are you going now?"

"I have a college friend who has a ranch in the north valley. I called her and told her I needed to hang out for a while. I'm scared. It's the doctor, I know it. He knows who I am, and he's on to me." Carlene sounded out of breath.

"Slow down. Tell me everything that happened, and start at the beginning."

Carlene sighed and began again. "Yesterday I got this call from Joe, the manager at Mastro's where I did Jared's bachelor party. He said a friend had called him, some VIP who works with a lot of celebs. Joe didn't tell me who, only that whoever was calling was working with some actor who had been in the restaurant the night of Jared's bachelor party. He left before all the excitement, so I guess he didn't know Jared had died. He only saw the setup and said he liked it. Anyway, this actor wanted to know if whoever had planned the party might be available to plan a classy event—a birthday party—for the guy's wife at their home in Malibu. It was all kind of mysterious, but then, that's Hollywood, right?"

I agreed it wasn't unusual. The really big stars had personal assistants who seldom used the star's name when booking hotels or checking out potential contractors for various events. Often times, not until there was a real need to know, was the celeb's name revealed to the potential hire.

"Anyway, Joe wouldn't give me the name, and I didn't think much about it. He set up a meeting at Geoffrey's in Malibu at seven p.m. and told me he'd given my description to whoever it was. He said I'd recognize the client when he walked in, and I could thank him later. Two hours passed, and when no one showed, I gave up and started back down the canyon. That's when my brakes gave out. The police said it was a miracle I hit the mountainside and didn't drive off the cliff."

"I assume you told the police you thought someone had tampered with your brakes."

"A lot of good that would do. I couldn't prove it, and even if I could, you think I'd risk bringing charges against the doctor? The police asked me if I'd been drinking, and when I said I'd had a drink at the bar while waiting for a client, they did a sobriety test. I wasn't drunk, but because I admitted I had a drink and was pretty shaken, they charged me with a lesser offense. Called it a wet and reckless and that it came with an automatic overnight at the gray bar hotel. Fun, huh?"

Carlene didn't have to be sitting in front of me for me to know she was still reeling from last night's experience. She had barely paused to breathe the entire time we talked.

"The thing is, I took Kanan Dune from the valley to Malibu, and the car was fine. But as I drove home, back through the canyon, something happened to the brakes. When I tried to slow down, my foot went straight to the floorboard!"

"And you're convinced it was Dr. Conroy?" I asked.

"I didn't see him do it if that's what you mean. I didn't have to. The doctor would never get his own hands dirty. He has people who do that kind of thing. Always has."

"But surely somebody would have seen something? What about the valet? Didn't you park in the lot?"

"No. I parked on PCH and walked up to the restaurant. I didn't want to pay a valet."

Not an unusual practice. Lots of visitors to the area parked along the Pacific Coast Highway to get a better view of the water and save the valet fee.

"I assume you locked the car?"

"I did, but I'm not the only one with a set of keys. The car was my mother's, a Mercedes diesel sedan, a gift from the doctor. It's at least twenty-five years old. My mother gave it to me when I graduated from high school. Dr. Conroy always kept an extra set of keys around, probably still has them in the desk in his office."

Everything Carlene told me fit like a piece to a jigsaw puzzle. Including the idea Conroy wouldn't have done his own dirty work.

"You think the doctor arranged to have you go out to Geoffrey's, had someone follow you there, and while you waited around, messed with the car's brakes?"

"I'd bet my life on it, and something else too."

"What?" I asked.

"He wanted me to know it was him."

"How do you know that?"

"Because of Jared's cologne. I smelled it when I got in the car. In hindsight, I should have gotten out right then, but I didn't think about it. Jared had been in the car with me a dozen times. I'd smelled that cologne off and on so often I guess it didn't register. But after the crash, I remembered the scent, and I knew it was no accident."

A chill ran down my back. Taste and smell can trigger a memory, and in the most traumatized state, crack open an awareness deep beneath our consciousness.

"I started to think back, and I realized there was no way the smell of Jared's cologne would have still been in the car. The only possible reason was that the doctor wanted me to know this wasn't an accident. Whoever he hired to tamper with the brakes had sprayed the cologne inside so that it'd be the last thing I smelled before I drove over the cliff."

My stomach dropped. "Do me a favor. Go stay with your friend, and don't tell anybody, even Amy, where you're going. I think it'd be a good idea if nobody knew where you were right now."

"But what about Amy?"

"I promise you, whatever's going on, I'll find out...and it's going to be okay. Until then, you need to go somewhere safe. I'll call you when it's over."

I hung up and wondered about the doctor and his hired hand. Had the man in the gray sedan also followed Carlene to Malibu and tampered with the brakes of her car? If so, I had a strong feeling that I hadn't seen the last of him.

Chapter 24

As soon as I hung up with Carlene, I went inside and found Wilson. He was, as I expected, in the study reclined in his chair, feet up on the desk, head bowed with his hands tented in front of his face. His pensive pose.

"Dare I disturb you?" I asked.

"You're here about Carlene."

"You know?"

"About the accident? Yes, my lady friends told me. We've been in touch."

I should have known. To my knowledge, this wasn't the first time Wilson had communicated with the luminaries without being in their presence. Unlike mortals, those on the other side of the veil aren't dependent upon mobile devices to facilitate their communications. It all happens seamlessly. Near as I can tell, it's like breathing. An idea can float from one mind to another with ease.

"You're getting good at receiving their thoughts," I said.

Less than a year ago, Wilson was like most new shades, unaware of his abilities and even more uncertain of his purpose. I had done what I could to educate him on his situation, but clearly, his lady friends had taken him a step further.

Wilson flicked a piece of lint from his shoulder.

"But that's not what's important right now. What is important is what Eli shared with me about Carlene and Matthew. Perhaps you'd like to sit down."

Wilson pointed to the window seat where Bossypants had

curled up, basking in the morning sun.

"Go ahead." I picked up my cat and curled my legs beneath me on the window seat. "What exactly did your luminaries tell you?"

"Matthew came by to see the doctor yesterday, right after we met with him outside Conroy's headquarters."

I rolled my eyes. If my mind hadn't been so full of questions about who had killed Jared, I might have seen this coming.

"Once Matthew arrived, he told his uncle some old-lady psychic had camped outside their offices and accused him of having something to do with Jared's murder. Then two of them went into the doctor's study to talk."

"I never accused him."

"Implicated then." Wilson took his feet off the desk and sat up straight. "Along with the doctor."

"So Conroy knows I'm up to something." I stroked Bossy's back.

"He does."

"And what about Carlene? How did the doctor know about her?"

"Amy told him," Wilson said.

"When?"

"After Billy's arrest. The doctor heard Amy talking on the phone and asked her who she was talking to. She confessed everything, told him all about Carlene, how they met, and became friends. How Carlene had set Amy up with Jared and, because the doctor blamed all of Jared's old high school buddies for his drinking, how Jared and Carlene made Amy swear she'd never say a word about Carlene to Jared's father. It didn't take much for Conroy to put it all together and figure Carlene was Carlita."

I could see how Amy, in her confused state, might have confessed all kinds of things to the doctor.

"But how did Conroy know where Carlene would be last night?" I asked.

"Once the doctor figured out who Carlene really was, he devised a plan to take care of her and asked Matthew to help."

"But how did the doctor know where Carlene would be last night?"

"Exactly as Carlene told you. She received a call from the manager of Mastro's that someone was looking for a party planner, and she accepted a meeting in Malibu. The doctor asked Matthew to arrange for said party planner to be there, and then the doctor called in a favor from one of his henchmen. Conroy instructed his henchman to followed Carlene, and he cut the brake hose on her car."

"What about Amy, where was she when Matthew arrived?"

"Napping in the solarium, she likes to go there to watch the sunset. Christina was with her. Turns out, Christina knew nothing of the plan Conroy and Matthew cooked up to take care of her daughter."

I didn't think so. I couldn't imagine a scenario whereby Christina would know about the doctor's plan to harm Carlene and not to try to do something to stop it.

"And Eli knew all this last night, and never said anything to Christina or reached out to you and insist you tell me?"

"Not a word."

I wasn't surprised. Luminaries are only loyal to themselves.

"Exactly how did Christina find out?"

"The old-fashioned way. She saw it on the morning news while Conroy was shaving. She recognized the car when the news cameras caught it being pulled from the canyon." Wilson put his elbows on the desk and leaned closer to me. "You're right about luminaries, Old Gal. They're self-centered to the core."

I bit my tongue. Wilson had heard enough from me from about how shallow and self-centered the luminaries could be.

"It seems Eli didn't think to mention anything about Carlene's accident to Christina last night because, well, it just didn't concern her."

"I see."

The fact that Eli and Christina had maintained a relationship, both in life and on the other side of the veil, could only mean one thing: Their vengeance for the doctor had bound them together. Much as they may have disliked one another, their joint dislike for the doctor was even greater.

"However," Wilson continued, "unhappy as my lady friends may be with one another, they've asked me to address another more pressing issue, which concerns you."

I was afraid to ask.

"They'd like me to remind you that up to now, you've discovered nothing you can take to the police as evidence concerning Jared's murder and that the clock is ticking. They want to know if you've given any more thought to their proposal."

I caught my breath. "You mean that I kill the doctor?"

"It is a plausible solution. A bit distasteful, I must admit. But if the doctor were simply to cease to exist, Eli and Christina would have to vacate the mansion, and poor little Amy," Wilson paused and looked up at the ceiling. "well, she'd be fixed for life. But you'd have to hurry. We both know the doctor plans to try to persuade the police she's involved with Jared's murder. And once he does that...it may be too late."

I felt as though I had been sucker-punched. I could barely catch my breath. Had all my efforts to help Wilson been for naught?

"The ends don't justify the means, Wilson. Despite the fact as your lady friends have pointed out, that we've learned nothing I can present to the police as evidence, I refuse to take justice into my own hands. I'm not some vigilante. That's not what I do, and you shouldn't either."

I felt the need to emphasize that, as a shade, Wilson's future soul might be in peril should he decide to do something on his own. While a ghost couldn't kill or facilitate any action that might result in the death of a mortal, a shade had more free will. It wasn't inconceivable Wilson might be persuaded to do something for which, I worried, he might be harshly judged.

Wilson dismissed my worry with a wave of his hand and told me I could think whatever I liked. "However," he added, "according to Eli, you're going to have an opportunity to test this vigilante theory of yours, and very soon."

"What do you mean?"

"It appears after yesterday's upset between the doctor and Amy, the two had that little heart-to-heart; she admitted how lost and lonely she felt and that she needed a friend. Someone she could talk to, and she asked Conroy if she might have you in for tea."

My stomach roiled. I knew where this was going.

"And surprise, surprise—" Wilson clapped his hands. "—the doctor agreed. Of course, if you ask me, it's all a setup. But then, what do I know?"

I doubted the idea for tea was Amy's idea alone, but one Eli had planted in Amy's head, and Conroy, seeing it as an opportunity to meet with me one-on-one, agreed.

I stood up. Aside from the luminary's desire that I poison the doctor, what might a tea mean? To Amy? To the doctor? To me? I placed Bossypants back on the window seat and got as far as the doorway when I turned and noticed a silver flask on Wilson's desk.

"Is that Jared's?" I asked.

Wilson picked up the flat silver flask and held it in his open palm. "Yes, lovely, isn't it?"

I closed my eyes and shook my head. "Please tell me it's not the one Raul came by to retrieve from Lupe?"

"Oh come now, Old Gal, you don't really think Jared only had one hidden cache in the guest house, do you?"

"So that's not the one Lupe gave Raul? You didn't somehow manage to steal it back from him?" I couldn't put it past Wilson's kleptomaniac tendencies to think he might not have wanted to lift the flask for his own collection of memorabilia. So much of the old craftsman was full of things I suspected he had obtained from similar habits while mortal.

"Please," Wilson tsked. "You witnessed it yourself. Lupe gave Raul the flask when he came up to the house. His flask had Jared's initials etched into it. This, however," Wilson tossed the flask in the air and caught it handily, "is a second Lupe kept in the kitchen for her own private use. Like you, when you palmed Amy's engagement ring, I thought perhaps she might be better off without it."

The idea Wilson continued to add to his collection of memorabilia convinced me he hadn't really bought into the idea of his temporary condition.

"You can't take it with you, Wilson. Not any of it." I gestured to the collectibles on the desk. "It doesn't leave here when you do. All that you see here is just temporary."

"Yes, that's too bad, isn't it? But it's no good stuffed away in some kitchen drawer. Lupe doesn't need it, and the police aren't interested. Unlike Jared's cologne, this has no bearing on the case, and I like it. Besides, perhaps when I'm gone, you'll take some comfort in seeing it on my desk. It'll remind you of me and this little discourse you and I always seem to have. Tell me, Old Gal, when I'm gone, will you miss me?"

"Like a headache," I said.

Chapter 25

Amy rang my cell phone later that afternoon, exactly as Wilson had predicted, with an invitation to tea the following day. In her mind, both she and the doctor had experienced a terrible tragedy and needed to do what they could to support one another. She pleaded with me to come and said she couldn't wait to see me.

I sensed the girl was in total denial. The doctor had painted a very different picture of events that, in Amy's current state of mind, she had substituted for the truth.

"We had such a good talk, Misty. I only wish Jared had been able to speak with his father like I did before he died. He told me so many stories. He and his wife didn't think they could have kids, and when Jared was born, it changed everything. All those wild parties they used to have here at the house? They turned into family get-togethers for the kids. Jared's aunt Elizabeth, and his uncle Edward and his wife Madeline, they'd come by with their kids, and there would be pony rides and games. They even had a puppet theater in the garden. He said Jared loved puppets."

Amy's willingness to accept Conroy's description of Jared's childhood smacked of denial and desperation—of a desire to believe in a world she wanted to be true, and one in which she hoped might mend her own fractured past. But when she mentioned Billy, my jaw dropped.

"The doctor even agreed Billy couldn't possibly be guilty of murder. He's offered to find him a lawyer. He thinks Jared was murdered by one of his competitors who wanted to hurt him. He said it could be a cut-throat business. Whatever happened, Dr.

Conroy's devastated, and he said we need each other now more than ever."

I knew right then exactly how easily the doctor had manipulated Amy, how he had gently coaxed the secret of Amy's relationship with his illegitimate daughter with a promise to help Billy. Amy had no idea as to the gravity of her confession or what the revelation of her secret might mean to her friend.

I felt it best I not let on. "I'm so happy for you, Amy. This must make you feel better."

"Yes, it's wonderful, isn't it? I even took Dr. Conroy with me for my ultrasound. And guess what? I'm having a boy. A boy! Can you believe it?"

As Wilson and I drove to the Conroy mansion, I had no idea what we might be walking into. Perhaps some cordial event where the three of us—Amy, the doctor, and myself—sat quietly, sipped our tea, and nibbled finger sandwiches while ignoring what each of us suspected about the other. A quiet visit full of pleasantries, whereby we'd shake hands, wish each other well, then bid one another goodbye.

Or maybe it'd be a much deadlier scenario.

I knew the idea for the tea had been Eli's, a thought she had planted in Amy's head in hopes that I would carry out the luminaries' plan to murder the doctor. But what if I didn't? What if, rather than spike the doctor's tea myself, the luminaries had convinced Lupe to sprinkle his tea with his digitalis medication or as Eli had said, the more organic version from Conroy's garden? With just the tiniest taste on our lips, one of us was doomed, certain to be dead before our tea cooled. What was I to do, just sit back and watch?

And what if I was wrong? What if the luminaries were merely goading me to see how far I might go? What then?

Was the truth even more twisted? Had the doctor agreed to have me to tea so that he might murder me? Or was it because he thought it might be the perfect opportunity to settle things quietly between us? After all, Matthew had told Conroy of our encounter. What the doctor didn't know was that I knew he knew about our meeting. He also didn't know I had been to the Conroy mansion, not once, but twice before, or that Lupe had given me Amy's ring. The possibilities of my death versus the doctor's death exhausted me. As a psychic, I can read many people. Unfortunately, my abilities end there, and I'm not able to read myself, and I could only hope for the best of all possible outcomes.

Despite my concerns for my personal safety, I needed to go. Amy's future, that of the baby, and Billy's future depended upon it. I knew the doctor was insane, that he had targeted Carlene, and I was just as certain the rumors he had murdered his wife and paramour were true. But was he disturbed enough to collude with his nephew and Madeline to kill his own son? Or had Matthew and Madeline manipulated the doctor, and he was nothing but a deranged and innocent bystander in his son's death? I didn't know, and like the luminaries said, I had no proof. My only hope was that now that the police knew Jared's death was no accident, they'd come up with some evidence connecting the doctor to Jared's murder. Unless, of course, the doctor convinced them Amy had been involved. After all, she did know about Jared's cologne and where he kept his EpiPen. In my mind, time was running short, and I had no choice. I had to act. So I tabled my worries and dressed in my best go-to-tea outfit, which was nothing more than a fresher version of what I already had on: a long skirt and a tie-dyed t-shirt. At the last minute, I clipped my wavy gray hair back into a fancy barrette, then checked myself in the hallway mirror, patted my growing mid-line—made a promise to myself once this was over I'd lighten up on the pasta and lose those troublesome twenty pounds—then sighed and grabbed a silk scarf and threw it over my shoulders. Voila! Wilson and I were ready to return to the House that Vanity Built.

*   *   *

Amy greeted me at the door dressed in a simple summer shift that hinted at her baby bulge. She looked rested and relaxed.

"You came," she said. "I knew you would."

Like a child, Amy threw her arms around me and hugged me close. I returned the welcome squeeze, then stepped back, and with her hands in mine, looked at her. The girl was glowing with new life, the color in her cheeks rosy.

"You look well," I said. My eyes traveled to the doctor who stood behind her, his hands clasped one on top of the other on his cane. He gave what I felt was a thin, obligatory smile, and nodded his head.

"I am," Amy said. "The doctor's been seeing to it." She gestured with her left hand to the doctor, and I noticed the sparkle of her engagement ring.

Dr. Conroy stepped forward. "It's nice of you to join us, Ms. Dawn. Amy's told me quite a bit about you. I apologize if I seemed a little overprotective of her at Jared's memorial. It was a difficult time for us both. I'm sure you understand."

Before I had time to answer, Amy took my arm beneath her own and led me down the long entry hall toward the kitchen.

With my head close to hers, I whispered, "I see you're wearing Jared's ring."

I wondered how much Amy had shared with the doctor about the ring. Had she told him it was missing and that I had given it to her? Or even worse, that Lupe had found it and given it to me? Either scenario wouldn't bode well for Lupe or me.

"Relax," Amy patted my hand. "I told the doctor I found it in the guest house. Exactly as you told me I had. I never mentioned anything to him about Lupe finding it, or that she gave it to you. If he even thought Lupe had anything to do with the ring, he'd fire her, and I need what friends I have around here to stay."

I was grateful Amy hadn't revealed my relationship with Lupe to the doctor or the housekeeper's connection to the ring. I deliberately hadn't called Lupe to tell her I'd been invited to tea. After my last visit to the mansion, I felt Lupe was in an emotionally precarious situation, and I didn't want to do anything that might rattle her. Best not to give her too much time to think about it.

As a result, I was relieved when I walked into the kitchen and Lupe, dressed in a crisp white housekeeper's apron, gave me nothing more than a slight nod of recognition that she might give any guest. My sense was that Amy had told her I was coming to tea, and Lupe had braced herself for the unexpected. Either that or Lupe was under the influence of the luminaries, comatose to the world, and following their instructions with no sense of self or understanding of what it was she was about to do.

I paused at the marble island, where Lupe stood with her eyes fixed on a silver tea service.

"May I?" I picked up one of the teacups, a lovely English bone china with a delicate blue and gold grapevine trim, and glanced over the rim at Lupe. Her eyes darted from me and back to the tea service, while her hands spread wide across her apron, smoothing it against her hips. Was it my imagination, or was there a slight bulge in her apron pocket? Big enough perhaps for a pill bottle? Had she done something to spike the tea, poison it perhaps?

I comforted myself with the knowledge a luminary couldn't plant an idea in the mind of a mortal and cause them to do something they wouldn't want to do on their own. However, luminaries were known to be very convincing. If Lupe were to kill the doctor, she might have easily been persuaded to think it to her advantage. No doctor. No challenge to her green card. No record of her past.

"It's Hammersley." Amy placed her hand on my back. "It belonged to Jared's mother. The doctor says it was her favorite. Beautiful, isn't it?"

"Ladies—" Dr. Conroy pulled Amy away and pointed with his cane in the direction of the solarium. "—shall we?"

As I followed the doctor and Amy through the kitchen and into the sunroom, we passed Wilson and his lady friends. They were sitting at the high-top cafe table, exactly as they had been before with a deck of cards between them. The doctor appeared to be totally unaware of their presence.

Which was not surprising.

Luminaries can choose to make themselves seen or heard when and where they like. It's entirely individual. As I understood it, it varied by circumstance. While Lupe had reported she had frequently heard the doctor talking to himself or someone whom Lupe felt was the doctor's wife, I had no reason to believe, based upon the fact the doctor didn't appear to react to their presence in the sunroom, that he had actually ever seen the luminaries. And he certainly wasn't acting like he saw or heard them now. Luminaries by their very nature were vain, and I doubted either would want the doctor to see them in death.

I scowled as we passed.

Eli raised a brow. "Such a lovely day for tea, don't you think? I wonder whose idea it was?"

"Does it really matter?" Christina asked. "People are in such a rush these days. Nobody just sits and visits anymore."

"Yes, such a shame," Eli gestured with her cards. "High tea's become a dying art, don't you think?"

The doctor and Amy settled themselves on one of two green-striped loveseats in the center of the room, while I made myself comfortable opposite them on the matching sofa. Between us, a glass table was set with a three-tiered cake plate on which scones, finger sandwiches, and small cakes had been carefully placed.

Dr. Conroy was first to speak. "I must confess, Ms. Dawn, after Amy told me about you, I googled you. You're quite the celebrity. Seems strange to me, you and I both living in the same city and knowing some of the same people, that we haven't met before. With all the parties I used to have here, I can't imagine why we never crossed paths."

"I'm afraid I've never been much for the party scene, Doctor."

"Yes, but you did have quite the Rolodex in the day. Big Hollywood names. Politicians. Not to mention your work with

LAPD and the FBI."

I smiled and stared back into the doctor's gray face and wondered if I were looking at that of a quirky genius or an evil magician who had orchestrated the murder of his own son. If the doctor had been a rational being, I might have been able to read him, but his diseased mind was too convoluted for me to even try.

"I have been busy," I said.

"It appears from those investigations you worked on that the police, particularly LAPD, hold you in high regard."

"Sometimes." I wanted to add but not at the moment. My recent fall out with the detectives had convinced me they thought me less than useful. Instead, I said, "Unfortunately, even psychics don't get it right all the time."

"Yes, but with your history and connection to Amy, I'm surprised they haven't invited you in on this case."

I shrugged. I wasn't about to give away my eroding connections with the case or the LAPD.

"You see, I find what you do interesting, and I hope you'll forgive me if I talk candidly, but it seems to me if you really are able to predict the future, you would have foreseen my son's death. And you might have at least warned Amy what was about to happen."

I was prepared for the question, and I knew it was the doctor's subtle way of undermining my relationship with Amy.

"The truth is psychics can't predict everything. Particularly life-changing events that don't happen to the person they're counseling. If it helps, a psychic is more of an intuitive. I can sense the wants and desires of those who come to me, but those close to them? That's another case entirely. Since I never met Jared, I can only tell you I was surprised to hear about his death and sorry for your loss."

"So you're telling me, even though you claim intuitive powers and spoke with Amy just days before my son's death, that you had no idea he was about to die, who might have killed him, or how it might have happened?"

The muscles in my back began to constrict. Both the doctor

and I knew I was aware of more than I let on.

"I'm sorry," I said, "I wish I could be more helpful."

The doctor's eyes narrowed like darts.

"As do I, Ms. Dawn. You see, despite my reluctance to accept what it is you claim to do, it would give me great comfort to know anything—anything at all—you think might be pertinent to the case. With all your past experience working with the police, you must have some idea."

"I'm sorry to say the police haven't shared anything with me."

"Nor with me. At least not since they arrested Billy." The doctor patted Amy's knee. "Which of course, we both know is foolishness. Unless, Amy dear, you've kept something from me." The doctor laughed as though he had been making a joke.

The irony of his statement wasn't lost on me. But the cunning manner in which he joked about what I knew was his intention to turn the investigation on to Amy, caused my mind to race.

Lupe interrupted. In her hands, she carried a large silver tray with a teapot, creamer, and sugar bowl. She placed the tray on the table between us,

"Tea?"

The doctor nodded, and I watched as Lupe filled each cup, leaving room for cream and sugar.

"I hope you haven't forgotten Amy's pills. The doctor winked at Amy. "Her OB insists she takes them every morning."

Amy put her hand on top of the doctor's hand. "You'll have to excuse Dr. Conroy. He's like a mother hen these days. He's developed his own concoction of prenatals. A super vitamin with a little melatonin added. He's convinced that I need it."

"And your OB agrees," Conroy said. "They won't hurt you, and goodness knows with all you've been through, you need them to calm your nerves. Don't want to have a colicky-baby now, do we?"

Amy rolled her eyes. Lupe reached into her apron and produced the bottle I had noticed bulging from her pocket. Three oatmeal-colored capsules, exactly like those Lupe had shown me just the day before. She placed them on the table in front of Amy.

The fact that Lupe didn't look at me or even so much as blink as Amy picked up the pills convinced me Lupe was under the luminaries' influence. I glanced back at Eli, who shrugged as though she had no idea about the pills or why I should be concerned.

"Sugar?" Lupe spooned a teaspoon of sugar from the bowl and held it above Amy's cup.

The doctor shook his finger. "Not for her. She needs to watch her sugars for now, at least until the baby's born. But for me, yes. Two spoonfuls, please. Load it up." The doctor held up his cup for Lupe, and I watched as she spilled the sugar into his cup.

Eli sat forward and pointed a long finger in the direction of the doctor. "Oh, yes, dear, take as much as you like. Sweeten your tea. It'll help you sleep. Just like it did me."

Christina slapped Eli's hand, and the two giggled so hard for a moment it looked like they might fall off their chairs.

The poison was in the sugar! It had to be.

The luminaries were aware of the doctor's budding concern for Amy's welfare and weren't at all concerned he would allow Amy to sweeten her tea. But for the doctor, they knew of his sweet tooth and had no concern. And if the pills in Lupe's apron were nothing more than Amy's prenatals, then Lupe had to have found another way to poison the doctor. I had a vision of Lupe, standing over the kitchen sink, wearing long rubber gloves to protect herself while mixing clippings from the foxglove in the garden with the sugar in the bowl.

"And you, Ms. Dawn," the doctor nodded to the sugar bowl, "would you have sugar with your tea? Or are you sweet enough already?"

I shook my head.

"Then perhaps a wee bit of lemon? Can't have tea without lemon, now, can we?" Insisting, the doctor took a lemon wedge from a silver bowl on the table and dribbled some of the juice into my tea.

Then with his cup to mine, he smiled at Amy, and toasted, "To

Amy and the baby."

I had to do something. If the sugar had been poisoned as I suspected, the irony of the doctor killing himself unknowingly, exactly as Jared had, wasn't lost on me. Nor was the fact the doctor had insisted I have lemon with my tea. Had he poisoned the lemon? Was that his plan all along? Agree to a tea so that he might taint my cup with enough digitalis to cause a heart attack? The very thought of it caused my heart to race. I dared not take a sip. I felt clammy. Before either Amy or the doctor could put their cups to their lips, I dropped Eli's expensive Hammersley china teacup on the table and stood up.

My move, so sudden and abrupt, not only knocked over the glass table and the tray with the silver tea service, but I also bumped the doctor, causing him to drop his cup to the floor. In front of me, the silver tea service and the delicate bone china tea set with its beautiful hand-painted gold and blue grapevines was shattered. The cups and saucers destroyed, smashed to smithereens.

"I am so sorry." I put my hand to my head. "I...I don't know what's gotten into me. I feel faint. Please, you'll have to excuse me, I need air."

I stumbled around the table and moved as quickly as I could toward the back door. I needed to get outside. Once there, I stood with my hands against the porch's cool railing and took a deep breath. The air never tasted sweeter.

Chapter 26

"Are you okay?" Dr. Conroy joined me on the back porch. Like a vulture, he leaned on his cane, with his shoulders scrunched up around his ears.

I reminded myself I needed to be strong.

"I'm sorry," I said. "I don't know what came over me. I felt as though I couldn't breathe and needed fresh air. Is Amy okay?"

"She'll be fine. I told her to go lie down."

The doctor nodded to the sculpture garden and suggested we take a stroll.

I could only hope Wilson's attention was not solely focused on his lady friends and that he noticed my absence. I took a deep breath and moved ahead. I wasn't about to be intimidated or let the doctor know how uncomfortable I felt.

As we walked, the doctor explained the path was part of his daily workout. "A mile-long loop," he said, "two-thousand steps, twice around through the garden and the pool area. Sufficient enough to keep these old bones in shape, despite my need for a cane."

Then taking my arm beneath his own, he pointed to the marble statues and referred to each as a former friend: Mansfield, Taylor, Gabor. All of whom had either aged out of favor or died.

Once beyond the marble garden, we went through the hedge, dividing the backyard from the pool and tennis area, and the doctor dropped my arm.

"You and I don't like each other very much, do we?"

I refused to let the abruptness of his statement shock me. I kept my eyes on the path ahead.

"I don't believe we really know each other well enough for me to say."

"No?" The doctor stopped and took a silver monogrammed cigarette case from his jacket. "Are you telling me the rumors about my wild parties, my wife's death, or that of my housekeeper haven't caused you to wonder? And now, with the death of my son, that you haven't formed an opinion about me?"

"I try not to listen to gossip, Doctor."

The doctor took a cigarette from the case and tapped it lightly against the cover. "But you do read the papers. You know I promoted Matthew to replace Jared as my choice for vice president." The doctor paused and glared at me. "You were waiting for him outside my offices, like a trap." Conroy lit the cigarette, inhaled, then blew a ring of smoke from the side of his mouth. "In fact, I'd bet the reason why you were there was that you think he killed Jared. Or maybe you think I did, and Matthew rushed back here to tell me."

There it was—the gauntlet. The challenge thrown down by the man who only thirty minutes ago had winked at Amy as we prepared to sip tea together. His charming persona now calculated and chilling, waiting for my response.

I stepped back. Alone and confronted by my suspicion, I feared an honest response would not be my best defense. I feigned ignorance and hoped I might buy some time to compose my thoughts. Better than risk an unpredictable response.

"I'm afraid you'll have to excuse me. I'm an old lady, and I sometimes get caught up in my conspiracy theories. Women my age," I laughed, "we're just a bunch of old busybodies. We don't have much to do. I'll admit, I was intrigued when Amy first came to me and I realized who she was engaged too. When she told me about Jared's death, I got caught up in it. I also thought you were right."

Now the doctor was off guard. My response had surprised him.

"In what way?" He cocked his head.

"You insisted Jared's death wasn't an accident, that someone had murdered him."

"And you agreed with me?"

"I did then, and I do now too."

I walked ahead, the sound of my heart beating in my ears as loudly as the incessant tapping of the doctor's cane against the cobblestones behind me.

"So beyond thinking the murderer might be my nephew or perhaps me, who else do you think might have murdered my son?"

"I'm sure there are many," I said. "But after visiting with Amy and seeing how you care for her, I can't imagine how you could possibly be involved."

"I'm a rich man, Ms. Dawn, and I have a lot of enemies. A lot of competitors who would wish me ill, not to mention certain members of my board who have wanted me to step down for some time. Jared's death was no surprise, particularly for those who knew of his addiction. And no disappointment for those who didn't want to see him advance within the company. My nephew was a natural. If anyone were happy about it, it was my sister-in-law. She's been after me for years to promote him." The doctor paused and lit another cigarette. "Hey, maybe it was my nephew, along with his mother. Maybe they killed Jared."

I stopped on the walk and looked back at the doctor. I had no idea if he was playing with me, was on the level, or if he even knew the difference. Only that in the morning light, leaning on his cane with a cigarette in his mouth, he looked drawn and so different from the handsome, gray-haired cosmetics genius that graced his ads and billboard campaigns.

"Listen to me." Conroy chuckled, then took the cigarette from the corner of his mouth and blew a ring of smoke into the air. "Maybe it's me who's the clairvoyant. Do you suppose that's possible?"

"Anything's possible."

Conroy glanced at his watch. "Look at the time. It's getting late, and I need to get back to the house. If you like, you can continue your walk. It's a lovely day. Just watch out for the bees behind the garage. You wouldn't want to get stung."

The doctor headed back to the house, then stopped as though he had a second thought.

"I'll tell Lupe to let you out. There's no need for you to bother Amy. She needs her nap. I'm sure you'd agree it would be best if she weren't disturbed."

I felt a huge sense of relief. If the doctor had agreed to invite me to tea for the purpose of poisoning me, I was certain after our short jaunt in the garden that I had convinced him I was nothing more than a self-proclaimed psychic, a lonely old lady, a busybody, fascinated by urban legend and the stories surrounding the House that Vanity Built. There was no need for him to worry about my relationship with Amy or pursue any threats against me. I was nothing. Which was exactly what I wanted him to believe.

Much as I wanted to turn back to the house to collect Wilson and go home, I felt drawn to the garden. The smell of fresh lavender and wild rosemary filled my senses and calmed my frazzled nerves. The walk I felt would do me good. I followed the path through a rose-covered trellis that led to a koi pond with lily pads and blue and white lilies-of-the-Nile. Next to the pond was a small wrought-iron love seat. This was the doctor's private garden, evidenced by the presence of a gold ashtray, mounted on a stand next to the seat. I was about to sit down when I tripped over a small hole in the ground. Gophers! Like landmines, their small holes pockmarked the landscape surrounding the path leading to and from the pond. This had been Eli's work. Her communication with the rodents to sabotage the doctor's garden was everywhere.

I picked my way carefully along the path so as not to trip again in one of the holes, and headed toward the far end of the property. Heeding the doctor's advice, I avoided the far side of the garage where I could hear the sound of bees humming, and picked up a dusty trail behind the garage that paralleled a security fence with a back gate that offered a private service entrance for property maintenance. The fence was covered with a hedge of tall flowering plants with lavender, bell-shaped flowers. Anyone else might have thought the plant a weed. But I knew different. This was foxglove. Deadly to the touch and whose poison could stop the heart and cause instant death.

I quickened my pace and headed up a slight incline toward the guest house, then paused to catch my breath. From here, I looked back at the garage, and beyond it, partially hidden behind a tool shed and between the security fence, was the back end of an old gray sedan. Not the type of car I would have expected to see on the doctor's property, but surprisingly familiar.

I looked over my shoulder to make certain no one was watching from the house, and took the pathway back toward the tool shed where I could get a better look. Could this be the car I'd seen parked in front of my house the day the masked man returned my cat?

Cautiously I approached.

The car, an old Toyota with Nevada license plates, wasn't locked. The front window on the driver's side was down. I poked my head inside. The car smelled of heat and chemicals I couldn't identify. The leather interior had been torn. Candy wrappers were scattered on the passenger seat and floorboard, and a man's shirt and a pair of paint-marked pants were rolled up on the backseat. Next to them was a travel crate, the type one might use to transport a cat.

From behind me, a pair of mourning doves winged above my head. I froze. Something had frightened them. Then the sound of heavy footsteps. From behind the garage, someone or something was coming my way. I didn't wait to see what it was or who. Instead, I backed away from the car, and fast as I could, made my way back to the main house.

Lupe had been looking for me. She spotted me as she was about to get into the cart. "You okay? I've never seen you move so fast. You look like you've seen a ghost. What's the matter?"

I put my hand to my chest to try to control my breathing and pointed in the direction of the garage. "Who owns the gray sedan parked behind the garage?"

"Why?"

"Just curious," I said.

"It belongs to the handyman. The doctor hired him to take care of some gophers. He's been here a couple of times, but far as I can tell, he hasn't done any good."

"Is he here now?" I asked.

"Probably. It's not my job to keep track of him. But I don't mind telling you, the man gives me the creeps."

Chapter 27

When I got back to the car, I found Wilson sitting behind the steering wheel of the old Rolls, dusting the wooden dash with his kerchief. I got in and crouched down beneath the window.

"Drive!" I yelled. "We need to leave, and quickly!"

No one could have seen me through the darkened glass, but I felt safer cocooned in a fetal position. I had already cheated death once that morning by refusing to drink tea with the doctor. I wasn't about to push my luck with the doctor's handyman. I worried he may have been lurking in the bushes and spotted me looking into his car. I wanted to make a quick escape.

"Someone after you?" Wilson's eyes searched the rearview mirror.

"The masked man," I said. I put my hand to my heart. It felt like it was about to jump from my chest. "I found the gray sedan. It's parked out behind Conroy's garage. I just hope he didn't recognize me."

Without waiting for further instructions, Wilson put the car in gear, and we rolled out of the drive like molasses. Despite my age and arthritic hips, I could have sprinted faster. Note to self: a 1952 Rolls Royce is hardly a getaway car. The car's top speed was only slightly faster than a snail's pace.

As we cleared the guard gate, I sat up and took a deep breath. "I need to see Detective Romero, and that Detective Williams kid too."

"Williams?" Wilson flinched. "You think just because you've seen a gray sedan parked behind Conroy's garage—which is probably one of a hundred thousand cars exactly like it in the city—that you're going to convince that young skeptic the car's owner is your masked man?"

"I do," I said.

"Really? And that our masked man is somehow tied to the doctor and Matthew?"

"I have a plan."

"Eli and Christina had a plan too, and they think you blew it. They're furious with you."

"Because I broke a couple of cups from Eli's ridiculously expensive tea set? Or because I failed to sit back and watch the doctor drink the poison brew they convinced Lupe to prepare?"

Wilson shrugged. "They believe the poison was an easy out."

"Yes, well, I wasn't convinced, and it would still leave Matthew and his mother unaccountable."

We drove along in silence with Wilson deep in thought, while I tried to imagine my next step.

Finally, as we pulled into the drive at home, Wilson turned to me. "You do know, even after all your efforts today, the detective's not going to believe you."

In that regard, Wilson was correct. I didn't expect Romero or his team of detectives, Williams, in particular, to believe I had been in contact with the doctor's late wife and his paramour or that I had learned that the rumors surrounding their deaths were true and that they blamed the doctor for their passing. Nor could I share anything about my very convoluted conversation with the doctor. Half the time, I wasn't sure if he was baiting me, shifting blame onto Madeline and Matthew, or confessing he was responsible for Jared's death.

But I did have one solid piece of evidence.

"The detectives may think I have nothing admissible, but that's because they haven't found the gray sedan parked behind Conroy's garage. When they do, and Williams finds a cat crate in the back seat—which he will—and he has his forensics people test whatever cat hair they find inside and compare it to Bossypants, they'll find it a match. And that is evidence there's a connection between our cat-napper and the gray sedan parked behind Conroy's garage."

I marched into the house ahead of Wilson. Convinced I had the evidence I needed to rally the detectives to piece my argument together and find Jared's killer. Wilson excused himself to do some research, while I headed to the kitchen to make myself a cup of tea. As I waited for the water to heat on the stove, I put in a call to Detective Romero. The call went directly to voicemail. The problem with today's modern methods of communication was nobody ever really talks to anybody anymore. We simply messaged each other.

Despite the inconvenience, I left a voicemail and marked it urgent. I told Romero I believed I had made a break in the case and that I needed to see him in person. I also suggested he bring along Detective Williams.

Two hours later, I got a call back.

"Sorry, Misty, I'm—"

"I found the gray sedan," I said. "It's parked behind Conroy's garage."

I didn't wait for Romero to explain why he had taken so long to call me back or why he hadn't chosen to see me in person. I expected him to be elated.

Instead, I was blindsided.

"We have a problem, Misty."

"What?"

"Dr. Conroy's filed a restraining order against you."

Me? I was stunned.

"How could he? I was just there this morning. Amy invited me to tea, and—"

"He says you've been harassing her, that she's intimidated by you. That you convinced her to invite you to tea today so you could get onto the estate."

"I did no such thing. You know better than that, Detective."

"I'm afraid I really don't." Based upon what I told Romero concerning my covert visits to the mansion, I couldn't blame him. "And it's not up to me. The doctor was quite persuasive and insisted we investigate his claim."

"Claim? What proof did he have?" I asked.

The words had barely escaped my lips when I realized what he might be talking about. The tea set. The exorbitantly expensive Hammersley china tea set I'd knocked to the floor. The doctor had no doubt shown the detective the accident scene. Perhaps even staged the site to make it look worse than it had been. In my mind's eye, I pictured the tea set, not just those pieces I had caused to fall to the floor, but the entire set, worth thousands of dollars broken into slivered pieces on the floor.

There was no point in trying to explain my actions. The detective would never believe that the doctor's dead wife and his paramour were haunting him, or that they had subconsciously convinced Lupe to poison the doctor's tea. Or that by upsetting the tea service, I had actually saved the doctor's life. I could only move forward and hope the presence of the gray sedan hidden behind the doctor's garage might help to prove my case.

"Do you want the license plate number or not?" I asked.

"The car's not there. I got your call before we visited the estate, and we looked. It's gone."

"But—"

"Relax. It's not as bad as you think, and you may have Detective Williams to thank for it."

I took a deep breath. I couldn't imagine Detective Williams being any help to me at all.

"Detective Williams? And how is that?"

"That bottle of cologne you brought back from Conroy's guest house?" Romero said.

"The one Detective Williams said couldn't be admitted into evidence?" My stomach tightened.

"We tested it anyway, turns out you were right. Williams got the results back from the lab this morning before we got the call from the doctor requesting we come by the house. The bottle had three times the amount of bee venom of any commercial product approved by the FDA. Williams thinks you might be on to something."

"Really?" I sat down on the sofa. "So the young detective believes I might be psychic after all."

"I wouldn't go that far. At least not yet, but it was Williams' idea once he learned about the concentrate of bee venom in the cologne that we play along."

"I don't understand. I thought you said the doctor filed a restraining order against me."

"He has. And for the record, it was Detective Williams who suggested the doctor file the order. But in truth, it was more for show," Romero said.

"It's not real?" I asked.

"Oh, it's real all right, and you can't go back there. Not under any circumstances. You need to stay at least one hundred feet away from the doctor and Amy."

Somehow being slapped with a restraining order didn't feel like a closed door, but more like a preemptive strike.

"So, if I'm correct in my thinking, it sounds like the young detective may have bought us some time to continue the investigation."

"Not us, Misty, or not you and me anyway. You've done everything you need to do. If you can give me that plate number, my team and I'll take it from here."

I wasn't thrilled Romero had cut me out of the investigation, but after nearly being poisoned by the doctor that morning, I didn't mind taking a step back and letting Romero and his team wrap things up.

"It's a Nevada plate," I said. "Personalized. The letters are X-T-R-M-N and the number eight."

"Exterminate?" Romero said.

"Clever, huh? Dr. Conroy hired the man to take care of a gopher problem. But if you ask me, I think he's a hitman, hired to do the doctor's dirty work. And if I might make a prediction, when you find the car, you'll not only find a cat crate in the back seat, but you'll also find something to connect him to Jared's murder as well."

"We'll see. In the meantime, no matter what happens, don't go back to the Conroy Estate. Promise me."

I promised. A promise I fully intended to keep.

But things happened.

Chapter 28

Later that evening, Wilson and I were in the study discussing this morning's near double murder. How I had foiled both Eli's and Christina's attempt to get Lupe to poison the doctor, and dodged my own death when the doctor attempted to drizzle a drop of toxic lemon into my tea. I'll admit, having escaped death, I was in a celebratory mood.

At Wilson's behest, I opened a bottle of Chateau Mouton Rothschild, a gift he had received from a producer for his work on an award-winning Broadway production of *The Drowsy Chaperone*. While Wilson couldn't imbibe—shades can't eat or drink—my description of the dark, rich, full-bodied wine seemed to suffice. Together, despite Conroy's restraining order against me, Wilson and I got silly while reenacting what I felt was one of my better investigations.

Maybe it was the wine, but I was confident that by now, Romero and his detectives had found the gray sedan along with my masked man and that his connection to Conroy, and Matthew and possibly Madeline, were all they needed to determine who and how Jared had been murdered. I had visions of the three of them sweating it out while the police questioned them. As for me, my part was done. I had led the police to my masked man—the missing link—and I was certain they would put the pieces in place. It was just a matter of time. Soon Billy would be free and Amy out from under the doctor's influence. I toasted Wilson to our victory and to Amy's happy-ever-after. To the baby, and Billy's release. I was savoring my success when my cell buzzed.

"Misty." Amy's voice was but a whisper. "I need you to come back to the house. I have to see you right away."

"Are you okay?" My first thought was that the police had been there, arrested the doctor, and Amy was alone, distraught, and in need of support. My second thought was darker. The police had yet to arrive, the doctor was still there, and based on the strain in Amy's voice, holding her hostage.

Time in the psychic world is easily confused. Past, present, and future can fold on top of one another, and in my stupor, I had confused what I wanted to believe with the reality of the moment. All was yet to come.

"Please, Misty, come quick." Amy's voice quivered. "I'll meet you at the guest house, and don't tell anyone. I don't know who I can trust anymore.".

"I'll be there," I promised.

I gave a quick thought to calling Romero and pressed the auto-dial on my phone. When his voicemail answered, I left a brief message that Amy had called, and I was headed her way. In my mind, despite Romero's warnings, I couldn't forsake Amy. Not now. Not in her moment of need. My overwhelming sense was that Amy felt she was drowning. I was her lifeline, and I needed to act.

I had no idea what to expect as Wilson and I approached the Beverly Park guard gate. For each of my previous visits, I'd had an excuse or an invitation and sailed through security without a problem. But tonight, in my haste to come to Amy's aide, I hadn't considered what I would say to the guard. Fortunately, as we pulled forward to the kiosk, I didn't need to think about it. Amy had left word she was expecting a delivery. The guard checked his clipboard for my name, then did a double take as he glanced back at the Jag.

"Nice car for deliveries. What year is it?"

"Fifty-four," I said. Wilson had insisted after our last slow getaway in the Rolls that we take the Jag. "It's a surprise for the doctor." With my fingers to my lips, I pantomimed twisting a key in a lock and smiled.

"Nice," the guard said. "Amy asked me to tell you to use the back road." Then waving us through the entry, he pointed to the utility road that footed the back entrance to the Conroy Estate. The same road I suspected my masked man had used to access the property in his gray sedan.

As we approached Conroy's back gate, Wilson dimmed the Jag's headlights and parked as close as he could to the fence.

The security fencing surrounding the back of the estate was complete with cameras and automatic lights triggered by a motion detector. I could only hope Amy had thought to unlock the gate and turn off the security lights long enough for me to sneak onto the property. Wilson would be no problem, but for a mortal like myself, one false move, the lights would go on, and I'd be discovered.

"You wait here." Wilson slipped out of the car and checked the gate.

The lock sprung open in Wilson's hand. He pushed open the gate and motioned for me to join him.

I left my bag in the car so that I might be more agile, and tiptoed toward the gate, ready to spring as best I could in any direction should the security lights come on. When the lights didn't respond to my passing, I paused and looked up at the Conroy mansion. The House that Vanity Built stood like a castle on the hill, a black silhouette beneath a full moon, dark but for a dim yellow light in the solarium. Whether Amy had thought to cut the power to the backyard's security lights or the luminaries had somehow shorted the power, I wasn't sure. Only that I felt a heavy sense of foreboding as I stumbled through the gate.

Wilson caught me. "I've got you, Old Gal, don't worry."

"It's not me I'm worried about, Wilson. It's your lady friends." I pointed to the solarium window where Eli and Christina sat, looking down at the backyard like fans at a football stadium with front row seats, waiting for the games to begin. "I sense they've upped this morning's ante."

"Don't worry about them. You go ahead and find Amy. I'll take care of them, and if I see the doctor, I'll warn you." Wilson started up the path to the house, then stopped and looked back at me. "And if you see Conroy first, snap your fingers, and I'll coming running."

It seemed like a plan, or at least as much of a plan as I could think of at the moment. Amy needed me. And Wilson? I could only hope he was smart enough not to be part of whatever end game the luminaries had in mind.

I continued in the dark along the pathway in the direction of the guest house. I had gone maybe twenty feet when I heard a sound.

"Psst. Misty, over here."

Amy appeared from behind the guest house. Dressed in a robe and slippers, she held an unlit flashlight in her hand. With her finger to her lips, she whispered for me to follow, then tiptoed around to the back of the house and slowly opened the door to the kitchen. Inside, the house was dark, the only light coming from a small digital clock above the kitchen stove—10:43 p.m.

In a voice little more than a whisper, she said, "I found something. I don't know what it is, but I think it might have something to do with Jared's murder."

"Where is it?" I asked.

Amy checked to make sure the shutters above the kitchen sink were closed tight, then turned on the flashlight and pointed it in the direction of the kitchen counter. In front of us was a thin, rectangular wooden box, like nothing I had ever seen before—no more than an inch-and-a-half high, and about ten inches long and six inches wide. Wires had been strung across the top about an eighth of an inch apart, and on the side was a small off-and-on switch taped to a battery.

"I'd turn it on," Amy said, "but I'm afraid I'd electrocute myself."

"Hand me the light. I want to get a closer look." With the light in my hand, my gnarled fingers traced the wires, then stopped. Caught between two of the wires was a small, scaly, winged creature. "What do you think this is?"

Amy leaned over my shoulder. "A bee maybe?"

Carefully I held the creature's remains up to the light. "It certainly looks like it to me."

I put the dead insect down on the countertop and looked back at the box. The top portion was removable, and beneath it was a small thin cookie sheet. I slid the sheet out from beneath the box and noticed what looked like razor blade scrapings across the bottom and the remains of a thin crusty residue along the sides. I closed my eyes and hugged the sheet close to my body. With the pan against my chest, I sensed the frenzied buzz of a thousand angry bees like tiny pinpricks against my chest. This had to be bee venom.

I put the cookie sheet back on the counter. "Where did you find this?"

Amy pointed to the kitchen door.

"It was sticking out from beneath the steps outside. I nearly stumbled over it when I came in. I didn't know what it was, but something about it didn't look right."

"You've never seen it before? It wasn't there last time you and Jared were in the house?"

"Not that I remember. Jared and I seldom went out that way, and I haven't been down here since he died. I can't help but think that somebody was trying to hide it under the house."

I had the same feeling and wondered if that might have been what Conroy's handyman had been up to when I had discovered his car behind the garage.

"Whatever this thing is," I said, "I believe it has something to do with Billy and his bees and was used to collect bee venom."

Amy squinted. "But how?"

"I'm not an expert on bees, and far as I know, only two people on the property were: Dr. Conroy and Billy."

Amy put her hand on top of the box. "You think it's the doctor, don't you? You got a reading off the box, and you think he had something to do with Jared's murder."

"The box can't tell me who killed Jared. I only know it's

connected to bee venom and that Jared died as a result of shooting himself with an EpiPen full of it. I'm not saying the doctor did it, but I do know he's not a well man, nor is he innocent of some of the things that have gone on around here. I'm not a doctor, and I can't tell you what form of mental illness the doctor has, but on some level, close as you are to all this, you must suspect something."

As an intuitive, I found people frequently knew things about themselves and those around them, whether they were conscious of it or not. Deep down, they always had some understanding. My job was to help them see it. To open those doors they may have been too afraid to look behind and to accept the truth so they could move forward. Amy had been hanging on to the idea that a baby and a new start for the doctor would help them to create a perfect family—something she desperately wanted. It was all within her reach if she would only trust herself.

Amy bit her lip.

"I'm not sure what I think. With Jared gone and Billy not around, I've been so confused. Jared always said his father was odd. I know he's not emotionally balanced, but when Dr. Conroy offered to help Billy with a lawyer, I guess I wanted to believe he was going to look out for me like a father might. He kept telling me how it was only the two of us now. That once the baby was born, we'd be a family. I needed to believe that. I needed to feel like I fit in somewhere."

"I know you do," I said. "I also know you're stronger than you think, and there's a reason you came down here tonight in your bathrobe and slippers. What made you sneak out of that big house and come down here all alone? What was it?"

Amy brushed a tear from her eye.

"After you left today, the doctor surprised me. He said he'd been collecting things for a nursery, and he wanted to show me what he had done. He thought it might make me feel better." Amy put a fisted hand to lips and quivered. "Misty, he's got a room upstairs made up for the baby. He never mentioned anything about it before. I had no idea. But the room has everything. A crib. A bassinet. A rocking chair. He said if I didn't like it, I could send it all back. It was entirely up to me. Then tonight, after dinner, the doctor went into his study, and I decided to go back upstairs to spend some time in the baby's room. I was sitting in the rocker, thinking how strange it all was when I got this craving for chocolate. I remembered that the week before Jared died, I'd made brownies. The kind with a gooey marshmallow-swirl inside, like my mother used to make. I could have eaten them all. Jared told me if I didn't stop, I wouldn't fit into my wedding dress, so I wrapped them up and put them in the freezer."

"And that's why you came down here? Because you had a craving for chocolate?"

"I couldn't help myself. But I didn't want to disturb the doctor; he'd probably tell me chocolate wasn't good for the baby, so I decided I'd sneak down and come in the back door. If he didn't see any lights on, I figured he wouldn't know."

I could relate to both Amy's cravings and her concerns about the doctor's unpredictable response. But in the end, chocolate had won out. I was about to suggest we sit down and split what was left of the brownies when I heard a thump outside.

"What's that?"

Amy's eyes widened. "I don't know."

"Sounds like footsteps," I said.

Amy grabbed my hand, and we huddled in the dark. Outside, somebody had inserted a key in the front door and was trying to come in.

"Is Lupe here?" I whispered.

"Not this time of night."

"Anyone else?"

"No. It's just the doctor and—"

"Amy?" Dr. Conroy's voice cut through the dark silence of the house as he pushed open the front door.

I ducked down below the counter and backed into the pantry.

"Dr. Conroy?" Amy looked nervously at me then moved toward the living room. "What are you doing here?"

"Why I'm looking for you, my sweet girl. Is everything okay? You shouldn't be down here all alone in the dark this time of night. You could have a fall. Something could happen."

"I'm fine," Amy said. "It's just, I've had this craving for chocolate all day long, and I remembered I made Jared some brownies a while back. I froze what we didn't eat. I couldn't help myself." Amy laughed nervously. "I'm sorry if I worried you."

"Nonsense, child. Cravings are expected. Go get your brownies."

I held my breath as Amy walked back into the kitchen, opened the freezer door, grabbed the brownies, and returned to the living room.

"Come now," the doctor said, "let's take them back to the house, perhaps we can have a little late-night snack together. Wouldn't that be nice?"

I didn't dare breathe until I heard the front door close tight and lock shut. I waited a good five minutes to be sure neither Amy nor the doctor would return, then slipped quietly from my hiding place in the pantry and back into the kitchen. I needed to get back to the car—more importantly, to my bag where I'd left my phone—and call Detective Romero. I paused at the kitchen counter, considered whether or not to take the bee venom collector with me, then thought better of it. Not only was it bulky, but I wasn't about to make the same mistake Wilson had made with Jared's cologne, and have the police tell me it wasn't admissible. I left it where it was and quietly tiptoed out the back door.

Chapter 29

I was halfway down the path from the guest house when I heard the doctor's voice behind me.

"What are you doing here?"

I froze.

"I don't suppose you'd believe I got lost on our walk earlier this morning?"

I turned around, and the doctor hit me with a beam of light, the glare so bright I could barely make out the shape of a human form behind it. If I hadn't recognized the doctor's voice and the silver tip of his cane in the moonlight, I might not have known who it was.

"Nice try, Ms. Dawn, but I don't imagine when the police find your body they'll believe it, and neither do I. What matters is that I've caught you on my property. It's dark, and the cops will think I mistook you for an intruder." The doctor moved the light away from my face and tipped his head in the direction of the garage. "I've had it with all your snooping around, and I don't intend to put up with your influence on Amy any longer. I tried to ask you nicely, but clearly you don't have any intention of leaving her alone." The doctor took a gun from inside his waistband and pointed it at me. "Put your hands up. I think it's time you and I finished that little walk we started this morning. Don't you think?"

Now would have been a good time for me to snap my fingers and alert Wilson to my situation. The problem was, with the gun aimed at my back and my hands above my head, my fingers were shaking too nervously to comply.

"How did you know I was here?" I couldn't imagine Amy had told him. Not voluntarily.

The doctor laughed. "The security lights. Amy must have turned them off before she snuck down to the guest house. When I realized she wasn't in the nursery, I went looking for her and noticed the lights weren't working. It was a dead giveaway something was up. The lights go on automatically after ten p.m."

I shuffled ahead.

"I thought doctors took an oath to do no harm?" I tried to keep it light. I figured as long as I kept Conroy talking, I had a chance.

"That's a medical doctor. I'm not an MD. I have a doctorate in chemistry and pharmaceutical science. I'm a scientist. Not a healer."

"Obviously," I said.

"And you?" The doctor scoffed. "You call yourself a psychic? You make me laugh. If there really was such a thing, you would have seen this coming."

I rolled my head, shoulder to shoulder, and tried to release the tension in my back as I stumbled ahead. "Unfortunately, much as I can predict for others, it's not possible for me to read myself or those of weak mind. No offense, Doctor."

"Is that what you think I am? Of weak mind?"

"Not my words, Doctor, your wife's."

"My wife's?" Conroy chuckled. "You're really going to try to convince me you're spoken to my wife?"

"Oh, yes. And Christina too. I believe the term she used was addled."

Conroy poked me in the ribs with the nose of the gun. "Keep moving, Ms. Dawn. I've no time for any of your tricks."

"Oh, come now, Doctor, it's just you and me out here beneath the stars. I know you hear their voices. They're quite the chatterboxes. And Lupe? She'd be the first to admit she doesn't believe in such things, but she has heard you talking with them too. Although she thinks it's just your guilty conscience talking. All those wild parties and—those rumors."

"I thought you didn't listen to rumors."

"Oh, I don't, but when confronted by the actual spirit, it's a bit hard to ignore them." I rattled on as we walked down the path toward the garage. I wasn't strong enough to overpower the doctor, but if I could keep him talking, I felt I had a chance. "Frankly, I think it's Eli that haunts you most, and rightly so. She's convinced you added something in with her sleeping pills. Perhaps from the foxglove you grow in your garden down behind the garage? As for Christina, she agrees with the reports that claim she was standing on a ladder, stringing Christmas lights before she died. Only she says she didn't fall accidentally. She says you pushed her."

"You really think anyone's going to believe some hand-to-mouth psychic who strung a few rumors together in hopes of making a name for herself? No wonder you latched on to Amy. The police will never believe you, and you'll never get a chance to tell your story. Move on."

"But you've heard their voices, and now that I've told you I've seen them and what they've told me, you're wondering if maybe it's possible. Maybe it's not just your imagination."

"It's getting late, Ms. Dawn."

"But you are curious, aren't you? Somewhere in the back of your mind you're wondering if it's really possible. And even more than that, you wish you could gaze on Eli's face, just one more time. You fell in love with that face. She was beautiful, and you built an industry around her. Look at all this—" I glanced over my shoulder to the house. "The House that Vanity Built."

Conroy scoffed. "I never called it that."

I allowed myself to breathe. He was giving me time. Time I hoped would work in my favor.

"Maybe not, perhaps it was your critics who coined the term."

"They were jealous. Half-baked talents who couldn't stand to see my success."

"Either way, you made a fortune selling your magic serum, keeping your fans young. The same way you gave Eli youth and beauty. Others wanted your serum as much as you wanted their respect and money that came with it. But the more successful you became, and the more Eli retained her youth and beauty, the vainer she became. Her youth and beauty were an obsession you both loved and hated. Eventually, her vanity drove you apart and into the arms of your housekeeper. I can't imagine how you did it. Balanced both families here on the estate."

"Stop! I don't need to hear this."

"Perhaps not, but still, I can tell—no, I can feel it here in the dark of the night—the idea you could see them again, it intrigues you. Like a young lover attracted to a beautiful woman, you can't help yourself. You want her, or in this case, you want them both. And it's possible. That is if you really want it."

"You're playing with me."

"Not at all. You've heard their voices. You know they're real. I've had other clients who, like yourself, could only hear the spirits around them. Like you, they were frustrated by their inability to see them. However, if you were to ask me, I could help you."

"You really think I believe you? For all I know, you've read through a bunch of old tabloids and made up a story because Lupe told you she heard me talking to myself."

"You really think that's all it is? How else would you explain what I know? The police never reported Eli's death a homicide, or your housekeeper's, as anything but an accident. How could I know any different? How could I know about the foxglove? It's never been talked about, never reported on. The only possible way I would know is because I've spoken with them, and they know what you did, and why."

The doctor looked over his shoulder, back to the house. "I suppose you're going to tell me they're here now?"

"Absolutely. They were in the sunroom this morning when we were at tea. And they're up there right now, looking down at us." I waved slightly with the tips of my fingers, my hands still above my head. "If you don't believe me, snap your fingers."

"What are you nuts? You think if I snap my fingers, a couple of ghosts are going to appear out of thin air?"

In truth, I hoped at least Wilson would.

"Not ghosts, Doctor. Luminaries. There is a difference. Ghosts are harmless spirits who visit us from time to time. I actually find their presence quite reassuring, like revisiting a pleasant memory. Luminaries, on the other hand, are nasty, vengeful creatures. Like your wife and former housekeeper, who are only here because they're seeking justice, which is why they've been so hostile toward you. They've made your life here miserable."

Conroy glanced down at his ankle, the result of one too many falls in his garden.

"If what you say is true, why would I want to snap my fingers?"

"Because in the back of your mind you wonder, what if she's right? What if I could see them one more time? Maybe you could reason with them. You've always been very good at that. And if you could, perhaps you might get rid of them, once and for all."

"I could do that?"

"Of course you could do that. It's really very simple."

"And I suppose you would help me?"

"Under the right circumstances, I might be persuaded."

"Meaning I let you go."

"Meaning if you were to rid yourself of them, you'd be happy. And if you were to let me go, so would I. After all, I've no proof you had anything to do with Jared's death, and I believe the cops aren't going to believe me if I try to tell them I think you murdered your wife and paramour."

"You amuse me, Ms. Dawn, but you're right. I do hear their voices, and for the sake of my sanity, I'll humor you."

The doctor took a step back, looked up at the moon, and snapped his fingers above his head.

And waited.

"See? Nothing. No ghosts. No luminaires. You're a fraud. Just an old hack, trying to make a name for herself. Now move ahead. Let's get this over with."

I took a few more steps. Where was Wilson?

"Keep going. There's no point in dragging this out. No one's going to come to your rescue."

What about Amy? Surely by now she knew the doctor wasn't planning to join her for a late-night snack. Had she called the police, or had the doctor drugged her and locked her in her room?

The closer we got to the garage, the more aware I became of the stillness of the night, the sound of my footsteps on the path, the tapping of the doctor's cane against the cobblestones, like the popping of gunshots.

When we got to the garage, the doctor flashed the light on the wall.

"Over there," he said.

I backed against the wall. A bee flew in front of my face. Strange. I didn't think bees flew at night. I waved it off, blocking both the light and the bee from my face, and squinted into the light.

Behind the doctor were Billy's hives. Over the doctor's shoulder, up the hill, I could see the back of the big house; the house that vanity built, with its yellow lights from the solarium, shadowed the figures of Eli and Christina and Wilson. They were waiting and watching.

A cold chill trickled down my back. I started to shake. Why wasn't Wilson coming to my aid? Had I lost him to the luminaries? Had they convinced him he could do without me? Was this how I was going to end?

With one hand on his cane, the doctor pointed the gun at me.

"Please," I said, "if you're going to kill me, at least give me the satisfaction of knowing if you killed your son, and why." I stood my ground. If I could keep Conroy talking, maybe by now Romero would have heard my voicemail, and the police would be on their way.

"You're the psychic. Why don't you tell me what you think?"

"All right," I said. "The night Jared died, Matthew and his mother came to the house. You had ordered a party bus, a nice gesture because you were concerned the boys might be drinking. Matthew went down to the guest house to join Jared and his friends, while you and Madeline went into your study to talk. I don't know what you talked about, only that Madeline was there, and Lupe told me the two of you spent quite some time together in the study alone."

"Lupe." Conroy looked up at the sky and shook his head. "I should have gotten rid of her long ago. That's what you get for doing favors for people. They take advantage of you."

"Actually, Lupe's been very loyal. She believes you had nothing to do with Jared's death."

"And you?"

"I don't know. I think your sister-in-law may have had something to do with it. I think she wanted to see her own son advance, and maybe she planted the idea in your head. Maybe she managed to sabotage the EpiPen and gave it to Matthew, along with a bottle of cologne that had been deliberately mislabeled to say venom free. Matthew put the bottle on Jared's dresser, and the pen in the drawer where he knew Jared would find it."

"Madeline?" Conroy chuckled. "Small chance. The woman's as allergic to bee venom as was Jared. The reason she was at the house the night of Jared's party was that she had visited a doctor for botox injections and had a reaction. Her face was swollen. She wanted my help."

"Then you did it," I said.

Conroy exhaled and gave me a crooked smile. "Pretty good, Ms. Dawn, but if you had planned on telling the police that story, you're missing one thing."

"What's that?" I asked.

"I'm Jared's father. I insisted on the investigation. If I had killed my son, why would I be foolish enough to turn what looked like an accident into a homicide investigation?"

"To throw the police off," I said. "And because you thought you could get away with it."

"You're making no sense. Jared was my son, an heir to my empire."

"But he wasn't your only son."

"What?" Conroy jerked his head back.

"Didn't think I knew?" Ever since Carlene had first told me about Matthew and how close he was to the doctor, I had a feeling there was something more to the relationship. "Matthew's your son too, isn't he? Different mother, but all the same, a son by your brother's wife. Family features are similar enough between you and your brother that nobody ever noticed, but you knew, or at least you suspected. Particularly when Matthew and Jared started school, and Matthew became the intellectual between the two. You figured Matthew had to be yours. It was a secret you and Madeline kept, much as you have your continued affair."

"So what if he is my son? Jared wasn't up for the business, never was."

"Which worried you. The board was pressuring you to name a new vice president, someone who could succeed you and keep the company profitable. A long time ago, you thought that might be Jared, but you knew Jared didn't want the job, and you were afraid if he were promoted, it'd only be a matter of time before he'd mess up. The closer Jared got to his birthday, and that five-million-dollar trust fund you put in place for him, the more concerned you were about it. Five million dollars was a lot to lose, and rich as you are, you didn't want to lose it. Jared had done everything you asked him to. Stopped drinking. Settled down. Found a nice girl. All of which made you suspicious Jared was playing you. You were convinced all he wanted was access to his trust fund, and once he had it, he'd be gone. But when Amy got pregnant, and you got to know her, you actually started to think—at least for a little while—that maybe things might be different. That something good could come of this after all, and you started to plan for a future. Only Lupe ruined it when she told you she had found a flask in the guest house. You knew right then Jared was never going to be different. He was an alcoholic, and he'd never change. You could never trust him. Not after all you'd been through with his drinking. You could never put him in charge of your company, and what kind of father would he be? So you decided to make Matthew vice president. He was everything Jared wasn't. Smart. Dependable. With Matthew as VP, you could step aside, and with a baby on the way, and Jared out of the picture, you could make up for your past and start over. You knew the police would never suspect you. Not the father. Not the man who pushed for the investigation."

"You spin a good yarn, Ms. Dawn." From behind the doctor, the bees began to hum. "Too bad the police aren't around to hear you. You almost convinced me."

Almost? Had I misinterpreted the facts? Was Matthew more or less than an accomplice? There wasn't time to ask.

The doctor stepped back and raised the gun.

I looked back at the house. Wilson and the luminaries had moved from the solarium to the patio. The three of them stared down at us like we were some type of exhibition. Then Wilson stood up, climbed on to the railing, and put his hands in the air. His Ninja pose, exactly like when he had communicated with my cat. The hum of the bees grew louder. So loud, I was forced to cover my ears.

Conroy took aim.

"No!" I yelled. "Don't. Please don't!"

It was too late. A cloud of bees swarmed the doctor like a tornado. Their frenzied masses covered him as he fell to the ground screaming. Fuzzy bodies with their comb-like wings smothered him, beating against each other as they fought to pierce the doctor's thin skin with their barbed stingers.

Chapter 30

I don't know how long I lay huddled on the ground, too afraid to look up for fear I'd be staring down the barrel of a forty-five. For however long it was, the world blacked out to me. Curled up in a fetal position with my eyes shut, I heard the sound of swarming bees, their angry buzzing, and the faint wail of sirens in the background.

It wasn't until I felt Romero's steady hand on my shoulder that I knew I was safe.

"You okay?" Romero helped me to my feet.

I brushed myself off, thankful to be alive. Conroy's body, like a heap of rubble, was covered with foam and surrounded by firefighters in yellow jackets. The hoses of the firemen's extinguishers aimed at the last desperate winging of the dying bees, their scaly bodies crusted against the doctor's skin like bubble wrap.

"Is he dead?" I asked.

"If he's not, he's going to wish he was. You were right, Misty. Conroy murdered his son."

"How do you know?" I looked at Romero, then back at the house silhouetted beneath the moonlight. The lights in the solarium were still on, but the windows where Wilson had sat with the luminaries were empty.

"This afternoon, after you and I spoke, we put out a BOLO alert and found your gray sedan along with your masked man. We were on our way to talk with the doctor about what we learned when Amy called."

"Is she okay?"

"She's more worried about you. She told us she had asked you up here to show you something. She was afraid the doctor would find you. Turned out her timing was pretty good."

"Thank goodness," I said.

"She's inside talking with Detective Williams now. Why don't we join her? I have a few questions I need you to answer as well."

I knew the minute I entered Conroy's house, Eli and Christina were gone. The chairs at the table in the solarium were empty, and the air in the house felt cool, like the night air outside, as though a gentle breeze had swept the house clean. As for Wilson? I didn't see him anywhere.

Romero shut the kitchen door behind us and told me Amy was in the living room with Detectives Williams and Smiley, and Carlene.

"Carlene?" I was impressed but not surprised. When I had first met Carlene, I thought her to be a shallow, self-centered girl with little concern for anything beyond her own well-being. Carlene's concern for Amy had convinced me otherwise.

"Amy didn't want to be in the house alone. After she called us, she called Carlene and Lupe. Can't say I blame her," Romero said. "The girl's been through a lot."

Romero led the way to the great room that up until now, I'd only passed on my way to the kitchen and the solarium. The room was stunning, equal in size to the entire first floor of Wilson's house, and divided into three distinct areas, with French doors and huge windows that looked out onto the vast expanse of the Conroy estate. Amy and Carlene sat in the center of the room on one of two facing sofas, with Detective Williams on the other.

Amy stood and came running to me. "Misty, are you okay? I was so worried."

"I'm fine." I hugged her tight, as much to reassure myself of her well-being as my own.

"And the doctor?" Amy asked. "Did...did he find you? Is he—"

"He's dead," I said.

Amy took a step back and grabbed her stomach. I reached out to take her hand, and Carlene rushed to her side.

Carlene put her arm around Amy. "The doctor killed Jared, didn't he?"

Detective Williams interrupted. "Why don't we all catch our breath and sit down?"

I sat in the middle of the couch with Amy and Carlene on either side of me. Both women grabbed a hand and held me tight while Romero brought us up to date.

Romero explained that because I had been able to identify the plates on the gray sedan that morning, the police had arrested Anthony Toscana on his way to the airport with a one-way ticket to Belize. Romero described Anthony as a hired hand with a record for petty theft and wanted for jumping bail in Las Vegas.

"Anthony confessed the doctor had originally hired him to take care of a gopher problem in the doctor's backyard. He also admitted the day of Jared's memorial that the doctor ordered him to follow you home. And when you didn't stop talking with Amy, Conroy arranged for Tony to do a drive-by, toss a rock through your window, and later to come back and pick up your cat." I wanted to say, I told you so, but I kept quiet. I knew Romero wasn't finished. "Then the day after Jared's party, Conroy approached Anthony about getting rid of the EpiPen."

"The same EpiPen Jared used the night he died?"

"We think so. Forensics is running tests now. We should know shortly."

"What about Matthew?" I said. "Did you find his prints on the bottle of cologne I gave you? He's involved, I think the doctor used him to get to Jared."

"I may be able to help with that," Williams said. "You were right about Matthew's prints being on the bottle of cologne you gave us. But Matthew didn't bring the bottle into the guest house, Anthony did. The bottle you found—the one you brought home, and we took from you—the doctor had given it to Anthony to sneak into the guest house before Jared's party. It looked exactly like one we found in Anthony's car this afternoon. He admits he had exchanged it for the bottle on Jared's dresser. And according to forensics, Matthew never touched that bottle. It was venom free. The type Jared would have used."

"So Matthew's not involved?"

"We still have some questions we'd like him to answer. I asked Amy to call Matthew and tell him the doctor needed to see him right away. We've got a news blackout on the house. Nobody knows what went down here tonight. Not yet anyway, and nobody's going anywhere until we do. Meanwhile, I've asked Lupe to make us all something to drink. Could be a long night."

I wasn't about to gamble with another cup of Lupe's tea. Not that I felt it was spiked with anything more potent than chamomile or lavender, but after this morning, I wasn't about to tempt it. "No, thank you. I think I'll pass."

Twenty minutes later, Matthew arrived at the house. He must have known the second he arrived that something was wrong. Outside, the motor court was jammed with police cars, a couple of unmarked detective's vehicles, an ambulance and a firetruck. Rather than ring the bell, he pounded on the door.

"Amy?"

Lupe answered and showed Matthew to the great room, where he immediately spotted Carlita sitting next to me on the sofa.

"Carlita?" Matthew stopped short of entering the room. He looked confused. "What are you doing here?"

Amy did a double take, from Matthew to Carlene. "Carlita?"

"I'll explain later." Carlene stood up and strode across the room and offered Matthew her hand. "My name's Carlene Muller now. I changed it after I graduated from college, and for your information, Amy asked me here."

"But why?" Matthew's eyes swept the room and spotted Romero and Williams in front of the bar. "I don't understand, why are the police here, what's going on?"

"Because in case you haven't figured it out," Carlene said. "The doctor's dead."

"Dead?" Matthew took a step back, his hands up. "Wa-wa-wait a minute. What are you talking about? You don't think I killed him?"

Romero stepped forward. "Unless you unleashed a colony of angry bees, I'd say it was an accident. But we do have a couple of questions.

"Me first, Detective." I was anxious to get a few answers for myself. "After all, I am the one who kept pushing your department to investigate. If you're not going to Mirandize him, and don't think he's guilty, I have a few questions of my own."

Romero raised his brows. "Go ahead, Misty."

"Matthew, the day we met in Burbank, outside your offices, and you and I spoke, if you weren't involved in Jared's murder, why did you leave in such a rush?"

Romero looked at me. *Another meeting you didn't tell me about?*

I shrugged.

"Why did I leave? Are you kidding me? Lady, you freaked me out. After the coroner had ruled Jared's death a homicide, I didn't know what to believe. I didn't know if the doctor was guilty or not. I had just been named the company's new VP, and people were talking. All the company needed was more gossip about the doctor and the house. I figured the least I could do is warn him."

"What did he say?"

"He told me not to worry, that you were just some street-freak who had probably read about Jared's death in the papers and was trying to blackmail me or something."

"That's all? He didn't say anything else?"

"Not about you, he didn't. Instead, he asked me to do him a favor. He said he had a friend who wanted to surprise his wife with a party. That his friend had been at Mastro's the night of Jared's bachelor party, and he wanted to know who had planned it."

I looked at Carlene, paused, then asked my next question. "And did you find out who planned Jared's party?"

"Yeah, sure. It was some girl named Carlene." Soon as

Matthew said the name, his jaw dropped, and his eyes went to Carlene. "Was that you?"

"Oh my God! I don't believe it!" Carlene stood up. "It was you. You're the one who nearly got me killed!"

I grabbed Carlene's arm and held her from charging Matthew.

"Me? What did I do?" Matthew looked at me, confused.

"You confirmed the doctor's suspicion that Carlene, or Carlita as the doctor knew her, was working with Jared. The doctor had warned her long ago he didn't want her anywhere near Jared. When you gave Dr. Conroy her name, he figured she was Christina's daughter, and he used you to set her up. He had someone tamper with the brakes of her car when she was in Malibu." I looked back at Romero. "Detective, you can call this a psychic hunch if you like, but if you check Carlene's car, you'll find the doctor's handyman's prints on it as well."

Romero took out his note pad. "Just a few more questions," I said. "In fact, my next concerns both Matthew and Detective Williams. If you allow me, Detective Romero, I believe what I'm about to ask may help to clarify exactly how my masked man ended up with the EpiPen you found in his glovebox earlier today."

Romero nodded at me. "Go ahead."

I started with Matthew. "The night Jared died. After he had the attack and the paramedics arrived, do you remember who was there?"

"Just us guys. We had a private room upstairs, off from the bar."

"And the doctor?" I paused and made sure both Williams and Romero were following. "Where was he? I was under the impression he might have stayed home. I know your mother had come by with you when you brought the party bus, perhaps they went to dinner?"

"No." Matthew shook his head. "That's not right. My mother wasn't feeling well that night. She went home. The doctor and my father decided at the last minute to go out to dinner together. They were at Mastro's as well, downstairs."

"So Doctor Conroy was there, in the restaurant?" I looked at Detective Williams. I didn't have to by psychic to know the young detective was uncomfortable.

"Yeah."

"And he must have noticed the paramedics when they came in."

"I guess."

I turned to Williams. "Did you know Jared's father was at the restaurant that night?"

Williams looked at Romero and Smiley. He was obviously uncomfortable.

"No. Detective Smiley and I met with Dr. Conroy here at the house. He said he had just come from the hospital. That his son had died, and the ER docs thought Jared's death was accidental, but the doctor was insisting we investigate. He felt certain his son had been murdered."

"So you didn't know the doctor had been at the restaurant?"

Smiley dropped his head.

Williams looked away. "It wouldn't have made any difference if he was. We talked to everybody at the party."

"Except for the doctor, who you assumed had been home that night. But he wasn't. And it was the doctor, who in all the confusion, picked up Jared's EpiPen and later gave it to his handyman."

I could see it all in my mind. The young detective had been eager to please both the chief and Detective Smiley and had missed the obvious.

Romero made another note on his pad than pointed to the bar where Williams had placed the bee venom box.

"Have you ever seen that box before?"

Matthew walked over to the bar and looked at the box, his brow furrowed. "Where'd you get this?

"Amy found it behind the guest house," Romero said. "She called Misty here tonight to show her. Do you know what it is?"

"Sure, it's a type of bee trap, a venom collector." Matthew

started to touch the box, and Williams stopped him. "Looks homemade to me."

"How does it work?" Romero asked.

"It's a simple process, really. It fits in front of the entrance to a beehive. The wires here," Matthew pointed to the wires strung across the top of the box, "they're connected to the battery which generates a small electrical charge. The charge doesn't hurt the bees, it just excites them, and causes them to go into a kind of stinging frenzy, dropping their venom onto the plate below. The bees aren't harmed. Their stingers don't detach since there's no soft tissue involved like they would if they actually stung a human being."

"The doctor could have used this to collect the venom?" Romero asked.

"He could have," Matthew said. "But why? If he wanted venom, he just as simply could have ordered it from his factory in Europe."

"Except that would have left a paper trail," I said.

Matthew paused. "Yeah, I suppose."

"But if he wanted to set somebody up," I said, "a trap like this, amateurishly made, might do just that."

Amy got up and went to the window. "Was the doctor trying to set Billy up? To make it look like he had killed Jared?"

"Not just Billy," Carlene said, "don't you get it? He wanted to set you up too, Amy."

"Me? But how?"

Carlene went to the bar and pointed to the box. "It's simple. The doctor makes some silly, homemade trap. Makes it look like Billy made it, then sets him up and reveals to the world that you and Billy were lovers."

"But that's not true." Amy shook her head.

"Maybe not, but you have to understand how the doctor thinks. Believe me, I know." Carlene looked at Amy. "He would have said you were from the same small town and that you and Billy went to school together and were involved. Later, after you graduated, you came to LA intent on finding a rich husband. You met Jared and got engaged, but that you got cold feet and didn't want to go through with the wedding. So you stole the engagement ring Jared gave you. Figured you'd get at least fifty, sixty grand for it, but Jared figured it out, and Billy killed him. The doctor would have testified against you. He had big, high-profile attorneys, and what did you have? Nothing. Before you know it, you would have been in jail for murder, and the doctor would have taken your baby."

"My baby?" Amy put her hands on her stomach. "Is that why he put the nursery upstairs? Because he never planned for me to move it to the guest house?"

"You may not need to," I said.

"What do you mean?" Amy looked at me. She had no idea how the doctor's death was about to affect her.

"If I recall correctly," I said, "the doctor changed Jared's trust and transferred everything from Jared to the baby, and named you as the acting trustee—"

"Unless," Matthew said, "something was to happen to Amy. Which, in such a case, the doctor would become the baby's guardian and executor of the trust. I remember because I had gone with Dr. Conroy to his lawyer's to sign paperwork for the company and overheard the doctor and his attorney chatting about it."

"But if the doctor were to die first," I said. "Then what would happen?"

From the corner of his eye, Matthew looked up at the ceiling then back at Amy.

"Everything in the trust, the house, the money, the doctor's personal property, a percentage of the company, would flow through to the baby with you, Amy, as the executrix."

Chapter 31

"Me?" Amy sat on the couch and rested her hands on her stomach. "I don't understand, how could I inherit all of this? How could this happen?"

The lights flickered in the great room. Romero went to the French doors and looked back out on the property. The detectives had turned on the security lighting. Nothing to worry about, the outage was only a momentary power glitch.

But I knew better.

Spirits can be slow to show up, but they invariably do when those they love are faced with big, life-altering decisions. Jared, I was pleased to see, was no different. Understandably, he had waited until the house was clear of his mother and his father's paramour before deciding to make his presence known. But when the lights flickered back on, I saw him, cool and relaxed, sitting on the couch next to Amy.

I took a seat next to her.

"Because, Amy, sometimes the universe has a way of setting things straight. I think when the doctor reworked Jared's trust fund and named himself the baby's trustee, he inevitably signed his own death warrant." I couldn't share with Amy the concern the luminaries had shared with me about the baby's trust, how they had tried to convince me to kill the doctor. Or that they had successfully persuaded Wilson to carry out their plan. All that mattered was that I convince Amy it was nature's way of balancing out good and evil.

"But what am I supposed to do?" Amy asked.

I looked at Jared, I knew without his saying what he wanted.

The power of thought, like light, can transfer from a spirit to a human mind, and the words came from me as though they were his own.

"Live here," I said. "It's what Jared wants."

"Jared? Is he here?"

I nodded. "He is. And he will be, temporarily anyway. He wants me to tell you he's sorry. He says he was selfish, and he feels like he interrupted your life. He wants you to be happy."

Amy's eyes started to well with tears.

"He's asking if you would help him."

"How?" Amy shook her head.

"He's anxious to make amends, to you, and to those he harmed, but he needs your help. As I said before, he's only here temporarily, and the sooner you can help him, the quicker his transformation can take place."

"I don't understand."

"You don't need to. All you need to do is follow his instructions,"

"Like what?"

"He'd like for you to help Lupe, keep her on as your housekeeper. He's always liked her. Says she's a good woman. And if you don't mind, he thinks it'd be a good idea if you'd let Carlene move into the guest house."

I looked at Carlene. I didn't feel it my place to fill in the blanks about Carlene's history or how she had set Jared up with Amy. I'd leave that to Carlene to explain when she felt the time was right.

"And, he says it's okay if you let Billy move in." Amy looked puzzled. "Jared knew you were still in love with Billy. You may not have known it, but he did. It's why he accepted Billy as part of his rat pack. He knew the two of you weren't going to last. He needed you to secure his trust fund and get away from his father. The marriage would have been a sham. You didn't know it, but Jared felt that maybe one day you might need Billy again, and he wanted Billy to be close by to pick up the pieces. Jared wants you to know you have his blessings."

Romero crossed the room and squatted down in front of Amy. I wasn't sure he had heard any of my conversation with Amy or if he had if he believed it. But the message he had for Amy was reassuring.

"Amy, there's no reason for the police to hold Billy any longer. After we arrested Mr. Toscana, we started the paperwork to release Billy. My guess is by now he's free and on the way back to Carpinteria. That is unless you call him."

I stood up. My job was done here. Amy, Carlene, and Matthew had a lot to talk about and a lifetime ahead of them to figure it all out. I knew Jared would hang around for a while, but not for long. As for Wilson, I wasn't sure if his job was done as well. I didn't see him anywhere. Had he left with the luminaries or had the universe snatched him up because he had interfered with the doctor's plan to shoot me?

I wandered back to the kitchen. I hoped I might find Wilson in the solarium. Instead, Williams joined me.

"Mind if I have a word?"

"Not at all." I took a glass from the cabinet and filled it with water. I knew before Williams asked what it was he wanted to know.

"You busted me back there."

"It wasn't personal," I said.

"All the same, I made a mistake. I didn't ask Dr. Conroy where he was the night Jared died. How did you know that?"

I thought about telling him the truth. That I had seen the whole thing in my mind as soon as Matthew started talking about the party and Jared's final moments, but I knew Williams wouldn't believe me.

"The police chief," I said. "You're young and new on the job. Smiley gave you too much leeway, and you were anxious to impress him. He probably should have been looking over your shoulder more, but the doctor was an influential friend of the department. Neither of you was about to challenge that. You aren't the first detective to make a mistake on an investigation, and you won't be the last. But you won't make the same mistake twice. I'm sure of it."

Williams pointed back to the great room. "One more question. Out there, with Amy, did you really see Jared's spirit, or were you just telling her to make her feel better?"

"You think I'd do that?"

"I'm not sure what I believe anymore, not after what I've seen tonight. But I don't buy that those bees attacked the doctor accidentally. You had something to do with that, didn't you?"

I finished my water and put the glass down on the counter.

"If I answered that you'd have to arrest me. Although, I suppose it wouldn't matter if you did. As Romero's so fond of saying, unless it's something he can carry into court and convince a jury with, he's not interested. But in answer to your question, no, it wasn't me."

Romero joined us in the kitchen.

"Misty, you going to need a ride? I saw the Jag out beyond the back gate and called Denise. I thought maybe she might drive you home."

I knew better than to let Denise drive Wilson's Jag. I grabbed my bag off the kitchen counter. If I pushed the seat forward, I felt certain I could drive myself.

"I appreciate the concern, Detective, but I'm fine. You needn't worry. If it's all the same, I'll bid you goodnight and be on my way. It's been a long day, and I think I'd enjoy the drive home alone. Lots to think about."

I was pleased Romero didn't argue. In hindsight, I felt Denise would be pleased as well. I knew she would be anxious to spend time with the detective alone and full of questions I'd rather not answer. Better him than me.

I took the path back toward the garage. The firemen were still cleaning up, and the guard gate that Wilson and I had come through earlier that night was wide open. Beyond it, the Jag sat beside the fence. In the moonlight, with the top up and windows rolled down, it looked deserted.

I stopped at the gate and glanced back at the house. There's a toll on some missions. It's not possible to stay focused on the other side of the veil without feeling drained. I felt empty, dehydrated of my energy, and tired beyond what I knew sleep could repair. This was more than mission-exhaust. This was something else. This was loss. A deep personal loss. Wilson was gone.

I walked through the gate, and as I approached the Jag, the headlights flickered.

"Wilson!"

I quickened my step and put my hand on the door. When I opened it, Wilson was behind the wheel, looking very pleased with himself. "How could you!"

"Nice to see you too, Old Gal."

"You know you shouldn't have done that," I scolded.

"What? Free the bees? Sic them on the doctor? Is that what's got you all in a dither? Would you have preferred I let the doctor shoot you?"

"He might have missed," I said. "And the police were on the way. I could hear the sirens."

"Sorry, Old Gal. Couldn't risk it. There wasn't time." Wilson put the key in the ignition.

"You may have risked more," I said. "Ordering the bees to kill the doctor was against the rules. Ghosts can't interfere. They must never cause the death of a mortal. You know that."

"Yes, but I'm still here, aren't I? And as you've pointed out so many times, I'm not a ghost. I'm only a shade, a temporary being at best. Perhaps your universal spirit wasn't watching or will count it a learning experience and forgive me."

I fastened my seatbelt.

I didn't like it when Wilson parroted back to me my own words. He had changed. I wondered if he felt it too. When we started out, he was nothing but a thorn in my side—a self-centered being whose life revolved around his fancy cars and expensive collectibles. But now, judging from his actions—saving me from the doctor—he was no longer the same man. There was a newness about him, a selflessness. All shades change. Our time together was growing short. I should have been happy, but instead, I was worried. Our next time could be out last.

"I hope so, Wilson. I really hope so."

NANCY COLE SILVERMAN

Nancy Cole Silverman credits her twenty-five years in news and talk radio for helping her to develop an ear for storytelling. But it wasn't until after she retired that she was able to write fiction full-time. Much of what Silverman writes about is pulled from events that were reported on from inside some of Los Angeles' busiest newsrooms where she spent the bulk of her career. She lives in Los Angeles with her husband, Bruce, and her standard poodle, Ali.

Mysteries by Nancy Cole Silverman

The Misty Dawn Mystery Series

THE HOUSE ON HALLOWED GROUND (#1)
THE HOUSE THAT VANITY BUILT (#2)

The Carol Childs Mystery Series

SHADOW OF DOUBT (#1)
BEYOND A DOUBT (#2)
WITHOUT A DOUBT (#3)
ROOM FOR DOUBT (#4)
REASON TO DOUBT (#5)

Henery Press Mystery Books

And finally, before you go...
Here are a few other mysteries
you might enjoy:

PILLOW STALK

Diane Vallere

A Madison Night Mystery (#1)

Interior Decorator Madison Night might look like a throwback to the sixties, but as business owner and landlord, she proves that independent women can have it all. But when a killer targets women dressed in her signature style—estate sale vintage to play up her resemblance to fave actress Doris Day—what makes her unique might make her dead.

The local detective connects the new crime to a twenty-year old cold case, and Madison's long-trusted contractor emerges as the leading suspect. As the body count piles up, Madison uncovers a Soviet spy, a campaign to destroy all Doris Day movies, and six minutes of film that will change her life forever.

Available at booksellers nationwide and online

Visit www.henerypress.com for details

PUMPKINS IN PARADISE
Kathi Daley

A Tj Jensen Mystery (#1)

Between volunteering for the annual pumpkin festival and coaching her girls to the state soccer finals, high school teacher Tj Jensen finds her good friend Zachary Collins dead in his favorite chair.

When the handsome new deputy closes the case without so much as a "why" or "how," Tj turns her attention from chili cook-offs and pumpkin carving to complex puzzles, prophetic riddles, and a decades-old secret she seems destined to unravel.

Available at booksellers nationwide and online

Visit www.henerypress.com for details

www.ingramcontent.com/pod-product-compliance
Lightning Source LLC
Chambersburg PA
CBHW060551260626
47161CB00003B/1153